I0675880

UGLY

A

Rod Cornelius

Novel

ISBN 0970851790

An Akirim Press Publishing

Ugly

There are many ugly things in this world, but Julius Graves is considered one of the ugliest of those things. His Big Lips, Big Nose and Jet Black Skin have always been the perfect recipe for nasty stares, cold shuns, and violent beat downs his entire life.

Once Julius moves to a new neighborhood, the torment he thought he escaped gets far worse when he becomes targeted by a menacing crew that's led by an egomaniac that's determined to make Julius' life a living hell.

Julius finds refuge in an unlikely ally that sends his life spiraling even more out of control at the cost of losing someone he loves the most.

UGLY

Acknowledgements

This novel is dedicated to the loving memory of

Mrs. Doris Cornelius Bowen

UGLY

More Akirim Press Books

Books by Rod Cornelius

Diggin' Gold

The Trusted

Single Again

Ghetto Eyes

The Best Kept Secrets

When It Comes Around

Books by Mirika Mayo Cornelius

Secret

Colored Lily: Poppa Took My Innocence

Ain't Quite What I Thought

Ain't Quite What I Thought 2

Sunny Sides of My Shade

Murders At Gabriel's Trail: The Complete Series

First Degree Sins

Paton

<u>Books by Cyan Deane</u>

Dead Man's Mayhem

Execution's Karma

TABLE OF CONTENTS

A Man Without A Plan Is A Man Without Direction...

UGLY

Chapter 1

He stood in front of the mirror with his head hanging down as he hovered over the bathroom sink with both arms stretched out against the wall. He had been positioned that way for a little bit over a half hour. He was fully dressed in his usual attire–black hoodie, baggie blue jeans and boots. It was another first day and another new school with a brand new group of potential tormentors. Julius had been dreading this day for months–three to be exact–ever since the day him, his mother, and his good for nothing stepfather moved into this new place.

Although his mom provided her best efforts to talk up the new school, there was no hiding the fact that Washington High was known for being one of the worst schools in the entire district, and possibly the whole state. But the rent here was good and his mother was hopeful that this school would be different for him than all the rest.

The neighbors told her many positive changes had come to the troubled institution near the end of the previous school year resulting from the successful basketball program there. They also told her that the school board had brought in a mostly new staff and a hardnosed veteran principal that didn't take any shit and that he was calling all the shots.

It made Julius no difference because he didn't play any sports, and he did his best to stay out of people's way, more specifically school staff. This was his senior year, and as with every school year, he was determined to do what he had to do to make it go by as quickly and as smoothly as possible. Of course, with his looks, he often found that task extremely difficult to accomplish.

He slowly lifted his head and gazed into the mirror. He had hoped when his eyes returned to the reflection in that spotty old bathroom mirror another face would appear. A handsome face. A likeable face. Any face but his.

Big nose, huge lips, jet black skin and a bumpy forehead. He knew he was stuck with three out of four of those features for life, but even a complete surrender on drinking sodas and eating sweets did nothing to smoothen out his rough skin.

He swiped a towel hanging from the shower rack and began dampening it. He gently applied the cloth to his face and then began to violently scrub his face with it. His intention was to wipe his face completely off of his head, but he was unsuccessful again. He tossed the towel across the shower rack and sorrowfully stared at himself in the mirror once more. *Why me?*

****

Vince sat at the table with his legs crossed and a newspaper hanging over his lap in the center of the small kitchen. The hair on his bronzed colored head and face looked like an army of buck shots was etched onto it as he hadn't done anything with himself in the past two weeks. Most days he didn't even make an effort to slip out of his wife-beater and jogging pants–his normal around the house attire.

"They say Michael Jordan is gonna redeem himself this season. His ass shouldn't have left in the first place," he said as he flipped to the next page in the sports section of the paper. "Talkin' about he wanna go play baseball. I guess he found out quick that shit wasn't for him."

"You know he was going through some things with his father's death and all. He just needed some time to sort things out," Felicia said. She was posted at the sink, scrubbing a frying pan amongst the pile of unwashed dishes that were spread out across the counter. It wasn't unusual for her to be the last one to get to bed and the first one up in the morning, just in time to have Vince his morning ham and cheese omelet ready so he could stretch out and read his morning newspaper.

In addition to making Vince his breakfast every morning, the middle aged, brown skinned woman was responsible for doing the previous night's dishes and all the housekeeping duties also. Despite Vince being home all day, every day, he did absolutely nothing but wait for her to come home and get supper ready.

The petite woman was clearly a fox in her day, with her slanted eyes, full lips and flawless brown skin, but working a full time job and taking care of the house was beginning to take its tiresome toll on her. A few days ago she began noticing small clumps of her hair falling out. She simply blew it off as a result of aging and the stress from the extra burden of having to take care of all the bills while Vince was out of work.

"Hell, I need some time to sort things out," he said while closing the paper and slinging it across the table. "Like what am I gonna do if these people don't call me back for some more hours on this damn job? Tucker nor none of them niggas called me about working any routes since we moved here."

"They'll call. They always do."

"How the hell they gonna call if the phone get cut off? We keep going this direction they gonna get cut off any day now. You asked them people for some more hours yet?"

"I've been asking for weeks now, but everybody is in the same crunch we're in, and they ain't trying to get up off their hours. I may be able to fill in for Rita today, but Lance has to call me and let me know something first."

"Well, something needs to give. Shit!"

Julius walked into the kitchen toting his notebook. His notebook was like an extra arm to him, and he rarely went anywhere without it. He strolled to his mother and gave her a quick peck on her cheek. "Good morning, Ma."

"Hey, baby," she replied as she leaned into his kiss, not removing her hands from the sudsy dish water.

Vince's face transformed into one of disgust the very second Julius walked in. His eyes zeroed in on the boy as he moved from his mother to the refrigerator. Julius grabbed a carton of milk and poured himself the remaining portion from the carton. He could feel Vince's beady eyes cutting through his back as they did every morning. He made certain not to make any eye contact with the old grouch, but it didn't matter because Vince had all eyes on him.

"I saw kids walking to school about twenty minutes ago," Vince griped. "It's not gonna be the same shit you pulled at Hampton down here. That's a good ten minute walk to that school, so I suggest you be there on time, every morning. Ain't nobody got time be talking to no teachers and no counselors this year. Your momma ain't gonna do it, and I'm damn sholl ain't gonna do it."

Julius simply guzzled down his milk as if Vince wasn't even there. He knew the guy wanted a fight, but he decided it was best not to even follow the old man up. An argument with him would only lead to a bigger squabble between him and his mother in her efforts to keep peace

16

between the two. He understood his mother had enough on her plate with working a full time job and cleaning up behind practically two grown men, than to have to go through another unnecessary war of words with Vince again.

"You can act like you don't see me. You can even act like you don't hear me. But you better damn well remember what I say goes around this here place."

Julius sat his glass in the sink as he cut his eye at Vince. The temptation to spit fire back at his common law stepdad was there, but he reneged. "Later, Ma."

As Julius made his way towards the side door to leave, Vince shot across the room and grabbed him by his arm. "Boy!"

"Vince," Felicia called out, wanting the dispute to end as fast as it started. She grabbed a towel from off the counter to dry her hands and approached the two.

"Man, what's wrong with you?" Julius questioned.

"Don't you ask me what's wrong with me," Vince grunted. "It's gonna be a lot wrong with you, you keep on playing with me, acting like you don't hear me. You gonna make me stomp a mudhole in your deformed looking ass."

"Vince, leave him alone. Please!" Felicia begged.

Vince looked over to Felicia with a scowl as he continued to place his firm clutch on the boy's arm. He looked back at Julius and gave him an inviting smirk, practically daring him to do something as he tightened his grip.

"Get off me!" Julius yelled as he snatched his arm away.

"Oh, I ain't on your ass, yet," Vince warned him, his eyes piercing through the young man like a savage lion on the brink of attacking some unexpected prey in the wilderness. Even though Vince hovered over Julius by an entire foot, the old bully was ready for certain victory. He yearned for the day that Julius would swing back at him. That would be the same day he would unleash severe pain on the teen, the day he'd been attempting to trigger for years. Fortunately for Julius, he never bit.

"Go ahead and head off to school, Julius," Felicia said as she gave her son a small pat on his back directing him towards the door.

Julius stood firm, contemplating smashing Vince in his grungy face a few good times with his notebook, but the chance of him swinging and missing frightened him. Vince's smirk transformed into a chuckle. He knew Julius didn't have enough nerve to make a move, and he rejoiced in that knowledge. Julius pulled his hood over his head and reluctantly left the house, slamming the door behind himself. Vince happily looked on as Felicia stood before him infuriated.

"I thought I told you to leave him alone in the morning."

"Ah, I ain't did nothing to the boy," he said as he waved her off and reclaimed his seat at the table. "He needs to be toughened up a bit anyway. Won't have to be crying about what them people at that school got to say about him all the time."

****

Washington High was a much bigger school than any Julius had attended in the past. Despite the school's notoriously bad reputation, the outside of the institution was well kept and the halls were spotless. He could smell the new paint from the freshly painted walls as he moved through the halls.

The halls were filled with students laughing and joking with each other, just like any school. Some kids were wandering down the long halls, staring up at the room numbers plastered over the door of each room to find the right class. Others stood posted up alongside their lockers as if they didn't have a care in the world. Julius briskly walked down the hallway with his hood covering most of his face as his eyes stayed glued to the floor. No eye contact always meant no problems.

"You gotta take that hood off in the building, son," said a man pointing a walkie-talkie straight at Julius as he approached him from the other end of the congested hallway.

Julius stalled with his movement for a moment as he looked up and made brief eye contact with the stout man. He didn't look like a teacher with his cheap pleated slacks and black sports coat, but he was making demands like he was a figure of authority. Julius thought he was just a hall monitor or somebody, so he quickly swiped his hood from over his head and heeded to the man's request. The man made his way past Julius, and he continued on his way down the hall once he recognized Julius obeyed his command. Julius kept his stride in his own direction, and after realizing the man was well on his way down the hall and not paying him anymore attention, he quickly whipped his hood back over his head. Julius felt naked walking around the school grounds without his hood covering up most of his face. He hated the feeling of people staring, pointing and laughing at him as they did so many times in the past.

Julius strolled into the classroom that was assigned to be his home room. He didn't have to wander around for any of his classes because when his mother signed him up to the school earlier in the summer, he surveyed all the spots most of his classes would be. The only class that wasn't in the same vicinity as the majority of his courses was his art class. His art class was on the other side of the building near the cafeteria.

He made it his business to get into the school's art class over gym. Art was his first love, and although he was in good physical shape, he wasn't very athletic. Art gave him an escape from how he felt about himself on the outside, and it was an opportunity for him to release the beauty he sustained on the inside. Not for anyone else, simply for himself.

Only a handful of students were sitting in the room, and they paid him no attention as he sought out his destination to the desk in the back of the room.

Julius immediately opened his notebook and began working on a sketch of a street hoodlum he had started the night before. With each stroke of his pencil, his mind reflected more and more on Vince. How he longed for his mother to drop Vince and kick his worthless ass to the curb. It pissed him off to see the old man reclining on the sofa each day while his mother worked her butt off to pay the bills without any help from him. It irked him even more because he was too scared and too undersized to put Vince in his place.

"Hey, is anybody sitting here, man?" asked a voice from the desk to his right.

Julius looked up and noticed a frail boy wearing a bright orange polo shirt had claimed the chair beside him.

This shocked him because in all his years of public education, no one had ever sat beside him freely, they'd always have to be assigned the seat. "Nah, nobody sitting there." Julius went back to his artwork and despising Vince.

"You must be new here. I never seen you before," said the boy.

"Yup," he said, not removing his focus from his artwork.

"Well, my name's Trey," said the boy as he extended his fist.

Julius looked up, puzzled by the boy's kindness. He glanced at the boy's hand, dropped his pencil and gave him pound. "Julius."

"Nice to meet you, Julius. What school you coming from?"

"A couple of different spots."

"Your family military?"

"Nah, poor."

The boy chuckled. "I'm familiar with that. Man, that's some smooth artwork you got going on there."

"Yeah," Julius answered, still puzzled by the boy's kindness. The boy had a low, box haircut and was as thin as a dime. He didn't look like a playboy nor a jock, so Julius figured him to be a nerd or some type of outcast. But even nerds and outcasts normally strayed clear from Julius due to his looks.

"I know you gotta be in Mr. Bass's art class with skills like that."

"Yup," Julius answered as a young lady walked in with a couple of girls at the front of the class. The moment he laid eyes on her it was like everything had started to move in slow motion. The small talk Trey was shoveling became mute as his eyes followed the pecan brown tanned girl to her seat. She walked in with two other girls, both were cute, but neither could hold a match to her beauty.

"That's Simone Wilson." Trey's last statement broke through Julius' deaf ears. "Finest chick in the school."

Julius focused back on Trey, "She a cheerleader?"

"Was," Trey answered. "They say she stopped because she wanted to just focus on her books and get ready for college, but she's fine *and* smart as hell. I think she was just trying to stay out of the view of that asshole, Ricky Smith."

"Who's Ricky Smith?"

He chuckled. "Nobody but the pride and joy of Washington High. He's the star basketball player that thinks his shit don't stink."

"Oh, one of those types."

"Yeah, he's bad news man. He wanted her but she didn't want him, and he can't seem to get over it. Dude thinks he owns the place. I can't stand his ass."

Julius takes another glance at the beautiful girl that's managed to captivate his mind in the matter of seconds. He knew he would never have a chance with her, but he couldn't help but think, *what if?*

Chapter 2

Felicia darted off of the porch dressed in her light gray housekeeping uniform with a small purse clutched underneath her arm. Her supervisor had finally given her the call she was waiting on all morning. Although her boss waited until the last possible minute to contact her for the extra hours, he needed for her to come in immediately.

The rusted car door to the '85 Chevy Cavalier barked as she swung it open and jumped in. She was in a panic to get on the road because she knew if she drug her feet, Lance, her slick mouth boss, would quickly disperse those hours he promised her to another housekeeper. As long as he didn't have to do any work and his slots were covered, he didn't care who worked those hours.

She turned the ignition and the engine began to stall. "Oh, not this mess today," she said nervously to herself. She gave the ignition another turn, and it failed to start again. She glanced out of the back passenger window and noticed the city bus was making its way towards the house. A bus stop was positioned on the corner, just two houses down. Although she wasn't very fond of the crowd the city bus attracted on her route, she wasn't above getting on it. When Julius was younger, there was no other alternative for them to get around but public transportation.

She gave the ignition one final try with hopes that she would just get one break today, but the engine failed again. She began beating on the steering wheel, not just because the car wouldn't start, but because she just gave Vince some money to take the car in to have the mechanic check it out last week. Obviously, he didn't do it, because now the car wouldn't start at all, after weeks of it cranking up after a couple of tries.

She glanced at the street from the rear window again and noticed the bus had just left the stop on the corner and was about to pass her.

"Damn it," she said as she grabbed her purse and jumped out of the rusty blue car. "Hey," she yelled as she made an attempt to flag the bus driver down before he passed her.

The bus driver looked directly at her but didn't decrease his speed as he continued the trek down the street. She continued towards the bus. "Hey…. bus driver. Stop, please!" she screamed. The bus passed right by her as if she wasn't even there. "Bus driver, please!" she begged as she began to run behind it. She stopped her pursuit as she realized the bus had increased its speed even more and the gap between her and the vehicle had gotten even greater. The next stop was about a mile down the road, and the bus wasn't going to stop before reaching it. "I know you saw my ass." She shook her head and made her way back home.

Vince was stretched out on his recliner in front of an old wooden television set. He comfortably had a bottle of Budweiser beer in one hand and a Black & Mild cigar in the other. The house was dark as it had no streaks of sunlight coming in as he had thick, dark curtains smothering the windows and thick comforters nailed over the curtains. He had a smile on his face from the shenanigans on the Jerry Springer show, his favorite midday pastime.

"You know you been sleepin' with that girl's sister," he yelled at the television with a chuckle. "I know my ass would. That broad fine as hell!"

The daylight from the outside crept in as Felicia swung the door open. She stopped at the door and looked over to the den as Vince didn't even acknowledge her entry. She slammed the door, but he didn't budge. She sighed and trudged through the den and into the kitchen to grab the lone phone in the house. The phone rested on the wall in the kitchen that was adjacent to the den. She dialed her job as she stood in the doorway, staring at the back of Vince's nappy head.

She couldn't believe he didn't have anything to do all day but sit in front of the television and drink himself in and out of consciousness. It made her skin boil just to see him relaxing, while chuckling at the nonsense on the tube.

Someone picked up on the other end.

"Hello, Lance?"

"Yup," he answered with a high pitched tone.

"This is Felicia…"

"Felicia…" he interrupted. "You were suppose to be here like twenty minutes ago."

"Lance, I know. I'm sorry. My car won't crank and…"

"Hey, tell it to somebody who cares. I've already given those hours to Connie, besides I told you to get that piece of shit car of yours fixed weeks ago. Just make sure you're in here later, when you're scheduled to be." He hung up the phone.

She closed her eyes and angrily gripped the phone to her ear as she was ready to explode in anger. She needed those hours to give her a little breathing room with the bills. She slammed the phone back on the wall and stomped into the den and stood between Vince and the old floor model television.

"I thought I gave you money to take the car to the mechanic," she pouted with her hands on her waist.

"What?" Vince asked, somewhat annoyed, as he tried to look around her in fear of missing something on the television.

She spun around and slapped the power switch off on the television set. "The car won't start, Vince. I gave you some money to take it to a mechanic."

"Ah, yeah, the car," he mumbled as he set his bottle of beer on the floor. "It's the alternator. Don't need to pay no mechanic for that."

"Then why ain't it fixed? I gave you some money to get the thing fixed."

He laughed while running his fingers through his peasy head. "You need more than thirty dollars to get that alternator fixed. Besides, ol' Mason is suppose to come over here this weekend and put one on it from the junkyard for me."

She was lost for words. She didn't even want to ask him what he did with the money because she couldn't handle the dumb explanation he would give her as to why he didn't have it anymore. She just stared at him as he sat dumbfounded. *What happened to the man I fell in love with so many years ago*, she pondered.

"What?" he asked.

She simply shook her head as she retired into the bedroom. His eyes trailed her until she was no longer visible.

"Shit," he expelled from under his breath as he hopped up and flipped the television back on. He swiped up his beer before his bottom hit the recliner and began chuckling at his show again.

****

Julius walked into his art class with a positive outlook on his new school. After this class was over, it was onto lunch and he had managed to go the entire morning without anyone picking on him or bashing on him about his looks. He thought for once maybe his mother was right. Maybe things were going to be different at Washington High.

Once he entered the class he was shocked that the room wasn't setup in a traditional classroom setting. The room was filled with conference tables lined up in a "U" with two chairs at each table. What he suspected to be the teacher's desk resided in the front of the class at the top of the formation.

One thing he always enjoyed about his art classes in the past was the fact that he didn't have to sit next to anybody. It was always just him, his pencil and his art pad–public solitude at its finest.

Julius moved to a table at the back and whipped out his pad. A few other kids began filing in. The art teacher, Mr. Bass, closed the door and looked over the class. He shook his head at the fact there was only five students that reported. There were two students on each side of the room at the first two tables in the front of the room and then there was Julius, sitting in the far back.

"Son, come on up here and sit closer," Mr. Bass requested as he walked in front of his desk and leaned on it before the students. "And take that hood off your head."

Julius broke away from his artwork and looked to the front of the class at the art teacher. Mr. Bass was an older man, maybe nearing his sixties, dark skinned with a completely bald head and a scruffy, graying beard. What stuck out to Julius the most about the instructor was the fact that he only had one good arm. His left arm was severed at the elbow joint.

"An art teacher with one arm," Julius mumbled.

"What's that, son?" Mr. Bass asked.

"Nothing, sir," Julius answered as he swiped his hood from his head and made his way towards the front of the class.

Julius was happy to see his new friend, Trey, was in the class, also. He sat at the desk next to him as Mr. Bass began the normal teacher introductions to the course.

"Hey, Julius, what's up, man?" Trey asked, barely moving his lips. He released his words just low enough for the teacher to not notice.

"Nothing," Julius whispered. "I didn't know you were an artist, too."

"I'm not. It was either this mess, Gym or Home Ec. I don't do dishes, and I don't jump rope," he joked.

"Gentlemen, do you have something you would like to share with the rest of the class," Mr. Bass questioned them.

"No sir," they answered in unison.

"Alrighty then," Mr. Bass replied. After a brief stare down of the boys, he continued on with his rambling.

"How is this dude suppose to be an art teacher with one arm?" Julius whispered.

"I don't know. That's probably why the class is so small. This should be an easy A, though, so I'm not trippin' about it."

"Yo my bad, Mr. Bass," yelled out a tall light skin guy with a huge Kid N' Play box on his head and a part in the front. He slowly eased into the class with his Karl Kani jeans barely hanging onto his butt. "I got lost on my way here."

"Ah, Mr. Nelson," Mr. Bass replied while shaking his head. He expected to see the boy again this year, but he had secretly held out hope the troubled student wouldn't show up at all this semester. "I'm not sure how you could get lost with this being the sixth year of you reporting to my class."

"You know what they say, Mr. Bass, six times is the charm," the boy laughed. "What you put me on blast for like that anyway, Mr. Bass? You got jokes and all."

"Just take your normal seat, son," Mr. Bass directed him to the other side of the class.

"You got it, Mr. Bass," the boy said as he trekked to the desk opposite of Julius on the other side of the room. He looked over to Julius and immediately burst into laughter. "Daaaaamn, Mr. Bass, you got some rough looking cats up in here this year. Boy, you from Uganda somewhere? Man, you got some big ole' lips."

The other classmates snickered as Julius held his head down at the boy's question.

"Boy, haven't I told you to watch your mouth in my class?" Mr. Bass said, furiously. "Just go 'head and get out of my class, right now. I don't have time for your foolishness this year. You're fifteen minutes late anyway!"

"Mr. Bass, what I do? Damn ain't even a curse word," the boy said while holding out his arms, declaring his innocence.

"Boy!"

"Alright, alright, Mr. Bass, I'll chill out. Just be easy. I need to pass this class this time," the boy pleaded. "I pass this year, and you won't see me no more."

Mr. Bass debated for a moment and opted to let the boy stay. "Alright, just sit down and shut your mouth, son. Don't interrupt my class again."

"Thank you, thank you, Mr. Bass," the boy said as he quickly grabbed himself a seat. He looked over to Julius with a big smirk on his face.

Julius knew it was too good to be true. The boy's crack had swiftly brought back memories from his past, from other schools and other bullies. He almost went half the day without anybody making fun of him, and in the blink of an eye, the streak had come to a brisk halt. He slid out a blank sheet of paper and began sketching a new drawing.

After a short introduction of himself and a short list of his expectations of his six students, Mr. Bass handed the class the immediate task of sketching a bowl of fruit he had positioned in the middle of the class.

While the other students favored the simple chore of drawing the bowl of plastic oranges, apples and grapes, Julius had too much love for his craft to be wasting it on emulating a bowl of artificial produce. Julius remembered a page he had tucked away in his notebook, torn out of a hip hop magazine the night before of his favorite rapper, Tupac Shakur, and he began the task of putting an image of him to paper.

"Hey," Trey whimpered. "He told us to draw fruit."

"You can waste your time drawing that mess, but I'm not," Julius replied, not removing his focus from his drawing.

Trey glanced at the torn magazine page and then at Julius' artwork. "Damn, looks just like him—show off."

"Mr. Graves," said Mr. Bass as he hovered over the boys. The old man managed to ease up behind them without either of them noticing.

"Wha–," Julius expelled nervously looking up at his teacher.

"That's the most peculiar drawing of a bowl of fruit I've ever laid eyes on."

"Well, Mr. Bass…"

"Uhm, no need to explain, Mr. Graves. See me after class before you leave."

"Ha ha," laughed Travis Nelson from the other side of the room. "You in trouble now, boy."

"Uh, Mr. Nelson," Mr. Bass yelled at the boy with an angry scowl.

"My bad, Mr. Bass. My bad," the boy answered.

Julius had already sized up the comedic thug several times during the class and figured the boy could take him easily, with his large frame and muscular build, but it still didn't stop him from wanting to sock the brute one good time, with all his snide remarks. He just remembered Vince's warning about not coming up to the school this year for anything, so he did his best to hold his tongue and his temper.

Although Julius rarely won any scuffles against most of his bullies and haters throughout his school tenure, it never stopped him from barking back. With his mom being the only working body in the house, he didn't want to add to her stress level of having to come up to the school and deal with the latest altercation he found himself in. And although Vince constantly made remarks about not coming up to the school for anything he gets into, he never does anyway. It just pissed him off because whenever his mother has to deal with his issues it would most likely cause him to have a late meal. Julius always thought for a man to rarely keep a steady job, Vince always managed to keep a consistent schedule for his laziness.

The bell rang and the students quickly scattered out of the class. Julius slowly gathered his things as he dreaded the reasoning for Mr. Bass wanting to speak with him before he left. He reluctantly stumbled to the front of the teacher's desk.

Mr. Bass had his head down as he thumbed through a binder of papers before him. "Ah, Mr. Graves, that was some fine artwork you were putting together earlier," he looked up at the boy. "Who was that, Snoop Doggy Dogg?"

"No sir, Tupac," Julius replied nervously.

"Oh, the one that's always on the news," the teacher laughed. "Do you always take it upon yourself to set your own lesson plan for your classes, Mr. Graves?"

"No sir, just to be honest with you, I just didn't find drawing some bowl of fruit very interesting."

Mr. Bass smiled and looked over to the fruit, "Yeah, drawing a bowl of fruit should be quite boring for an artist with your skill set, I imagine. That's actually the reason I wanted to speak with you son. Your artwork is exceptionally good."

Julius sucked in huge glob of air and stuck out his chest little from the praise he received from his teacher about his work. He quickly realized the instructor wasn't about to scold him for not doing the assignment he asked of him, and that instantly calmed his nerves.

"I don't know how, but it seems as though you have the basics of art pretty much figured out, young man. I can clearly see that you have an extraordinary gift, so I don't want you to do the same work everyone else will be doing. If you allow me, I will give you a few assignments here and there that I would like for you to complete, but for the majority of our time together, I would like to give you the opportunity to be as creative as you'd like to be and for you to hand in projects that you'd like for me to see."

"Wow, really," Julius asked.

"Yes, really," Mr. Bass answered. "I think you possess a special talent Mr. Graves and I would like to assist you with broadening it. Now by no stretch of the imagination does this mean that I'm providing you with a green light to get lazy and waste time in my class. I expect a newly completed project from you every Friday before you leave this classroom and run off to lunch. If I sense that you are slacking off, or that you are taking this unique opportunity for granted, well then I guess it will be back to drawing boring old fruit for you and trust me, over the years I've acquired an extraordinary collection of artificial fruit bowls. Do you understand?"

"Yes sir, I understand."

"Very well, Mr. Graves. Enjoy the remainder of your day." The old teacher went back to thumbing through his binder.

"Yes sir. Thank you, sir." Julius was ecstatic as he rushed out of the classroom. He couldn't believe he received permission from the teacher to do just about anything he wanted to. The news from Mr. Bass immediately overshadowed the rude remarks made by the class thug earlier.

"So what did the old fart want?" asked Trey as Julius passed him. He stood outside of the door.

"He just told me that I could draw and work on whatever I wanted to. He gave me free reign." They began walking down the crowded hall.

"No shit!"

"Yeah, whatever I want."

"Damn! Must be nice, but with the skills you got, I don't think there's much that old fart can teach you," Trey said. "Oh yeah, don't worry about that guy, Travis Nelson. His dumb ass is damn near twenty years old and rounding out his second term as a senior. Every year it's the same thing, he comes to class for the first few days, and then you may not see him for a couple of months. I don't know why his dumb ass even comes at all to tell you the truth."

They entered the crowded cafeteria and paced to the end of the long lunch line. The cafeteria was packed with students eating food, standing around in different cliques and arguing aloud about sports and a litany of different subjects. Julius surveyed the lunch room and was impressed by how large it was.

He was still hyped up about the news Mr. Bass had given him and the diarrhea of words coming out of Trey's mouth was simply entering into one ear and quickly out of the other. He was too excited to even think about the back story on every high school senior that popped up in the cafeteria that Trey felt the urge to tell him about. Julius always kept to himself, and other people's business never did anything for him.

Out of nowhere Julius felt a hard bump on his shoulder, and his notebook went flying across the floor with his school work and drawings scattered all over the place.

"Outta my way, scrubs," said a tall light skinned student wearing an all black Adidas sweat suit and a large gold herringbone resting around his neck. He had two equally tall guys walking behind him.

"Hey man, what's wrong with you?" Julius questioned him with his fist balled up.

The six feet two tall boy turned around and shoved Julius so hard with both hands, him and Trey went tumbling to the floor.

"You got a problem, lil nigga? You want some of Ricky Smith?" The boy yelled in a fighting stance.

"I don't give a damn who you are. That's my stuff you just knocked all over the place," Julius barked.

Ricky smiled, "Oh, this shit?" He kicked Julius' notebook across the cafeteria floor and even more of Julius' papers and drawings flew out.

"Hey man, what the hell?" Julius tried to get up and charge at the tall bully.

"Julius, Julius, hold up man," said Trey as he pulled Julius back onto the floor with him.

"Bring it, little nigga. Bring it. I need to sock me a nigga today," Ricky said as he bounced around and threw his fist around like a boxer.

"Nah, man, I'm not taking this crap from this dude. I don't know who he think he is." Julius argued while trying to pull away from Trey.

"Let the lil' ugly nigga go, Trey," said one of the two boys standing behind Ricky, laughing at the situation.

"Yo Trey, where you find this ugly nigga from with them big ass Roger Wood sausage lips?" Ricky asked. "This your new homeboy or something? You fighting with this nigga?"

"Nah, nah, never that, Rick. I just met him. Dude's new and all, you know. Just showing him around, that's all."

Julius was shocked by Trey's betrayal and jerked away from him.

"Man, leave that lil nigga alone, and let's get something to eat," said one of the other boys standing behind Ricky. "I don't feel like hearing coach bitchin' about us starting no trouble today. Besides, I'm hungry as hell," he said while rubbing his belly.

"Look here lil' nigga, I'ma do you a solid and not fuck you up today, but if you ever get it in your mind that you want a bout with the champ, that's gonna be your ass," said Ricky.

"Man, whatever," Julius said as he started gathering his stuff from the floor. He kept his eye on the boy while picking up his things, just in case he tried to sneak him.

"Yeah, it's gonna be whatever on your ugly ass," said Ricky as he kicked some more of Julius' papers across the floor. "You better watch it new nigga." Ricky moved through the line, passing by the other students that had all become an audience to the commotion.

Julius was on his hands and knees gathering all of his drawings and school work. Trey bent down on one knee to help him.

"That dude is such a buster, man." Trey whispered from under his breath.

"Nah, man, I don't need your help," Julius said, shunning Trey away from his stuff.

"What's up with you man?" Trey asked. "Why you trippin'?"

"I don't roll with a lot of people, that's all. Especially people like you."

37

"Word?"

"Yeah, word," Julius nodded.

"Alright then," Trey said, standing upright. "Cool with me." He stood up and pushed on through the lunch line.

Julius felt like crying as he gathered his things, but he didn't want to attract any more laughs from the onlookers. All hopes of Washington High being different than all his other schools were finally put to rest. This school was just like all the rest of the schools he attended in the past, full of bullies and people that weren't going to like him just because of his looks. Looks that haunted him every day. Looks that people laughed at, made fun of and didn't want to see. Looks that he, himself, didn't want to see.

The spectacle at lunch had Julius pretty down and he couldn't wait for the school day to end. In his final class for the day, he wandered to the last desk in the class near the back door as usual. He pulled out his drawing of Tupac but he was so down he didn't even feel like doing anything with it. This made him feel even worse because drawing had always been his escape. The times in his life where he couldn't draw had always been his lowest.

It was disheartening and unusual for him to feel the way that he did because he figured by now he'd be used to getting treated the way that he did. There hadn't been one school since kindergarten where he'd caught a break but somehow, secretly, he had hopes that Washington High would be different. That he could go a day without someone not even noticing he wasn't a very attractive guy. That he could just come in, learn and make some genuine friends, just like everyone else. He felt foolish for collecting those hopes because every year he gathered those same foolish aspirations, and every year he found himself disappointed. He knew no one would ever try to get to know him, because they just couldn't get pass how he looked.

He looked up and noticed the pretty girl from his homeroom class earlier had walked in. Simone Wilson, he remembered Trey had mentioned her name. Light brown skin, long dark hair and flawless face, she was a living beauty.

She was making her way to the back of the class also, and his heart began beating like a snare drum the closer she got. For some reason odd to him, she smiled at him. He nervously bowed his head, not acknowledging her greeting. Not looking anyone in the eye was a common practice he developed over the years. Eye contact always led to conversation or chaos, and he wasn't a fan of either. He just wanted to be left alone.

She sat at the desk in front of him and silently waited for the class to begin. She smelled as sweet as a bouquet of roses, and her being so close to him made him uncontrollably nervous. His hands were trembling immensely, and he couldn't get his right leg to stop jumping like a woodpecker's beak. He felt like a complete idiot for not saying hello, or just smiling back at her.

Truthfully, he never had any confidence in his smile. He remembered a class mate named George Sprewell in second grade, that stood in line behind him as they waited to take school pictures. George told him that he had an ugly ass smile with his jumbo lips, and his mother would be ashamed to put any picture up in her house with such an ugly smile just before it was Julius' turn to get his picture taken. He told Julius he had the ugliest smile he'd ever seen and probably ever would see in a million years. Needless to say, Julius didn't smile on his picture, no matter how hard the photographer tried to get him to. He never smiled on any picture after that day, and rarely smiled at all in public. George's hateful words always found their way in the back of his mind whenever he felt relaxed enough to smile. Any slight twitch of his lips to smile would quickly vanish.

His concentration on her beauty quickly yielded when he caught a glimpse of Ricky Smith strolling into the classroom, yelling back at someone in the hall.

"Ah, shit," Julius mumbled under his breath as he flipped his hood over his head and slouched down in his chair.

"Simone… Simone," he called out as he made his way to the back and sat in the desk next to her. Ricky's eyes were so transfixed on the girl, he didn't even look Julius' way.

"Hello, Ricky," she answered reluctantly.

Julius could hear frustration in her voice when she spoke to him. He could tell she didn't care for the dirt-bag neither and that made her even more attractive to him.

"I called you all summer to take you out, and you didn't even answer a brother phone call one single time," Ricky told her. "Now, you know that ain't right."

"I've been busy. Real busy," she replied.

"Yeah, what's up with that? How come?"

"Been studying."

"Studying in the summer?" he laughed. "Who does that?"

"Ricky, everybody doesn't have a guaranteed scholarship for basketball."

"Damn girl, you can't make a little time for me?"

"And who are you suppose to be?"

Julius couldn't help but to let out a slight chuckle at her response. Unfortunately, it was enough for Ricky to take his attention off of Simone for a second and notice him sitting behind her.

"The fuck…" Ricky said as he looked back at Julius and bent down slightly to see his face. "What the hell are you doing back there? Your nosey ass. You find something funny monster boy? You laughing at me?"

Julius kept his head down and didn't respond. He was mad at himself for getting noticed by Ricky, and he immediately realized he'd just opened up a serious can of worms. People like Ricky loved to do wild things for attention, and what better way to get that attention than to punk out the new guy.

"Leave that boy alone, Ricky," she said.

"If I leave him alone will you let me take you out?" He turned to her with a smile.

"No!" she fired back while rolling her eyes in disgust.

"No? Then I'm 'bout to kick his lil' ass," Ricky said as he started to get up out of his chair.

Julius closed his eyes and tensed up, awaiting the boy's first blow. He wasn't about to hit back, not on the first day. He had too many first day brawls in the past, and he knew his mother would be disappointed if she had to run up to the school for another one.

"Good afternoon, class," said the teacher as he walked in. The sight of the teacher gave Julius a huge sigh of relief as he opened up one eye. He knew Ricky was the star basketball player for the school, and he wouldn't jeopardize his position on the team by starting a fight in front of the teacher.

"You're real lucky, lil' nigga," Ricky whispered to Julius with a mean stare. He turned away from him when the teacher started talking.

Simone turned around for a moment and gave Julius another smile. He had no idea what the smile was for, and he couldn't believe it happened. No girl had ever smiled at him before, and she did it twice in one day. Despite his heart racing a mile a minute from the near beat down he almost received, her acknowledgement of him blew his mind.

"Welcome to American History. My name is Mr. Rawls," the partially bald, Caucasian teacher announced. The frail teacher looked like a carefully designed nerd with his thick bifocals and his light beige suit jacket with dark brown elbow pads. He even wore a pen protector in his coat.

"Young man, can you please take your hood off?"

Julius didn't answer.

"Oh, you don't want to see what's under that hood, Mr. Rawls," Ricky joked.

The class laughed.

"Young man, I'm talking to you," Mr. Rawls said with a bit more bass in his voice. "I'm going to need for you to take that hood off right now."

Julius continued to act as if he didn't hear the man's request. He could feel the eyes of the other students zeroing in on him. He didn't want to take off his hood, but he knew if he didn't, there was going to be trouble. Trouble at this point, with Ricky Smith dropping an ensemble of jokes, he was willing to accept.

"I don't know if you're hard of hearing or what," said the teacher as he raced towards Julius. "But you, sir, will not sit in my class while wearing this hoodie like you're out on the street corner somewhere. This is a classroom, mister." The teacher flipped Julius' hood from over his head. Julius swiftly jumped up in a fighting stance, as if he was ready to pound on the teacher.

"DAAAAMN, you ugly, boy!" Ricky Smith yelled. The entire class burst into laughter behind him. Everyone was laughing, except Simone and Mr. Rawls.

The teacher stood in front of Julius, his face turning red with both fist balled up against his waist. He angrily waited to see if Julius was going to swing at him or not.

Julius looked over the laughing class, where other students were making their own hurtful remarks, some on the floor with their jeers as others pointed at him while clutching their bellies. His heart sank. It was one of the most embarrassing moments he'd ever experienced. He scooped up his notebook and stormed out through the back door.

He moved so swiftly he didn't even notice that some of his drawings had managed to slip out of his notebook. Drawings Simone picked up and stood amazed by the fine detail of his work. She shuffled through his sketches of Martin Luther King, Michael Jordan and the Notorious B.I.G. All of the drawings were spitting images of their real life counterparts. It was as if she was staring at real life photos that were somehow transformed into black and white pencil sketches.

"Alright class, settle down with all of this nonsense and horseplay," said the teacher as he swiftly paced to the front of the class. "Any more profanity in my class will lead to a trip to Mr. Benson's office, even if your name is Ricky Smith." The teacher issued Ricky a stern look.

Ricky simply rolled his eyes at the geeky looking teacher as he slouched down his chair. He knew the teacher wasn't going to do anything to him, and could care less about his harmless threats. In Ricky's mind, he was the principal of Washington High.

"I'm not playing with you people this year. You come to school to learn, not to joke and play," said Mr. Rawls.

Simone gathered her things and eased out of the back door with Julius' artwork. She knew nothing about him but she had to see if he was okay. When she walked out of the classroom she quickly surveyed both ends of the hallway to figure out which end Julius walked down. Then she noticed him stomping down the far end of the hall that led to the back of the school with his hood over his head. "Hey!" she yelled as she began to follow his trail. She was surprised he was still in the building by the way he dashed out of the classroom.

Julius heard her call, but he didn't bother to turn around to see who was calling him. He figured it was just someone Mr. Rawls had sent out to tell him to come back into the classroom. A request he would surely decline this day. He had enough of the basketball phenom, Ricky Smith, for one day, and enough of people making jokes about how he looked.

He wanted to burst out crying, as he was finding it extremely difficult to hold in his tears, but his pride kept them contained. He just wanted to leave and never come back. The burden of having his face was getting to be just too much. At home and school, he was getting badgered around the clock. He heard the girl's call again. Closer this time.

"Hey," cried Simone as she grabbed his arm.

"What?" he yelled as he spun around.

"You dropped these," she said as she held up his drawing. "They fell out of your notebook when you ran out of class. I was just trying to give them back to you."

He glanced at the drawings then back at her. Even though he was upset, he couldn't help but admire her attractiveness. She was the prettiest girl he'd ever laid eyes on. "Keep 'em," he said as he turned around and began walking away.

"Hey, wait!" she said as she tried to grab his arm again. He snatched his arm away and kept walking. She tried to grab at him once more but only snipped at his sleeve, "Hey, stop!"

"What?" he angrily snapped back around.

"What's wrong with you? I'm just trying to be nice to you."

He angrily flipped up his hood and yelled, "Do you see my face? Do you see…this...this ugly face?" he burst into tears while pointing at his face.

She was speechless. His outburst made her feel like crying herself. She was so sad for him, and she didn't know what to do to ease his pain.

"I'm so ugly." His words cracked from the back of his throat. "I'm so ugly, man!" He kicked a locker with the back of his heel and slid down the locker with his back. The flood gates were opened, and he couldn't control those tears he had so passionately tried to contain. He was balled up on the floor with his head buried in his knees.

She looked around to see if anyone was coming. "Hey…hey, looks aren't everything." It was the only thing she could think of saying. It felt stupid coming from her lips, but it was all she could come up with. She felt the need to say something.

"Just go away, man," he replied. "Just go away."

She didn't have any answers and she knew standing over him was only making things worse, so she reluctantly abided by his request. She slowly walked away, looking back at him several times until she returned to the classroom. She paused and looked at him down the hall one final time. He hadn't moved an inch, remaining balled up on the floor against the lockers.

Chapter 3

She pushed her laundry cart full of dirty sheets to the doorway of the hotel's laundry room where she was greeted by one of the men that worked the area. He thanked her and rolled the cart back into the room.

"Thanks," said Felicia. She stretched her back as she walked towards an older co-worker that was sitting on a bench outside of the women's locker room. "Girl, they know they got some nasty rich people staying in these rooms."

"Fee, you ain't never lied, child," said the woman. Her name was Barbara. She was an older lady. She looked up at Felicia while she rubbed her feet. "Nasty ass people."

"I just did a room on the thirteenth floor that had used condoms scattered all over the floor. You would think some of these jerks would have enough decency to throw some mess like that in the trash or the toilet. Nobody wants to touch no crap like that, not even with gloves. Disgusting!"

"They don't care, baby," she laughed. "They know they got somebody cleaning up behind their asses, and that's why they do it. Trifling ass people. That's why I don't never smile with any of 'em. I just do my thang with my head down and keep it movin'. Don't talk to me because I ain't got nothin' to say back to your ass."

"I know that's right, girl." The work calendar posted on the outside of her manager's office caught her eye. "Is that the new schedule," she asked.

"Yeah, child. His silly ass just put it up about an hour ago. Don't go in there trying to kick his ass after you see it, though."

"What?" When her eyes closed in on her name she became infuriated. "Oh hell, no!" She stormed into her managers office, slamming his door behind herself. "Lance, what the hell are trying to prove?" she yelled.

He was lounging in his chair with his feet kicked up on his desk. He had his office phone up to his ear. "...Faison, I'll call you back in a minute, hun." He removed his feet from the small desk and slammed the phone down. "Do you know how to knock? I was on a call."

"Why'd you cut me down to three days?" she asked, totally disregarding his question.

"You have transportation issues–duh! I can't rely on you to be here when your piece of shit car don't start."

"Lance, when have I ever missed a day? Huh? When?"

"How often are you on time?"

"If I'm late, it's only by a few minutes. No more than thirty."

"Late is late, and last week you were late by at least an hour four times. Four times, Felicia. You're lucky I don't fire your ass."

"And before that, how often have I been late or even called in? Whenever you need somebody to fill a shift, I'm always the one you can call."

"It doesn't matter. It only takes a few days to form bad habits. In this business time is money, so until you get a more reliable means of transportation, I'm cutting your hours. When things don't get done around here, it's my ass on the line, and I'm going to do what's best for my ass, sorry. I suggest you do the same."

"Lance, I can assure you I won't be late, again," she promised him while hovering over his desk with both hands. The wells of her eyes began tearing up. The back of her mind ran through bill after bill she wouldn't be able to pay if he didn't give her back her hours. "I need my hours. I'm the only one working right now, and I can't afford to have my check to be any less than it already is."

Lance repositioned himself in his leather chair and kicked his feet back onto his desk. He was a young, skinny white male, in his mid thirties with thinning brown hair. He loved seeing his female workers nervous and on edge. It made him feel powerful. He enjoyed it and gave him a cheap thrill. He took a moment to take what she had told him into consideration. "I'm going to give you back your days because I'm nice like that. But if you so much as come in a second late, I'm going to fire you. Do I make myself clear?"

She nodded while wiping her eyes. "Yes... Yes, I can handle that."

"Now get out of my office and clean yourself up."

She grabbed the door handle.

"One second, Felicia," he added.

She hurried out of his office and leaned backwards on his door with her arms rolled. She just had the scare of her life. Thoughts of not being able to pay her rent and being out on the streets again raced through her mind even after her supervisor agreed to give her back her hours.

****

Julius rushed through the front door and didn't even notice the dead weight laying on the sofa that he referred to as his common law stepdad. He marched into his bedroom, slammed the door behind himself and threw his books on his desk. He plowed onto the bed and buried his face into his pillow. He felt awful. Starting from the embarrassing run-in at lunch with Ricky Smith, all the way to his History teacher bringing him out in front of the entire class, it just wasn't a good day.

When Julius' door slammed, Vince's head popped up like a deer's head springing up over some underbrush in the wilderness. He awakened from his long slumber with his eyes red like a fire engine and a splattering of dried saliva etched around the corners of his mouth. He looked up at the clock on the wall and knew the only person coming in at this time would be Julius. Rubbing his eyes, he roamed down the hall to Julius' bedroom door and eased the door open.

The small room had almost every inch of its wall covered with sketches Julius had drawn since he began his hobby as an artist as a kid. The only parts of the walls that wasn't covered by his artwork had an assortment of torn out of magazine photos of Ice Cube, 2Pac, Biggie and Snoop Dogg.

"What the hell wrong with you?" Vince mumbled from the door. His legs were still wobbly from just waking up. "You ain't been fightin' at that damn school already, have you?"

"No," Julius answered with his head still stuffed in the pillow.

"Better not! I done told you I ain't got no time for that shit this year."

"What you worried about it for? It's not like you ever come to the school anyway."

"You right, and I ain't gonna start neither. But when your momma gotta go down there and have to deal with your shit, that's taking her time away from me, and I don't like it."

"Whatever, man."

"Whatever," he said to himself with a giggle. "Boy, you gettin' to have a smart ass mouth. Since your ass so smart, why don't you go down to that damn mini mart down the street and get me a pack of cigarettes. Some Newport 100s."

Julius gave him a brief glance. "Why you can't go get 'em?"

"Because I'm telling your ass to get 'em."

"Man, I got homework to do."

"You do your goddamn homework after you get my damn cigarettes, smart ass. Now, I'm tryin' to be nice about the shit. I'm not gonna ask a-damn-gain!"

He rolled over on his side and stared at Vince as he stood leaning in the doorway with his arms folded. The sight of the man sickened him. Every time he looked at Vince only one thing came to mind–what did his mother see in him? He knew she could do much better.

He wanted to tell him to go straight to hell, but he just couldn't gather up enough gall to say it. So he cowered, as he always did with Vince. He jumped off the bed and stood in front of him. He looked away from him, careful to not make any eye contact with him. "Alright."

Vince stared the boy down with a demented smile. He couldn't stand Julius, and he understood the feeling was mutual. He knew the boy didn't have enough balls to fight him. It brought him extreme pleasure to just pick and pick at the boy, pushing the boy's buttons, knowing good and well he was just going to take it. "Your momma ain't here to protect your ass now. You might want to watch the shit you say to me and how you say it. Once I get up on a nigga's ass, it's haaaaard to get me off."

"It's 'bout to get dark. Can I just get the money," he asked as he held out his hand.

"I should make your ass pay for it, but I know your ass ain't got no money." Vince dug into his pocket and dropped a crumbled up twenty dollar bill in his palm. "And bring me back all my change too, nigga. I know how much I'm supposed to get back."

"I'm not even old enough to buy cigarettes, man."

"Boy, ain't nobody i.d. for no mutha fuckin' cigarettes. Besides, you're a smart guy, you'll figure something out if they do. Now go get my shit before you make me mad." He shoved Julius down the hallway.

He didn't want to do anything for the man and he especially didn't like him pushing on him the way that he did. He was so enraged by the old man's bullying tactics that he punched the wall. His reaction triggered a chuckle from Vince.

"Gone and swell up and beat that wall's ass, 'cuz you sholl can't beat mine."

Julius stormed out of the front door. He went to slam the screen door, but Vince caught it and stood in the doorway as he stomped off of the steps and onto the sidewalk.

"And don't take all fuckin' day either, smart ass," Vince yelled.

He flipped his hood over his head and started his journey to the corner mart. After he took a moment to think about it, he figured a good walk could make him feel a little better anyway. His greatest fear was one day getting so fed up with Vince, he would snap and swing at him and do his best beat his ass, but his even greater fear after that would be to unsnap in the middle of snapping and having Vince beat him into a coma.

Rumor had it, Vince was a real bad dude back in the day, and he loved a good fight. Although he was currently a practicing couch potato and did some heavy drinking at times, he somehow managed to stay in good shape. Julius thought it must've been good genetics or something because he never saw him working out, unless you considered lifting a Budweiser bottle from his knee to his mouth exercise.

Other than a weekly push or shove, Vince never struck him nor his mother to his knowledge, but the threat was constantly there. He figured the only reason Vince never really struck him was because he knew that it would be the final straw that broke the camel's back, and that his mother would finally leave his good for nothing ass once and for all.

As he continued his trek down the worn down sidewalk, his mind skated onto things other than his normal quarrels with Vince. His thoughts quickly found its way back to his first day at Washington High. While thinking about the school he became upset and baffled at the same time. He was angry at the fact that he had not one but two run-ins with that jerk, Ricky Smith, and he was also baffled as to why the cute cheerleader chick had come out to check on him. No one ever bothered to check on how he felt about anything, let alone a gorgeous female. He was just so embarrassed that he broke down and lashed out at her.

"Well, well, well, if ain't black Picasso himself," said a voice as he approached the walkway to the corner mart.

It was Travis Nelson sitting on a stack of milk crates outside of the entrance. He was standing with a group of older men, all gripping brown bags he assumed to be alcoholic beverages.

Julius couldn't believe his luck in actually running into another bully. This time outside of school. He had come to the corner store several times since they moved down the street, and never saw Travis there before. He ignored the boy and grabbed the door handle to the store's entrance as another customer was exiting the place.

"Damn, you're one ugly mother fucker. Do you know that?" Travis got up and walked towards him.

The older men laughed, one of them even went as far as to yell out, "Leave that young buck alone, man. You always fuckin' with people."

Julius continued to ignore Travis as he entered the store.

"Hey! I'm talking to you," Travis said as he followed Julius into the mart.

Julius dug into his pocket and pulled out some change and started counting up some quarters as he made his way to the back of the store, towards the beverage section. The store had extremely narrow aisles and was consumed with more alcoholic beverages than any other products.

"You hear me, dude? I was talking to you."

"What, man, what? Dang! Yeah, I heard you. I'm ugly, I'm ugly, I'm ugly. I hear that every single day of my life. Say something I haven't heard. What do you want?"

Travis stood frozen. He was surprised the boy actually spoke up for himself. "Ah, man I was just playin' around, damn. You don't have to get all sensitive."

"And that's funny to you right? Picking on somebody that ain't did crap to you. You don't even know me." Julius shook his head, opened up the cooler door and grabbed a juice.

He walked right pass Travis without saying another word. Travis eyes trailed Julius to the line. He grabbed himself a bag of chips and took a place behind Julius in line.

Julius could feel the boy behind him as he quickly remembered his sole reason for coming to the store. He surveyed the cashier. He was a slender man that appeared to be of Indian descent. The man carried a bit of a frown on his face and didn't speak to any of the customers he checked out at the register. Judging by his unfriendly demeanor to the customers in front of him, Julius didn't expect the odds of the man selling him some cigarettes to be very good.

When it was his turn at the register, Julius sat his juice on the counter and looked over to the selection of cigarettes beside the register. As he stood nervously, the cashier stared at him with his unfriendly scowl. He knew Travis was behind him, and he didn't want to be embarrassed by the rejection he felt was certain, but he had to do what he had to do.

"Can I get a pack of Newport 100s?"

The cashier glanced over to the cigarettes and back at Julius. "Let me see some I.D." The man requested with a heavy foreign accent.

"I.D.?" Julius asked, trying to act stupid.

"Yes, I.D., I.D. You know what I'm talking about."

"Ah man, I don't have it on me," he said patting his pockets.

"No I.D., no cigarettes, brother. A dollar six for the drink."

"Come on, man," Julius pleaded.

"Nope, rules are rules. You don't even look old enough to buy tobacco in the first place."

"Shit," said Julius.

"Man , you know you're not old enough to buy them damn cigarettes," Travis laughed. "Move the line."

Julius didn't want to get him started again. He handed the cashier the change for his drink and slowly walked out of the exit. He knew Vince was going to be pissed. He looked over to the group of older guys that were standing at the front of the building and thought about asking one of them to buy the cigarettes for him, but he didn't know any of them and feared they'd take his money and run. They were all alcoholics and drug users, and they were not to be trusted. His neighbors warned him and his mother that a friendly smile was a deadly smile in this neck of the woods and to keep friends to a minimum.

Vince never jumped on him before, but coming back without his money and the cigarettes would guarantee Vince would do his best to put his foot in his ass. He started walking back home, dreading the argument that ensued ahead.

"Hey," he heard Travis yelling at him.

Not this dude again, he thought. "What?" he answered angrily.

Travis ran up to him and threw him a pack of cigarettes. The pitch caught Julius off guard as he nearly dropped the pack of smokes.

"You don't look like you smoke. Who you getting those for?"

"My momma's boyfriend," Julius replied.

"That nigga don't know you're not old enough to buy cigarettes?"

"Yep, he knows. He doesn't give a damn, though." Julius pulled the twenty out of his pocket that Vince had given him earlier. "You got some change?"

Travis shook his head. "Nah, don't worry about it. I figured I owe you that much. Crackin' on you and all."

"Thanks."

"I put in a word to Savit back there, if you need to buy some more next time. He got you. You're a new face, and he didn't trust you like that."

"Thanks," Julius said as he held up the pack of cigarettes and continued his walk back home. He thought it was odd the guy would bash him so freely and then turn around and look out for him the way that he did. Nevertheless, he was certainly ecstatic that he did what he did. The gesture was sure to make his night a whole lot more relaxing by not having to hear Vince's grumblings.

****

Felicia eased into Julius' room with a small bag of art supplies. The room was partially lit by the low watt lamp on his desk. She sat the bag on the desk and took a seat on the edge of his bed. He was fast asleep on his back, but once Felicia planted a gentle kiss on his forehead his eyes batted open.

"Hey, Mom," he mumbled.

"Hey, baby," she replied. "I didn't mean to wake you."

"I..I just dosed off. I just got finished doing my homework."

"You need a haircut," she said as she ran her hand through his nappy, mini afro. "I asked you to get one last week, before school even started."

"I know, Ma. I'm not really feeling any of these barbershops around here."

"Well, I do want it cut. I gave you the money last week, so that's what I expect."

"I will, Ma."

She smiled, "How was your first day?"

When she brought up school, he quickly thought back to how horrible it was. Sleep temporarily removed thoughts of the disastrous day from his mind. "Well, Mom, school was school. It wasn't good at all."

"I'm sorry, son," she rubbed his cheek. "You already know well enough that people are going to say things, and some are even going to try to do things. Just keep your focus on what it needs to be on and let them teachers handle any problems you might have with any other students. That's what those teachers are there for."

"Yeah, the teachers." He rolled over to his side, opposite of her. "Night, Ma."

She could only imagine what he goes through on a daily basis. She was privy to knowing the harsh names and mean things other kids had said to him in the past because of how he looked, but in her eyes he was her beautiful baby boy. It didn't matter what anyone else thought.

She left the room and was met outside of the room door by Vince.

"What a nigga gotta do to get some pussy 'round here," he said as he grabbed her wrist while making an attempt to kiss her on her neck.

She slid away from his lips, his breath reeking of alcohol. "Get a job," she said while snatching her arm away. She pressed on down the hall to begin her nightly chore of cleaning up the place.

"Damn, it's been six months girl," he said, his speech slurring. "Ain't good for a man to do without for that long. Shit!"

Chapter 4

As soon as Julius entered the art class he handed Mr. Bass the sketch he had completed the night before. He knew the work wasn't due until Friday, but he couldn't wait for the teacher to see his first completed assignment.

The teacher slid his glasses on and took a good look at the sketch. It was a drawing of a little black boy sitting on some cement steps with an umbrella over his head as it poured down raining. Julius eagerly awaited the teacher's response. He tried his best to read his facial expression as he stood before him.

"My," he started as he looked up at Julius. "This is one of the best pieces of work I've ever seen in my twenty-seven years of teaching. You are a very talented artist, Mr. Graves."

"Thank you, Mr. Bass," he smiled. After getting his desired response, he headed for his desk.

"Oh, Mr. Graves, I almost forgot," Mr. Bass stopped him. He held out a sticky note for Julius to retrieve. "Principal Benson, stopped by this morning. He asked that you would come to his office as soon as you got here. He's expecting you as we speak."

"For what," Julius questioned as he grabbed the small yellow paper with his name written on it.

"He didn't say. He just asked for you to report to his office once you arrived here. So run along and see what he wants, son. We're discussing different shading techniques today, and with artwork like this," he pointed at the drawing that was sitting on his desk. "You aren't going to miss anything important."

"Okay," Julius reluctantly responded as he exited the classroom.

Whatever Principal Benson wanted, he was hoping it didn't require his mother having to come up to the school and getting him out of it. He figured it must've had something to do with the altercation in his History class at the end of the day. Whatever the problem was, it had his heart beating a mile a minute.

He entered the office and approached the desk of the office secretary. She was a chubby, little lady with a mix of graying and dark brown hair. She wore thick glasses with gold eyeglass ropes hanging from each side of her face.

"I'm here to see Mr. Benson."

"Office to your right," she said, not even looking up.

He strolled to the office door and gently knocked. "Come on in," was Mr. Benson's response from the other side of the door.

Julius slowly walked in. He was shocked to discover that the principal was the man that told him to take his hood off in the hall the day before. He was standing at a window behind his desk, gazing outside through his blinds.

"Have a seat, young man," he pointed to the leather chair that sat in front of his long, oak desk. As he took a seat behind his desk, the principal said, "Julius Graves."

"Yes, sir."

He gave Julius a cold stare, like he was trying to figure him out. The stare down the principal issued him made him feel extremely uncomfortable. There was an uneasy silence in the room while he grabbed a thick green folder that was sitting on the edge of his desk and thumbed through it. He flipped through a few pages and looked up at Julius again. He repeated the process after every few pages he turned.

Julius sat nervously as his mind rambled away at about a million different things the chubby, brown skinned man was focusing in on those papers. He sported a neatly shaven goatee and beard, with a shiny bald head that had a nickel-sized light reflection bouncing off of it that Julius couldn't seem to take his eyes off of.

"I remember you," the man said as he closed the folder and flicked it over to the side of his desk. "You're that kid in the hall that I had to tell to take that darn hood off yesterday, aren't you?"

"Yes sir."

The man gave Julius a quick look over, "You wear hoodies everyday?"

"Yes sir."

He shook his head. "Don't walk around in my school wearing a hoodie over your head again. You understand?"

"Yes sir."

Mr. Benson dealt Julius another strong look as he twisted his lips. "Julius, I called you in here because we need to have an understanding. Now I pulled your file, and your grades look satisfactory to say the least, but it seems that you have an irresistible knack for getting into trouble from time to time. Your file is overrun with multiple incidents. A scuffle here, a scuffle there." He leaned back in his chair and scooted around in it for comfort. "Mr. Rawls told me about what went on in his class yesterday, and I feel the need to address it right away."

Julius took a big gulp as the fear of being suspended flashed through his mind.

"What happened yesterday can't and will not happen again," he continued. "If you do not feel the need to abide by the rules and regulations of this institution for learning, then it will become apparent that you do not feel the need to get a quality education at this school. I mean, let's be honest, despite your problems at other schools in the past, you're still a senior. No one needs to hold your hand, and at this point, no one should have to instruct you on how to behave in a classroom. I don't tolerate the foolishness here, Mr. Graves."

Julius focused in on his lips as he awaited his suspension length to be expelled from the man's mouth at any moment. The man sat up and placed both his arms on his desk.

"I worked too hard to clean this school up, son, and I will not have some new thug come in and screw up the very environment I'm trying to create. I got my eye on you," he said while pointing at Julius. "I want you to see this as your lone warning. As long as you are on this school's premises, you will keep that hood off your head. If I have to talk to you about anything at all, especially about wearing those ugly hoodies over that head of yours in my school again, the penalty will be severe. Do we have an understanding, son?"

"Yes sir."

"Good," he nodded. "Now that we both have an understanding of what's expected of you during your stay here at Washington High, you can return to your class."

"Thank you, sir," Julius responded as he held in his relief for not getting suspended. He got up and made his way towards the exit.

"Mr. Graves," Principal Benson called out.

"Yes sir," Julius answered with his hand on the doorknob.

"Don't disappoint me," he added with a straight face.

"I won't sir." He left the office feeling like a ton of bricks had been removed from his shoulders. The idea of being suspended on the second day of school sent shockwaves through his body.

****

Flex slowly paced himself behind the filthy garbage truck as it crept through the neighborhood. Each time the truck stopped, he grabbed a dumpster and attached it to the grapple to let the trash compactor do its thing.

"Flex!" was the call from a house he'd just passed. He turned around to see Vince jogging down the sidewalk towards him.

"Hold on," he said, calling from the truck to stop. "Hey nigga, where the hell you been hiding? Boss man been trying to track your ass down for weeks. Say if you don't come back soon he gonna fire your black ass."

"Ah, fuck him. His punk ass," said Vince. "My woman taking care of my ass."

"Word? You got it like that?" He looked towards the front of the truck and yelled, "Vince say he got his old lady taking care of his stank ass."

"That's what I'm talking 'bout," said a raspy voice from inside of the truck. "Gone 'head, Vince."

"Yeah, nigga. She wash my clothes, fix me breakfast every damn morning, cook my ass dinner and givin' it up. I'm living like a goddamn king. What the hell I wanna rush back to a dingy ass garbage truck for? Tucker ain't paying nobody shit."

"Say now, you say she doing all that and giving it up, too?"

"And givin' it up! Nightly and frequently, nigga."

"Oooooohhweee, you're a bad man, Vince. How can a nigga be like you?"

"You gotta put their ass in their place. That's what you gotta do first," he nodded. "Can't be no old scary nigga like your ass, that's for sho."

"Man, hell with you, Vince." Flex laughed, "I try some shit like that with my old lady and that bitch will probably kill my stankin' black ass. Nigga wake up with his drawers on fire."

He leaned into Flex and whispered, "Anyway, you got some more of that shit?"

"What, weed?"

"No, no, that other stuff. You know what the hell I'm talkin' about, nigga."

"Ohhh, that other stuff," he chuckled. "Oh, you want some of that candy."

"Yeah, nigga, pipe down with your loud ass." He looked around to see if anyone was paying them any attention. "This is my neighborhood. I don't want everybody to be knowing my business."

"My fault. My fault," he chuckled. "Well, um, I got some, but it's my own supply."

"Nigga, you act like I ain't never went in on some shit with you. What you talking about, your own supply?"

"Ah, nigga, you always bringing up old shit. Nigga, I know. Come on down around seven. The old lady going off to play bingo tonight. She'll be gone for a few hours. We'll hit it then."

"Alright." They shook on it.

"Seven o'clock, nigga. Seven o' clock. 'Cuz you're an ole un-prompt nigga."

"Yeah, yeah, I heard you the first time."

"Let's go," said Flex as he jumped on the back of the garbage truck and slapped the back of it with the side of his fist. The truck began moving down the neighborhood.

****

Julius sat at the table by himself. As he gazed through the window in the back of the lunch room, he was stuck in a trance with a group of students standing outside.

As he chomped on his chicken sandwich, he wondered what it would be like to be one of the them. One of the cool people. How it felt to be liked and admired. To look someone in the eyes while passing by and getting met with a smile.

It really didn't bother him that no one ever offered to sit with him at lunch since he started high school. Over the years he'd gotten adjusted to the solitude, and often looked forward to it. However, it didn't stop his fascination with being popular–just for a day.

"Anybody sitting here?" asked a voice. His chewing stopped. His eyes trailed their way up a black shirt with a Chicago Bulls logo splattered across it. It was Simone, and she was standing across from him holding her lunch tray. Surprised, he mindlessly nodded. "Good," she said. She took the seat across from him.

He looked left to right and all around to see if someone had put her up to sitting with him. He didn't notice anyone paying him any mind, but he remained suspicious of the girl.

"So, where did you learn to draw like that?" she asked as she began digging into her salad.

"Huh? What?" he murmured.

"Draw," she said as she pointed at his notebook at the center of the table. "Where did you learn to draw like you do?"

"Oh," he glanced at his notebook, still baffled by the girl's presence. "I taught myself."

"Wow, that's great. I've never seen anyone draw like that in person before. You really have a great gift."

"Thanks. Thank you."

"Are you planning to go to art school after you graduate?"

"Uhm, no."

"Why not? You could probably get a good job with your talents. You could become a cartoonist or something like that, I don't know."

He nodded, "Never thought about it." He began eating his sandwich again as his heartbeat began to slow down to a more relaxed rate.

"You know, he's hardly in class this time of year," she said.

"Who?"

"Ricky."

"Oh, that guy."

She rolled her eyes while shaking her head at the simple thought of the boy, "He's just stupid. You really can't pay him any mind. He thinks he's God's gift to the world because he's the star player on the Varsity team, but in reality, he really needs to work on his jumper and pass the ball a lot more."

Julius chuckled. "I guess you're a sports fanatic."

"Bulls fan for life," she pointed at her Bulls shirt with a giggle. "Who do you like?"

"No one really. Not a big sports fan."

"You're missing out. With Jordan coming back this season, his first full season back since baseball, I know the

Bulls are gonna take it all the way again. Never mind that fluke playoff exit last season," she said, closing with a frown.

"Wow, you're in it deep."

"Yup," she said. "So what's your name?"

"It's Julius."

"Hey, Julius," she said as she held out her hand. "I'm Simone. Nice to meet you."

"Hey, Simone," he said as he shook her hand. As she continued to talk about her favorite team he couldn't help but notice the calming feeling he had around her. He realized he didn't feel on edge with her.

On the other side of the cafeteria, Ricky stood in line next to one of his teammates, Tim.

"Dag, that ugly cat must got hella' game," Tim said as he nudged Ricky's arm and nodded his head toward Julius. "Looks like he pulled Simone in just two days. Your ass couldn't do it with a year and half," he laughed.

"What the hell?" Ricky said as he gazed over at the couple. "Shut the hell up, nigga." He gave Tim an angry stare that quickly wiped the smile on his face away. He set his attention back to Julius and Simone. "I don't understand this shit. What the hell is she doing with that ugly ass scrub with all the game I've been throwing at her?"

"Beats me, cuz," Tim replied.

"This ugly nigga is beginning to work my last damn nerve. Just like this chick is."

"Let her go, dude. You can have any chick you want in this school. Why waste all your time on her?"

"Because that's the one I want, nigga. It ain't worth it if it's too easy. She's a challenge. I know she wants me, she just don't know it yet."

Chapter 5

He sat on the stairs of an abandon building in a trance with the sign that hovered over the entrance of the barbershop across the street. Flip's Barbershop, the simple yellow sign with black wording read. He was debating over an hour about entering the joint as he placed the finishing touches on a sub he had picked up at the sandwich shop a few blocks down.

All he could hear playing in his head was his mother's voice demanding him to get a haircut. He knew she would never let up until he finally got one. She figured if he kept himself neatly groomed he would always maintain a positive outlook about himself. The problem was, he was far beyond the point in his life where how his wooly hair looked even made a difference to him anymore. He could care less if he ever got another a haircut ever again. A bald fade certainly didn't stop people from picking.

He tried to get a haircut at Flip's Barbershop from Flip himself the first week they moved into the new place, but his visit was spoiled with the sideways jokes Flip and a couple of the other barbers kept slinging his way. He finally booked up and left the joint after getting passed over by Flip with several customers that had come in after him. Flip claimed they all had appointments but he knew better. He vowed not to go back, but Flip's shop was the closest in the neighborhood and the neighbors told his mom they cut the best hair in town, if you could overlook all the loud music and playful atmosphere.

"And then this broad gonna tell me she tired and she just wanna be held," Flip said while pushing his clippers across the back of one of his client's neck. The middle aged man that was being serviced sat quietly with his eyes closed while smiling as Flip told his story.

Craig Mack's *'Flava in Ya Ear'* blasted from two speakers that were hanging from the ceiling in the back of the tiny barbershop. Hair was scattered all across the floor as one lone customer waited his turn for his cut in the row of empty chairs that sat across the two remaining barbers, Flip and Tadpole.

"Nooooo, she ain't say that, Flip. I know she ain't say that shit to you," said Tadpole, who was cutting hair at the booth next to him. Tadpole had his focus completely removed from his own customer and was more focused on Flip.

"Hell yeah, she sure did," Flip answered with a smirk plastered on his smooth golden face.

"What you do now, Flip? What you do? I know you ain't let her do a nigga like that!"

"I told her how it was and how it was gonna be." He let out a slight chuckle. "I said to her that you the one that called me over here, talking about you bored and ain't got nothing to do. My yellow ass was just fine at my own crib with my big ass bowl of Fruity Pebbles watching some Yo MTV Raps. I told her, hell, I could've stayed home and beat my own meat. Damn, running cross town in the middle of the night to Holland Lakes trying to get a night cap with your monkey ass."

"Not beat your own meat and monkey ass, Flip." said Tadpole, who seemed to be amazed by every word that spewed from Flip's lips. "You did not call that girl a monkey ass and told her that you can beat your own damn meat. Now just cut the foolishness."

"Like hell I didn't," Flip announced matter-of-factly.

"Boy, you lucky that chick ain't cut your wee wee off like that chick on the news that time, Bobby, Bonner, Bonita," Tadpole tried to recall.

"Lorena Bobbitt," Tadpole's customer interjected.

"Yeah, that crazy broad, Lorena Bobbitt . We wouldn't be calling your ass Flip no mo', we'd be calling your monkey ass Tip," he laughed. The guys in the barbershop burst into laughter also.

"Negro, you crazy as hell. Any chick come at me with a knife tryin' to cut my shit gonna get a size twelve timbo across her nose," said Flip.

The laughter came to a screeching halt once Julius walked through the door. All heads angled towards the entrance as Julius stood frozen and uncomfortable.

"Ah shit," Tadpole mumbled.

Julius gathered himself and made the short walk to a chair that was positioned directly in front of Flip. Flip took a brief glance at Julius and began to refocus himself on his customer's head.

"Alright," Tadpole said as he slid the barber cape from off his customer. The only other customer in the shop got up and approached Tadpole's booth as the previous customer paid and skirted out of the barbershop.

As Julius waited patiently he looked over the petite shop overrun with boredom. He glanced at the huge black speakers hanging from the ceiling that was now blasting 'One More Chance' by Notorious B.I.G. He observed the scattered clumps of hair–brown, black and gray that laid spread out and unattended to around all four booths of the shop. He zoomed in on the ripped out and taped up collection of Jet magazine 'Beauty of the Week' pictures Tadpole had plastered all over his booth mirror behind him.

He looked over every square inch of the snug barbershop all while repeatedly asking himself, *is this negro going to cut my hair tonight?*

"Man, you know it's gonna be an extra twenty for cuttin' the brillo pad, right?"

"What?" Julius answered as he broke out of his train of thought.

"I said it's an extra twenty bucks to cut that nappy head of yours. Looks like you ain't damn near do nothing to it in months. Ain't muckin' up my clippers with that ol' slave hair," Flip explained.

"Clipper killa," Tadpole blurted out as he tried his best to contain himself from bursting into laughter from his own joke.

Julius couldn't believe how difficult this guy was making it to get a simple haircut. He'd pay the money just to get the thing over with. Finally. "That's cool man," said Julius.

Flip snatched the barber cape off his customer and the man quickly paid. Before Julius could get out of his seat and claim a spot in Flip's barber's chair, Flip took the spot himself. "Oh, yeah, but I'm done cuttin' for the day. You gonna have to come back on Tuesday for a cut."

"Man what are you talkin' about?" Julius asked.

"We closed. That cat right there was my last for the day. I'm 'bout to ride on out," Flip said with a smirk.

Julius instantly looked over to Tadpole.

"Don't look at me, Kunta Kinte. My ass is ghost right after I get finished with this cut right here," Tadpole laughed.

Julius looked back to Flip. "And you couldn't tell me this before I sat down and waited all this time?"

"Hey," Flip shrugged his shoulders. "You didn't ask. You just came in, ain't speak to nobody and sat right down. I can't answer no questions if nobody's askin' 'em."

"Man," Julius said furiously.

"Hey, what can you do? See you Tuesday, boss."

Flip and Tadpole both started laughing. Julius, overrun with anger stormed out of the barbershop. All he could see was red as he stomped down the sidewalk.

"Hey!" he heard a yell. He took a quick look behind himself, thinking it was Flip or Tadpole with a change of heart, but to his dismay it was only Travis Nelson again. He couldn't believe how many more times he'd seen this guy roaming in the streets instead of Mr. Bass' art class. Travis buying the pack of cigarettes for him was a cool gesture, but not cool enough for him to stop and socialize with the guy. He ignored the boy's call and kept trekking down the sidewalk–still mad as hell.

"Hey dude,' you didn't hear me calling you?" said Travis as he eased off his light sprint once he closed in on Julius.

"What'cha want man?" Julius whipped around. "What do you want?"

"Hold, hold, hold on there, buddy. Exhale some of that air you sucking in. What the hell's wrong with you?"

"That punk ass, sorry ass barbershop, that's what!" Julius yelled towards the barbershop from the top of his lungs. He was hoping Tadpole and Flip could hear him.

Travis laughed. "Yo, you let them herbs back there clown you or something?"

"Whatever, man! I was just trying to get a haircut, that's all. Ain't nobody got time for all that b.s. all the time."

"What, they won't cut you?"

"Nah, man, I waited in there for over an hour, and the one they call Flip gonna tell me he done cuttin' for the day when he got finished with his last customer. He just had me in there, sitting there all that time and didn't say nothing. That's just foul, man."

Travis cut his eye at the barbershop. "Man, Flip is an ole' punk ass. My cuz used to whip his ass daily back in the day."

"Yeah, whatever, man," Julius said, not wanting to talk about it anymore. He started his trek back down the sidewalk.

"Hey, where you going?" Travis yelled.

"Home!"

"I'll cut you."

"What?"

"I said, I'll cut you."

"You know how to cut hair?"

"What you think I'm just a dumbass that don't know a damn thing?"

"I didn't say all that."

"You didn't have to. I heard it in your voice. Come on, I live right down the street."

Julius' feet remained firmly planted to the ground. He was reluctant about trusting him and thought Travis could be up to no good.

"Come on," Travis waved at him.

Apprehensively, Julius accompanied him.

"Yeah, that punk ass Flip, there ain't nothing to him," Travis explained. "He got his own shop, looking like an Al B. Sure reject, thinking he the shit now. Before my cuz got blasted on, Flip used to be his little bitch. Merc used to take me into that shop and make that nigga cut my hair and his, free of charge, every two weeks. Jump everybody, no matter how long they were waiting."

"Word?"

"Yup! I miss that nigga, Merc, too. He really held it down when he was here."

"What happened to him?"

"Got shot, messing around with some jealous nigga's trick. Niggas set him up when he had his guard down. Shot him right in the head. Them niggas got theirs the next day though, that's for sho. All of 'em.''

"Did you get 'em back?" Julius asked wanting to know how crazy Travis was before he got any further away from his home.

"Nah, I wish. His boys put in the work. Snuffed them clowns clean out with the quickness, too. They may have taken Merc out, but they didn't live long to tell about it.''

"Oh," Julius answered relieved that he wasn't walking with a proud murderer.

"Your name is Julius, right?"

"Yeah."

"Cool. Jules, I like that."

"I said Julius."

"Jules sounds better. That's what I think I'm gonna call you–Jules."

"Whatever, man," Julius said. "You serious about knowing how to cut hair?"

"Hell yeah, nigga. I cut my own head. You see how good this ma'fucker look, right?" Travis said while leaning his head down to swipe the top of his even flat top.

"Yeah, I see. How much you gonna charge, though?"

"Nothin'. Don't even worry about it."

"Why are you being so nice to me? A couple of weeks ago you were screaming about how busted I was all up in class, talking about I looked like I was from Africa somewhere."

"Awe, man." Travis fanned. "Why you still thinking about that? I was just trippin', that's all. I already told you that. Besides, I see a little bit of me in you."

"Really?"

"Well, not the looks," he laughed. "Just trippin' again. But, yeah, personality-wise, I can tell that you're a loner. Just like me. Real recognize real, dude."

Julius followed Travis off the sidewalk as they stomped across a yard with very little to no grass. Just grass spots with bottles, papers and cans scattered all across the lawn. A little white brick house with metal bars covering the windows rested on the lot.

Julius followed Travis onto the two-feet high cement porch. Travis started banging on the beaten down, wooden screen door. The screen at the bottom of the raggedy door looked like someone had been trying to yank it apart.

"Open the goddamn door," Travis yelled as he beat on the door again. The door rattled loudly each time he pounded on it.

An older, tall, heavy set dark skinned man with a jherhi curl opened the door and flipped the latch up on the screen door. "Your momma in here tryin' to sleep."

"Fuck all that," Travis said as he pushed his way into the house.

The house had an unpleasant stench that hit Julius' nose once he stepped his first foot onto the dingy wooden floor. Armies of roaches were running astray on every wall in the den–big, small and medium. Julius cringed at the site of the filthy bugs. His household was poor, but they never had roaches. His mother detested roaches, and made sure she fumigated every shack or apartment they ever lived in a week before they actually moved in.

"Who this little nigga is?" the man questioned. He gave Julius a quick stare down as he closed the door behind the boys.

"My man, Jules."

"I don't think your momma want no company," the man warned. "She wants some rest."

"What, nigga? I pay the bills up in this ma'fucka."

"What you say, Travis?" said an older light skinned woman sitting upright on a sofa on the other side of the trashy living room. Her hair was thin and grey and looked as if some birds were scratching through it. It was his mom, and she appeared to be spaced out with her head swaying round and round.

"You heard me, Ma. I ain't stutter."

"Boy, I put you in this world and…"

"Yeah, yeah, yeah" he interrupted. "Come on, Jules." He signaled Julius to follow him into the back of the house.

"You always talk to your moms that way?" Julius whispered.

"Hell with my mom. She gave me up for that crack shit a long time ago. She lucky I let her ass stay here."

"You really pay the rent?"

"How else is it gonna get paid? Her ass is a base head, and her sorry ass brother around there don't put in on nothin' with his disability check. I should throw his ass out, now that I'm thinking about it."

Travis dug into his pocket and unlocked his room door with a key. Julius was surprised by the look of his room when they entered because it was like an oasis compared to the rest of the house. The bedroom was neat with posters of half naked models plastered across the walls, a high end forty inch television set and VCR, expensive stereo equipment and classy silk linens covering his bed.

"Have a seat on the bed. Im'a go get a chair out of the kitchen. You want something to drink or something?"

"Nah, I'm good," Julius answered while surveying the cozy room.

Julius sat on the edge of the bed with his whole body tensed up. The room was exquisite and tidy, and he didn't see anything crawling on the wall, but he knew if the roaches were in the front room, they were definitely lurking throughout the entire house.

Travis returned to the room totting an old kitchen chair with his clippers wrapped up on the seat. He dropped the chair just outside of the area rug he had stretched out across the floor. He swiped his clippers and motioned Julius to the chair.

"Sit here. I gotta get right before I cut your shit."

Julius eased to the chair while observing Travis dig through his drawer.

"You smoke?" Travis asked, while giving Julius a side eye slightly over his shoulder.

"No."

"I ain't talking about no damn cigarettes," he laughed. He recovered a joint from his drawer and stuffed it in his mouth. "I'm talkin' about weed, nigga. You know, the chronic. That gunja."

"Nope."

"Shit, you don't know what you're missing," he said with his joint bouncing up and down from his lips with each word.

"I ain't never really messed with that stuff."

"Hey, it's all good, more for me," Travis said as he flipped the clippers on and off to make sure they had power. He gripped Julius' head and ran his hand through his hair. "Goddamn! Do you even comb this ma'fucker? You got all these damn sharecropper naps. I'ma need some more damn clippers after this."

"Man, the only reason I'm getting it cut is to keep my mom happy."

"No wonder Flip don't wanna cut this shit," he said as he grabbed a pick from his dresser.

"Man, if it's gonna be too much trouble…" Julius rose from the chair.

Travis gently pushed him back into the chair, "Man, sit your ass down. I'm just messing with you. Your problem is you wear your damn feelings on your sleeves too much. Anything somebody say to you, you get mad, ready to fight, or haul ass."

"You try living with everybody picking on you about how you look."

"Well hell, everybody think I'm dumb. They ain't gonna say it to my face because they know better." He started picking through Julius' head. "But I know what they say. I ain't worried about it as long as they don't touch me. That's what you better learn, dude."

"Man, you don't know me."

"Yeah, but ain't nothin' new up under the sun either, Jules. You learn how to pick your fights wisely, you won't have to worry about niggas pickin' on you about your looks. I mean, in all honesty, and I'm saying this as nice as I can say it, you are one ugly nigga, but you never let how you look define who you are."

"I guess you know everything."

Travis smiled while running his clippers through Julius' hair. "You know what, I lied about you not having to pay me."

"What?" Julius leaned away from the clippers.

"Not with money, dude." He chuckled as he pulled Julius back into the chair. "One day we gonna roll up in Flip's barbershop, and we gonna make that nigga give you a cut."

"Why?"

"Because you gotta learn that you don't wait for niggas to give you respect, most times, you gotta take it."

Chapter 6

As she marched through the house with a clothes basket cradled in one arm, she scooped up the trail of socks Vince had scattered along the floor. She looked over to the recliner and Vince was in his usual spot, knocked out with a beer bottle clutched in his hand and a pile of empty bottles underneath his feet. Felicia took a moment to stare at him as she shook her head in disgust.

She couldn't understand how she stayed with the lazy lug for so long. At one time she relied on him so much to be her crutch throughout her tumultuous younger years, but as the years flew by and the older she got, the less she relied on him and the more dependent he became on her. She fell out of love with him a long time ago, and often wondered if she ever really loved him at all, thus simply fooled by the false sense of security he provided by merely being there.

She once yearned for the day he would sweep her off her feet and make their relationship truly official before God and her family, but those days, too, were long gone. Then it hit her, just when she began stuffing his clothes into the raggedy old washer. Loyalty. It was the only thing that kept her from taking her son and leaving him for good when she had the first opportunity. Despite all of his laziness, the arguing and the fighting, she felt extremely loyal to him.

There was a loud knock at the front door. She set the timer on the washer and scurried into the living room. Even on the worn down recliner, Vince was a hard sleeper, and it would take something equivalent to a major earthquake to awaken him once he was well into his slumber.

"Vince, wake up," she said as she gave him a firm nudge on his arm in passing.

"Wha…what is it, woman?" he mumbled as he batted his eyes and repositioned himself on the recliner.

"Someone's at the door."

"Well, it ain't for me." He let out a yawn that resembled a lion's roar. "Must be somebody for you."

"Just wake up. You know how you get if you're left sleeping on that chair and company comes over." She glanced through the peephole. "Oh, it's Ma."

"Uh, shi…" He uttered lightly as he began scratching through his rough beard.

She swung the door open. "Hey, Ma. We weren't expecting a visit from you."

"You better damn well believe that," Vince mumbled from under his breath. He took a quick swig from his bottle, finishing off his brew.

"Felicia." The bronzed complexioned lady greeted her with a scowl on her face. She wore a classy navy blue dress suit and a large blue hat to match.

"Come on in, Ma," Felicia said, a bit unsettled.

The woman's three inch heels echoed throughout the house from the rough wooden floor as she slowly entered through the front door. She did a quick look around the place, still armed with the scowl on her face. Her observation of the room ceased when she laid eyes on

Vince, which triggered her to roll her eyes and let out a loud sigh. "Humph, Vince."

"Louise." Vince replied with a frown and a devilish look. He didn't like the woman, just as much as she didn't like him and he was waiting for her to say something out of the way so he could tell her about herself.

Felicia could cut the tension between the two with a steak knife. She knew the two never liked each other, and she didn't want to waste any time getting them separated. "Ma, why don't you follow me into the kitchen. I was just about to put something on."

"Hell, y'all can sit in here. I'm 'bout to go down to Flex's crib. Ain't got time for people to be rolling their eyes at me in my own damn house."

Louise folded her arms and shook her head as her daughter's common law husband fled to the back of the house. The bedroom door in the back slammed shut.

"Why, why, why, Felicia," Louise whispered as she took a seat on the sofa. She sat on the very edge of the chair as if she was uncomfortable with having her entire body seated.

"So, Ma, what brings you here today," Felicia asked as she claimed a spot on the recliner next to her.

"Well, I thought I'd take the initiative and come by and see my daughter since she never sets aside any of her time to come check on her dear old mother. Seems like you've forgotten that me and the rest of the family even exists anymore, Felicia."

"Well, ma, no disrespect, but I've been really working around the clock lately. I have to take whatever hours they give me at the hotel."

"Paying all the bills no doubt."

"Ma, why you gotta start? You haven't been here a good ten minutes, and you've already started judging people."

"Well, it's true, Felicia, and you know it. I bet that so-called man around there don't do a thing to help you," she said as she angrily cut her eyes toward the rear of the house where Vince retreated to. "It ain't right for a woman to be taking care of a grown, able bodied, man. It ain't right, I tell you."

"Good Lord, Ma!"

"And it ain't good to be shacking up together. I haven't seen a marriage license from you two till this day."

"Is that what you came over here today for, Ma? To preach?"

"No, but a good sermon would do this household some good. I just happen to call it like I see it. That's the only way I know how to do it."

"Julius is doing well," she said in an effort to switch gears.

"And."

"And?"

"Yes! And? You know good and well how I feel about Julius."

"And how do you feel about my son, Ma? Cuz' let's not forget, he is your grandson."

"Oh no he's not. That boy is no relation to me. It was your decision to keep that boy after that monster violated you. Your father and I would've…" She stopped herself.

"Paid for the abortion?" she said.

"Well!" The old woman was reluctant to proceed with her case, but she couldn't stop herself at this point. "What woman keeps a child from the result of a rape? Huh? What woman?"

"You…you…you!" Felicia was so upset she hopped out of her seat and walked towards the window. Louise's eyes followed her there. She ripped open the curtains to let the daylight in.

Uneasy by the sudden silence, her mother got up and walked up behind her. She was careful not to get to close. She wasn't sure what her daughter was capable of since she'd been with Vince for so long. She said, "Nobody would've blamed you if you would have just gotten rid of the child. It would've been the right thing to do, Felicia."

"The right thing to do?" Felecia whipped around and faced her mother. "Weren't you just talking about good sermons? Last time I checked, Ma, God don't like abortions, just like he don't like grown people shackin' up."

"This would've been the exception. With what you went through, Felicia, nobody would've faulted you one bit. Not one bit, I tell ya'."

"Yeah, well I guess not in your eyes." Felicia threw her hands up out of frustration and said, "Look, I don't care what you say about my son or how you feel about how he got here, he's my son. He doesn't have an ounce of that evil man, Herman Joseph, in 'em. And like it or not, if he came out of my womb that means he is still your flippin' grandson. Your flesh and blood, Momma–like it or not."

To have the name Herman Joseph slither from her lips instantly brought chills down her spine. It's been years since she last spoke the man's name, but he rests in the back of her mind every day since that night. That night that monster took advantage of a rebellious seventeen year old girl simply looking for a ride across town. It was one ride she would never forget.

After returning home from a weekend with her then boyfriend, Kelsey, all hell broke loose when she walked through her parent's door. The teen didn't tell her mother nor her stepfather where she was going for the weekend, and she failed to call and let them know if she was alive or not. Felicia, being the hot head she was at the time, didn't have the patience to be scolded about what she could or could not do, so she left. Her intentions were to make it back across town to her boyfriend's older brother's house where she had been all weekend with Kelsey, but she would never make it to that destination.

She remembered the night as if it just happened yesterday. It was dark and frigid, and the streets were wet. She flagged down the first set of headlights she saw coming her way. He stopped. She told him where he was going, and he advised her he was heading that same way. Dark skinned, cleaned faced, unattractive, muscular fellow, Herman Joseph was. He gave her the creeps as soon as they took off, but she was so determined to get as far away from her family and back into her boyfriend's arm, she neglected her reservations.

After a few questions about if she had a boyfriend or not and if she was sexually active, she had finally had enough, and asked to be dropped off on the side of the road, advising him she would walk the rest of the way. Joseph wasn't having it, and he pulled in behind a closed grocery store and violently raped her. He had every bit of intentions of killing her, but she managed to get away after kneeing him in his crouch at the very end of the assault.

If it weren't for an off duty officer that just happened to stop at the grocery store to pick up some diapers for his newborn baby on his way home, Joseph would've caught her and killed her, just like the other twelve of his known thirteen victims.

Her mother and stepfather indeed offered and later demanded she have an abortion when she discovered the serial rapist had impregnated her, but she couldn't do it. She felt connected to the tiny soul that was hidden snugly inside of her, and she declined to do what most women would've done without a second thought in such a scenario. She opted to keep the child whom would later become her Julius. Her only child. Once she broke the news to her parents, they responded by throwing her out on the streets for her to fend for herself and her child, a position she has accepted ever since.

Even though Joseph was captured and imprisoned five years and twelve sexual assaults later, she didn't get any form of peace of mind from being in the criminal's crosshairs until she was notified that he was slain behind bars when Julius was seven years old.

"Felicia, all I'm saying is…"

"I'm 'bout to go," Vince interrupted as he returned to the living room.

They both turned to him as he strolled to the front door.

"Okay," answered Felicia as she wiped the tears away from her eyes that had just begun to develop.

He looked at Felicia, then to Louise and back at Felicia again. "I suspect you'll have supper ready by the time you send Mrs. Ellison off on her way."

Louise frowned, crossed her arms and planted herself back onto the sofa. Vince looked back at her with a smile on his face.

"Yes, Vince."

"Good," he replied. "Louise."

"Goodbye, Vince."

He let out a short chuckle and then went on his way.

"You had a way out. But you didn't want to take it, and look where it got you–taking care of a grown bum of a man!" said Louise.

"Ma, you came over here for a reason. I know it wasn't to come see me. So what is it?"

"Well, as a matter of fact I did. I guess there's no reason to beat on a dead horse."

"Yeah, you're right about that. So what is it?"

"Your sister and Mike are coming down from Michigan, and I thought it would be good for you two to see each other since it's been so long."

"Now, stop right there, Ma. You know Kim and I don't get along."

"Well, she's your sister."

"So! Julius is your grandson. He's your family. How do you expect me to see a child of yours when you won't see a child of mine?"

"My word, what do you expect me to do, Felicia? Embrace a child that was conceived by rape?"

"If he's your grandchild, you should. No matter what you may think about the situation, Julius is a part of me. He's my son, and he's your grandson and if you expect me to be a part of your life, don't expect it to be without my son."

"Well, I guess you've said a mouth full."

"Yeah, I guess I did, Ma."

"I know you and I have had our differences in the past, Felicia, but all I'm asking you to do is come see your sister when she gets to town."

"It won't happen as long as you continue to belittle my son. It just won't."

"Well, I didn't come over here to ruffle anyone's feathers, and I most certainly didn't come over here to argue with you. If you come and you bring Julius along I will do my best..."

"You will treat my son appropriately, Ma."

The stubborn old woman let in huge glob of air. "That, I will do," she said. "Now if you would excuse me, I have to be getting home."

"How's Frank doing?"

"He's doing okay. It's getting harder for him to get around these days, but he's holding up."

"Is that why Kim is coming down and the real reason you want me to come?"

Louise nodded, somewhat emotional at the thought of her ailing husband. "The doctor says there's nothing they can do for him. The cancer's terminal this time. They say he has four months, but I know he'll do his best to prove 'em wrong. He always does."

"Why didn't you just say that, Ma? You should've told me about this sooner. I'm sorry, Ma," she said as she went to her mother's aid to embrace her. She could see her about to burst into tears.

"I'm okay. I'm okay," she said as she put her hand up to stop the embrace. "You know, Felicia, Frank never tried to replace your father. He knew his place. He just wanted the best for you, just like I did. He had nothing to do with throwing you out of the house when you decided to keep Julius. That was all on me. He loves you the same way he loves Kim, always have."

"I guess we both know we can't change what's already been done, Ma."

"You're right," the old woman said as she marched to the door. "I'll be looking for you."

"Okay, Ma."

Felicia's mom walked out the door. After shutting the door behind her, Felicia backed into the door and looked up towards the ceiling. She wasn't prepared for the emotions of seeing her mom and discussing the demons from her past.

****

Felicia sat the table in the kitchen with all the lights turned off. There was a plate of food sitting on the other side of the table. The jingling sound of keys could be heard from the front of the house as Vince made his entrance. After carefully closing the door behind himself as silently as he could, the man tip toed into the kitchen. When he flicked on the lights, he was surprised to see Felicia sitting at the table.

"What are you still doing up?"

"My mother left hours ago."

"And?"

"It's one in the morning, Vince." She could smell the stench of alcohol on him from across the room. It pissed her off even more.

"Last time I checked I ain't had no curfew."

"It's not about a curfew, Vince. It's about you being respectful."

"Respectful?" he huffed. He grabbed his food, threw it in the microwave and slung the door shut. "Maybe if a nigga could get a piece of ass around here he would be more motivated to come home early."

She rolled her eyes. "I had ninety dollars saved in my drawer, and now it's missing."

"And! Did you ask that boy around there about it?" he asked on wobbly legs.

"Yes, and now I'm asking you."

"Well, as long as you didn't jump to conclusions like you always do, and ask me first, your second guess would be right. I took it. I had to pay Mason to fix the alternator on that car you've been driving around in. Did you think it paid for itself?"

"It would just be nice if you tell me before…"

"And a piece of ass would be damn nice, too! I didn't even have to ask for it back in the day when you were turning tricks at the club. Now you wanna' get all stuck up and be Claire Huxtable on a nigga."

"You're drunk and you need to sleep it off."

"You don't tell me what I need. And I don't need nobody around here interrogating me like some damn police, woman! I'm a grown ass man. I come and go as I goddamn please."

"Whatever, Vince," she jumped up and headed for bed. He quickly grabbed her by her arm and slung her in front of him, not allowing to leave.

"Now, I done told that boy of yours about how you niggas be running around here talkin' to me like I'm some type of a lightweight," he explained in slurred speech, while wielding his finger in her face. "I ain't gonna be taking too much more of this bullshit. Now you talk about respect–you niggas gonna respect me or it's gonna start being some problems around here. Some major problems."

She snatched her arm away. "You done?"

"Am I done?" he laughed hysterically. "I'm just getting started, honey."

She furiously marched out of the kitchen.

"You niggas gonna learn. Believe that," he yelled. He spun a full circle in one place. "Now, what the hell did I do with that plate?"

Chapter 7

Simone entered the lunch room with her two friends, Tammy and Raven, trailing closely behind her. They always took their time getting to the lunch room because they knew by the time they arrived, the line of hungry students would be diminished and they could simply stroll in, grab their daily salad of choice and enjoy their lunch outside in the courtyard amongst all the cooler and popular students.

Julius sat in his usual spot at the far corner of the lunch room with his chair facing the entrance so he could catch a glimpse of Simone when she walked in. He had no idea why she even bothered with him, since nobody else in any school ever did, but for some reason she did. She seemed to genuinely like him, and he could tell. She sat with him at least two days out of the week, and he was hoping today would be one of those two days. When he saw her, his face lit up like a candle. As soon as she saw him, she gave him a little wave.

"Simone, what is up with you and that boy?" Raven asked. The light skinned girl with short hair frowned at the sight of Julius. She quickly turned to Simone for her answer.

"Who? Julius?" Simone asked.

"Yeah, really, Simone. Dude is like fright night," Tammy added.

"Hey, don't say that," said Simone. "Julius is a sweetheart."

"Yeah, well I hate to break it to you, suga, but your sweetheart is really nothing great to look at. I mean, really, Simone, I can't believe you've actually been ditching us to sit with him. What's up with that, girl?" Raven said. "I mean, I don't really have the heart to tell the other girls where you've been hanging out lately. It's just too embarrasing."

"Are you working on some type of charity case or something? You know that boy is beneath you. I mean, you got Ricky Smith begging to take you out, and he's the star basketball player and one of the finest guys in the school. You won't even give him the time of day." Tammy declared.

"Uhm hmm, Ricky is too fine! I'd put something on that boy he'd never forget. With his sexy ass lips" Raven said biting her bottom lip.

"What girl? I know I would," said Tammy as she exchanged high fives with Raven. "But Miss thang here acting like she too good for the boy."

"Well, how about you two screw Ricky. Together!" said Simone.

"Heeeeey!" Tammy did a little dance waving her fist in the air. "We may have to work something out with ole' boy, Raven."

Raven rolled her eyes. "Girl, please! I'm not sharing no nigga with any other heffa. I don't care how fine he is."

"Hey, just a thought, girl," Tammy replied. "Just a thought."

"Well, keep those kind of thoughts to yourself, for real," Raven said.

"Y'all crazy. Ricky's just not my type. He's arrogant, he's rude and he thinks he's God's gift to the earth." Simone responded as she grabbed a pack of salad dressing from the salad bar and placed it on her tray.

"The finest brothers are always the jerks, but we love 'em anyway," said Raven.

"Not me," Simone nodded. "Besides, I'm not trying to be in any type of relationship with anybody right now. With my dad losing his job at the plant, I have to make sure my grades are perfect to get the right scholarship that can cover most of my tuition."

"Well, obviously you're not looking for any relationship hanging around that ugly boy," Raven said as they exited the lunch line and entered the cafeteria.

"Raven, don't talk about him like that. Everything is about looks with you." Simone nudged the girl.

"Uhm! Well, it's true," said Tammy as she zoomed in on Julius across the lunch room. "That boy is uggggg-ly! My Lawd."

"Whatever, Tammy," Simone replied. "Hey, why don't you guys come sit with me at Julius' table. Once you sit and talk with him, you'll see that he's a really nice guy. You can judge somebody for what they offer from the inside for once."

"What? Uhm, that would be a no," said Tammy. "You can keep him and his insides to yourself."

"Yeah, girl, I know you're trying to be nice and all, but I'm not sitting over there him. He has like zero attractiveness, and I do have an image to uphold. I can't be seen hanging around with no scrub, and especially not an ugly one," Raven replied. "Feel free to enjoy your charity case on your own, Simone."

"Ha!," Tammy laughed. "I know that's right."

"Oh, wow, Raven, you guys are so mean," Simone replied.

"Hey, if you wanna be seen with some lame, that's your business, girl," said Tammy. "We'll see you next period though."

"Alright, ladies," said Simone.

The two girls went off on their way as Simone veered off and walked over to Julius' table.

"Hey, Julius," she said as she took a seat at the table.

"Hi, Simone," Julius nervously answered.

"How are you today?" she asked.

"I'm good. I'm good."

"Did you get that project finished you were working on for Mr. Bass?"

"Yep," he answered. He couldn't take his eyes off her.

"Cool," she said. She froze. "Everything okay?"

"Oh, yeah. Yes." He replied. "I got something for you, though."

"You do?"

"Yeah." He slowly pulled out a drawing and slid it across the table to her. It was a black and white sketch of her standing side by side with Michael Jordan wearing a number 45 jersey."

"Oh, Julius, this is amazing. I can't believe you drew this. Did you remembered how I look from memory?"

"Yes," he nodded. He was so nervous he didn't know if he should smile or keep his face straight. On the inside he was overjoyed by the smile on her face.

"This is so cool, man." she said in awe of the picture. "Now, my only complaint is that you put MJ in the number forty-five jersey." She flipped the picture around to face him and pointed at Jordan's jersey. "I'm pretty confident he'll be rockin' that old number twenty-three that we all know and love at the beginning of this season. That forty-five just don't look right on him."

"I can change it. Or do another one," he quickly offered as he reached for the picture.

"No!" she said as she quickly pulled the picture away and playfully poked out her lips. "I love this one exactly the way it is. Nobody's ever drawn me in a picture before, Julius. This is so cool. Thank you."

"You're welcome."

As she stared at the picture with a smile from cheek to cheek, Julius had a sense of pride for putting the smile there. She made him feel good. She made him forget about how the rest of the world saw him. Around her, he felt peace. For him to be able to put a smile on her face really made him feel warm inside.

"You're sitting in my seat, scrub!" yelled Ricky as he stood over the couple with two other guys behind them, all carrying trays of food.

Julius looked up at the three large figures as he quickly realized the day was just going too smoothly for his type of luck. He couldn't believe this guy was in his face again, harassing him.

"Ricky, why don't you just chill out," said Simone. "You know you don't ever eat your lunch in the cafeteria."

"I am today. And when I do, I eat it here," he bumped Julius' chair. "Now get your ass up, before I move you myself."

"Ricky leave him alone," she demanded as she threw a bread roll at him.

He quickly batted the bread away and laughed. "I'm not even talking to you," he said pointing at her with his eyes still piercing through Julius.

"Man, why don't you just leave me alone?" Julius asked.

"Yeah, Ricky leave him alone," mocked the taller boy hovering on the right side of the bully. His name was Jermaine. At first glance, with his tall, lanky frame, you could tell he was a basketball player also, but the guy on Ricky's left, Ice, was no baller at all. With his full, dark black beard, he barely even looked like he was suppose to be enrolled at any school. He stood silently behind Ricky while issuing Julius a mean look as if he wanted to beat his brains in.

"I'm not bothering you yet, punk. But if you don't move, things about to get real ugly fast," Ricky promised.

Julius glanced at the group and knew the odds were severely against him, and he certainly didn't want to get jumped in front of Simone. "Man, I don't want any problems. I'll go." Julius began gathering his things.

"Julius, no! You don't have to leave because he said so," said Simone. "Ricky, you're nothing but a bully!"

"Don't listen to her, Julius," laughed Jermaine. "She just gonna sit there and watch you get your ass beat. My man, Ice, has been waiting to give somebody a good beat down."

Ice continued to stare at Julius with his nostrils flaring. Ice took a step in front of Ricky, and Ricky immediately pushed him back. "I got this Ice. His ass know the routine."

Ricky's cocky demeanor infuriated Julius. He looked across the table at Simone and began to rethink leaving altogether. He did his best to keep a cooler head because he didn't want to get into any trouble, but Ricky was beginning to push too many buttons for him to back down this time. There were so many bullies at his previous schools that stuck out in his head before him, like Stretch at Sanders High, that would always call him Craig Mack Jr. when he saw him in the hallway, or like Big Kev at Eastshire High that would give him a hard bump in class from time to time and tell him to get the hell out of his way, yet none of them were like Ricky Smith. Ricky was different. Not only was he persistent, but he was also ruthless and hateful. He was quickly becoming the worse bully he'd ever crossed paths with. The more Ricky talked his trash, the more he became content with the idea of going down by a good ass whippin' than to run away and look like a coward in front of the only female that ever gave him the time of day.

"I don't see you moving, punk ass." Ricky said as he leaned into Julius' face while having both his fist smashed down into the table. "You hard of hearing?"

"No, I'm not. And I'm not moving, either." Julius said, looking the boy dead in his eyes. He knew what his words meant, and he was prepared for the consequences.

"Big mistake," said Ricky as he slung Julius' lunch tray off the table, across the lunch room floor. He attempted to grab Julius but he backed up in his chair and shoved Ricky backwards, making him loose his balance and falling into the arms of his two goons.

"You little bastard!" said Ricky, stunned that Julius had put his hands on him. Ricky balled up his fist and was about to hit Julius who had quickly moved into a fighting stance until–

"Gentlemen," Mr. Benson called out to the boys. They both turned their attention to him as he rushed towards them. By this time Simone was standing and the entire lunch room had all eyes on them. "Is there a problem over here?"

"No sir, Mr. Benson," Ricky briskly answered.

"Is there a problem, Mr. Graves? It certainly looks like there's one." The principal turned to Julius.

Julius looked over to Ricky who was squinting his eyes with a look that could kill. "No sir, Mr. Benson. There's no problem."

"Just want to let you know, as I'm sure Mr. Smith and his associates are aware of already, I take fighting very seriously at my school. Understand, Mr. Graves?"

"Yes, sir," Julius answered, reluctantly. It infuriated him with how Mr. Benson appeared to concentrate most of his attention on him only. He could smell the favoritism towards Ricky a mile away.

"Ms. Wilson," said the principal as he turned his awareness to Simone.

"Yes sir, Mr. Benson," she answered.

"You still haven't considered rejoining our cheerleader squad?"

"No sir," she answered.

"Alright. They need you, but we know studies come first," he said. "How about try and keep these gentlemen around here from losing their minds over you. It will make my job so much easier."

"I'll try Mr. Benson," she smiled.

"Well, since there isn't a problem over here with you gentlemen, let's break all of this up while the credibility of your responses are still strong with me." Mr. Benson said.

"Yes, sir," Julius answered.

"And Ricky, you're just the young man I was looking for," he said as he patted Ricky on his shoulder and put his arm around him.

"What's up, Mr. Benson?" he answered as he walked away with the principal and his buddies, leaving his tray behind.

"Julius, I'm sorry," Simone said.

He shook his head, "Don't worry about it. I'm used to it," he said. "I hope you enjoy the sketch." He grabbed his tray and his notebook and headed for the exit. She sadly looked on.

****

Julius stood in front of the restroom mirror with his hands stretched out over the sink. His heart was still racing, and he couldn't fix his hands to where they would stop trembling. The bell to his next class had sounded off ten minutes prior, but he wasn't sure about going to anymore classes for the day. Ricky had him on edge. He knew the boy wasn't going to let the altercation in the lunch room slide and eventually he was going to have to fight him. He suspected he would have to ever since the first day of school. He'd been in enough drama and schools to know which bully was going to pull his card, well before his card even got picked.

As he stared at himself, at the face he had grown to hate for so long, he couldn't help but ask himself the same question he always asked himself. *Why me?* He closed his eyes, placed both hands over his face and brought them down. His eyes opened and then he started punching the wall on opposite sides of the mirror. Anger, rage and exhaustion was all he could feel throughout his body. He was so tired of being everybody's punching bag, everybody's eye sore, everybody's joke.

He backed away from the mirror, into the closed door of a stall behind him, and slid to the floor. He began to cry. He simply sat there and cried to himself, while wanting to be somebody else. He wanted to be somewhere else. He wanted peace. To be left alone.

"You have got to be the ugliest piece of crap on this planet," declared a familiar voice from the door. It was Ricky. He strolled in carrying a half full bottle of Gatorade with his two cronies from the lunch room behind him.

Julius quickly wiped his eyes and jumped to his feet. He knew what the boy was coming for, and though outnumbered, he was going to do his best to fend for himself.

"Rick, I think the little nigga was in here crying," laughed Ice.

"Oh, he ain't crying yet," said Ricky. "Because I'm 'bout to give him something to cry about."

"Thought you were big shit in front of that cheerleader broad, huh, chump?" Jermaine added. "Not even Benson can save your black ass now."

"With your big ass pancake nose and your Roger Wood sausage lips, I can't figure out why she likes you so much...let alone be seen with your ugly ass," Ricky said as he came closer. "I mean, what is it?"

Julius stood in his fighting stance with both his fist balled up. As he awaited for Ricky to make his first move on him, he said, "Man, if we're gonna fight. We fight one on one."

Ricky laughed. "Negro, you don't make the rules around here. I do."

Another boy, Tim, ran into bathroom, out of breath and breathing hard. "Okay, you good, Rick," said the boy as he moved into a position to keep the door closed.

"Good lookin' out, Tim," said Ricky as he sat his bottle on the edge of the sink. "I told you, if you wanted a bout with the champ I would be right here, didn't I?" he asked, pointing at Julius.

"Man, whatever you say," said Julius.

"Oh, it's gonna be whatever, chump," Ricky replied. "Grab his ass." Ricky signaled his boys with a wave.

The boys charged at Julius. He did his best to fight them off, with swing after swing, but they were too big and too quick. They grabbed both his arms and slammed him backwards into the wall twice. With each pounding against the restroom wall, they knocked the wind right out of him.

"Alright, now hold him there," Ricky demanded. He slowly approached Julius and stood nose to nose with him. "Next time you get to a new place, you better check your references ahead of time. I'm not to be fucked with!" Ricky warned as he issued Julius a menacing left hook to his ribcage.

"Alright, no face, no face, Rick," said Ice as he struggled to keep Julius still and upright.

"I know what I'm doing," Ricky replied, slightly annoyed. "You hear that Julius, my boy Ice here wants to make sure we don't fuck up your face any more than it already is. Well, that's cool with me," said Ricky as he exploded with two more hooks to Julius' stomach.

The immense pain shot through Julius' abdomen like he was getting struck by a sledgehammer. No matter how much he squirmed and jiggled the boys had him pinned into a firm grip he couldn't work himself out of. He did his best to clutch his stomach as tight as possible to ease each fierce blow Ricky pounded him with, but it did very little to yield the pain.

"You don't have nothing to say, chump? You don't have nothing to say?" Ricky asked as he grabbed a handful of Julius' shirt and held him up against the wall to see his face. "Where's your smart ass mouth now? You ain't got nothin' to say? Say something smart now, punk?"

Julius didn't speak. His only response to Ricky was a wide smile which infuriated the bully even more.

"I guess you think this shit is funny. That I'm some type of joke. I see, I gotta teach your ass a real lesson," Ricky said. "Keep him right there," he instructed his boys.

Ricky walked over to the sink and grabbed his bottle. He dumped the remainder of his drink into the sink and eased into one of the stalls. The flowing echo of him urinating in the bottle could be heard distinctively. The two boys holding Julius still exchanged blank stares with each other. Ricky walked out of the stall carrying a bottle full of urine and a demonic smile on his face.

"Ah, man, come on now, Rick. You said we was just gonna beat his ass a lil' bit," said Ice. "You ain't say nothing about this, man."

"He's had enough, man. This cat is barely on his feet, Rick." said Jermaine as he struggled to hold Julius up.

"I'll tell you when this lil' nigga had enough," Ricky said, pointing at Jermaine.

Julius' legs were wobbly like some dangling strings of spaghetti. He was dazed and bruised but when he realized Ricky was carrying his urine in the bottle, he tried to scrape up all the energy he could to escape from the boy's clutches.

Ricky stood before him with a huge grin on his mug. "Since you like to walk around here, looking like you're pissed off, I wonder how you'll feel about being pissed on for a change," said Ricky.

"Don't do this, man. Don't do this," cried Julius.

"You don't tell me what to do," Ricky said as he began to slowly dump the urine over Julius' head.

"What's wrong with you, man!" Julius yelled as he yanked and kicked, trying to do anything he could to get out of the downpour of urine.

"Damn, Rick," said Tim as he put his hand over his face, turning away, disgusted.

"Ah shit, man, what's wrong with you," Ice asked as he tried to position his body away from Julius while still holding him to prevent getting any of Ricky's urine on him.

"You one nasty ass nigga, Rick," said Jermaine. "You cold."

Ricky threw the bottle down and smashed Julius chin with a quick right punch, knocking him out cold. The boys allowed the momentum to plow Julius onto the floor.

"Man, I told you no face, nigga," Ice angrily yelled. "We fuck up his face, he can prove we jumped him."

"His face already fucked up," Ricky said looking down at the boy, laughing. "How somebody gonna tell the difference?"

"Man, come on," Tim declared. "Rick your ass is crazy."

"Let's get the fuck up out of here before Benson finds us in here beating this lil' nigga's ass," said Ice running towards the door. "Ain't none of us got it like Rick ass do. He'll expel our asses in a heartbeat."

Ricky's crew quickly scattered from the restroom as he calmly remained hovering over Julius. Julius was curled up on his knees as he struggled to keep his eyes open. He looked up at Ricky as he only appeared to him as a blur. The pain he felt was excruciating. The smell of his urine drenched clothes was horrific. He could only wonder what he did to make this guy so upset with him.

"I guess you'll know better next time," Ricky said as he kicked Julius in his side.

Julius fell face first to the floor again. He clutched his stomach and moaned in pain. He couldn't fight back if he wanted to. He just wanted them to leave him alone. He had more than enough.

"Don't make me have to kick your ass again 'cause next time, it'll be worse." He let out a chuckle as he casually strolled through the exit.

****

Julius stumbled slowly down the sidewalk as he tightly clutched his stomach. His entire body ached with each step he gingerly took as he felt as if he was run over by a bus. The inside of his mouth was sore and his lip was busted. To add insult to injury, he could barely stand the smell of himself as he reeked of Ricky's urine. He couldn't believe the boy actually dumped piss over his head. It was by far the worst thing anyone had ever done to him.

He didn't even bother to stop by Mr. Benson's office to rat the boys out. He could tell by the principal's demeanor with Ricky at lunch, he wouldn't do anything. It didn't take him long to realize Ricky Smith was truly the pride and joy of Washington High, and Principal Benson was going to do whatever he had to protect his image, even if it meant allowing Ricky to run amuck on school grounds and do whatever he pleased.

As he cautiously crept onto the front porch, he prayed his mother wasn't home. The car wasn't parked out front so he figured she probably went off to work for some extra hours. Although the only wound that was visible to the plain eye was his bruised lip, he knew it was just enough for his mother to flip her lid. The last thing he wanted to do was burden his mother with anymore of his school problems.

He eased into the house, and at first sight the coast was clear. The home was completely mute. Vince's old dusty record player wasn't even left spinning, like he normally left it. Feeling completely relived, he started to limp his way to his bedroom.

"Julius!" he heard his mother's call out from the kitchen.

His body jumped at her voice as he instantly froze in his tracks. He stood at the edge of the hallway with his eyes shut closed. He could hear her footsteps approaching him on the rugged wooden flooring.

"So you're just gonna sneak in here and not speak?" she asked while drying her hands with a dish towel.

"Nah, Ma, I didn't even know you were here. I wanted to go 'head and jump into this assignment Mr. Bass got me doing for art class." The inner walls of his mouth burned with each word expelled from his lips.

"Okay, I know you gotta get your school work done, but it doesn't excuse you from not coming in here and speaking," she said.

"My bad, Ma."

She looked at him suspiciously. "And why aren't you facing me?"

"No reason," he said, continuing to his room.

"Julius, I'm talking to you," she said. "I don't know what you got going through that head of yours, but you better turn around and face me when I'm talking to you."

"Ma!" he growled. He debated between taking a few more steps into his room or turning around to face her. He didn't want her to worry, but the choice was simple. He knew he wasn't getting to his room without answering her request.

"Julius, turn around," she said as she took a step closer to him.

He slowly faced her, and her eyes immediately shot opened. Her towel hit the floor.

"Julius, what happened?" she asked as she rushed towards him.

"Nothing, Ma. Nothing. Nothing I can't handle on my own," he declared as he tried to back away from her caring hands.

"What do you mean, nothing? Your lip is busted, and you're holding your stomach like you're hurt. What happened, baby?"

"I'm okay, Ma. I told you. I'm alright," he claimed as he continued to dodge her hands.

"Baby, who did this to you? You've been in a fight. I can tell," she said as she gently held his chin. She tried to pull his face into hers to get a good look at him and to hold him as only a mother could, but he continued to back away. She sniffed his shirt before he completely backed out of her grasp. "Julius, what happened? You smell like…you smell like pee."

"Ma, I'm alright. I'm alright, I tell ya'," he yelled.

"No, you're not. You're holding onto your ribs like somebody's been beating on you, and you smell just like piss. What did them bastards do to you? You tell me, Julius! You tell me now."

"Nothing, Ma. Nothing. I'm okay. I got this. Just let it go!"

"Don't tell me to let it go," she yelled as he ran into his room. "Julius!" She tried to catch him by the edge of his shirt, but he slammed the door in her face. She heard the click from the lock on the other side of the door as she grabbed the stiff door knob. With her mouth balled up, she fiercely pounded on his door. "Open this door, Julius! Open it right now. I'm not done talking with you. You're gonna tell me what happened."

She couldn't hear a peep from the other side of the door as she continued to beg and plead for him to let her in. After a few moments of not getting any response from her son, she yielded her assault on the door and slowly backed away from it as she attempted to ponder her next move. "I know. I know what I'm gonna do. I'ma call that damn school, and I'm gonna get down to the bottom of this, right now!" She yelled into the door. "You hear me Julius, I'm gonna call that school, and I will find out what happened to you."

She darted into the kitchen and snatched the phone off its handle. She rummaged through her purse on the table and retrieved a business card with the school's number on it. She dialed and placed the phone up to her ear.

"Hello, hello," she glared at the phone base on the wall and began smashing down the phone's switch hook. There was no dial tone. The phone had been turned off. In a fit of rage, she threw the phone at the refrigerator, and it broke into pieces after it tumbled to the floor.

Tears began rolling down her face as she pulled out a chair and planted herself in it. Her son had gotten attacked, and he refused to tell her who did it. She couldn't call the school to make them tell her what happened because she didn't have the money to pay the phone bill. She felt extremely helpless, and it stung like hell.

Chapter 8

Julius hung over the railing of the second floor mall balcony as he did on most Saturdays. The mall was always a place Julius was very fond of because he could sit back and observe people and not have to worry about being noticed. He admired each unsuspecting patron from afar. The most attractive mall goers often caught his eye, as he wondered what their lives were like to be looked upon, not in disgust but with respect, trust and envy. He felt their worlds were a far cry from the reality he lived in each day where his dark black skin, brawn nose and thick lips were always the catalyst for discrete chuckles, slick insults and unpleasant stares.

As his eyes bounced around from one person to the next, thoughts of Ricky Smith crept from the back of his mind. He wanted to make the boy pay for what him and his goons did to him, but the idea of being in the same place with the boy again really unnerved him. When the thoughts of having another confrontation with Ricky came to mind, it made his heart race and his whole body quiver.

His mother badgered him for days for the identity of the culprit that assaulted him to no avail. When she finally scrapped up enough resources to get the phone turned back on, her response from the school was utterly unhelpful. They advised her that they couldn't fix an issue they could not identify as needing repair. By him not ratting the boys out about the beating, they were reluctant to do anything, and the school made it clear to his mother they weren't about to waste any time helping someone that clearly didn't want to be helped. As the week went on, his mother began to back off on the issue, but with the extensive stares she gave him whenever she was home, he knew the altercation was still fresh on her mind.

"Julius," he heard a voice calling out his name. He turned around and realized it was Simone walking with an older woman. Her companion looked like an older version of her, so he immediately figured the woman to be her mother.

"Hey, Simone," he answered, startled. He was taken off guard by seeing the girl anywhere other the school grounds.

"What are you doing in the mall? Shopping?" she asked as she pulled away from the woman, who was giving Julius a suspicious look.

"Nah, I'm just chillin."

"I never figured you for the mall type."

"Nah, really," he shook his head, "I'm not."

"Ma, I'll be right here," she advised the woman.

"Okay, I'm going in, and I'm coming right back out. I'll only be a few minutes," said the woman as she issued Julius one more look over with a bit of a frown before eventually walking away.

"That's your, Mom?"

"Yeah," she nodded.

"Cool, y'all look alike."

"No we don't," she giggled.

"Really, you do."

"I heard about what happened with Ricky."

"Really? What happened?"

"Come on, Julius, he's been bragging about it to the whole school. He's been telling people he dumped his urine all over you."

"Yeah, well, that's what dicks do," he mumbled as he returned to his leaning posture over the balcony railing.

"Julius, why didn't you turn them in for what they did to you?"

"Turn 'em in for what? So they can kick my ass again? Y'all principal, he ain't gonna do nothin'. They never do."

She took a spot next to him on the railing. "Julius, if you let him get away with this, you know he's not gonna stop bothering you. He gets off on hurting people. It's all funny to him. You gotta turn him in. Mr. Benson has to do something."

"You and your mom come to the mall and shop every Saturday?"

She paused, upset that he ignored her, but she wanted to respect his silent wish to change the subject. "We used to. Not as much as back in the day, though. Not since my dad lost his job."

He took a moment to take in the fact that she was standing so close to him. Not because somebody made her, but because it appeared she wanted to be there. No female other than his mother ever stood as close.

"Everything changed when he lost his job. That's how I ended up at Washington. We couldn't afford to live where we were anymore."

"Yeah, you seem way different than the people at Washington."

"How so, Julius?"

He let out a chuckle. "For one, you're talking to me. And nobody talks to me."

"Well, that's a shame, Julius. They don't know what they're missing out on."

"Why?" he asked.

"Why, what?"

"Why do you talk to me? I'm not cool. I'm not on the basketball team. I'm not..." He wanted to say that he was unattractive, but he decided not to. He didn't want her to know how much he didn't like himself.

"Julius, I don't judge people on how they look or what status they think they have. That stuff doesn't mean anything to anybody."

"Well, you're one of a kind, I tell you that."

"You are, too, Julius."

"Hey, what kind of grades do you make in Mr. Rawls' class. History has always given me problems."

"A's and B's. I kinda' like history. I don't really care for Mr. Rawls, though," he grinned. "I'm sure you remember why."

"Yeah, he's a bit of a character," she nodded. "Me and the girls…"

"You and the girls… noooo thank you."

"Awe, Julius, come on," she said as she gently nudged his arm with her elbow. "We wanted to start something like a study hall at the library after school for his class, and you're making better grades than all of us. It'll just be one day out of the week."

"I'm cool with studying with you, but your girlfriends, I don't know about that. I mean, I see how they be looking at me some times at lunch. I don't think they would too much want me around. I just don't know about that, Simone."

"Well, just think about it Julius. It will be on Thursday's, around six."

"Okay," Julius said. "I can't make no promises, though."

He looked at her and smiled. She smiled back as they both shared a view of the people below them, wandering about, enjoying their day at the mall.

Julius' ride on the bus from the mall was filled with thoughts of Simone. As he glanced out of a window in the back of the bus he couldn't take his mind off her gorgeous face and the sweet smell of her skin. She gave him a feeling inside he couldn't formulate words to explain, but he knew it made him feel good. When he was around her, he didn't worry so much about how he looked or what others were thinking when they saw him. She gave him a free feeling–free of stress and free of anxiety, feelings that had become as natural to him as breathing itself.

When the bus turned down the street near his neighborhood, he realized Travis was waiting near the bus stop. It had slipped his mind that he was suppose to meet with him a couple hours prior. He pulled the bus ringer and hurried off the bus. Travis was sitting on the stairs of the vacated city hall building.

"Man, there you are. What the hell?" Travis said.

"My bad, man. I lost track of time when I was at the mall." He bumped knuckles with Travis.

"The mall?" Travis asked as he looked down at Julius' empty hands. "What the hell you buy?"

"Nothing, I was just chilling out."

"You are one weird dude to spend all day at the mall and not buy shit." He shook his head. "I was out here waiting on you and shit, and you at the mall window shopping. Come on."

"Cool," Julius answered as he followed Travis down the sidewalk.

The sound of a police siren chirped for a second. They both turned to the street to notice a slow moving police cruiser easing up behind them. Travis stepped in front of Julius and bent down to look the young officer behind the wheel straight in his face. The officer was a clean cut white male, in his mid thirties. He wore big dark shades and had a straight face as he returned his own stare to Travis. His car crept along almost to a stop, but not completely.

"Can I help you, Officer Tillman? Were we doing something wrong?" Travis said while swinging his arms out. The cop didn't offer any response, just an unfriendly scowl. His car slowly moved on without incident. "Punk ass, pig," Travis mumbled.

"He know you?" Julius asked.

"Yeah, that's old punk ass Officer Tillman," he said as they continued their stride down the sidewalk. "He arrested my ass one time, and ever since then, every time his punk ass see me, he's always staring me down and shit, actin' like a nigga can't walk nowhere."

"Does he always slow down like that when he sees you?"

"Man, screw that pig. I ain't talking about his ass right now."

"Where we going."

"My spot, nigga."

"Your house?"

"No, dude, my spot." He said as they took a cut through a filthy alley between a row of worn down buildings.

Julius had never wandered into this part of his neighborhood. He was astonished to see so many homeless people sitting along the trashy walkway, sleeping between dumpsters, exchanging needles and even performing sex acts in broad daylight without any regards to anyone approaching them. He understood the area he lived in was rough, but he didn't realize the magnitude of the corruption and severe poverty that was right under his nose.

"This place is ragged, man," Julius said as he was careful not to make any eye contact with anyone they approached. They didn't look at him either. It was almost like they didn't exist in passing.

"I bet you didn't know shit was this messed up down here, did ya'?"

"Nah, not at all."

"It's all good, though. You don't bother them, they don't bother you."

"How'd it get this messed up?"

"Jobs, man. Everybody talkin' about Clinton fixing shit around the country, but he ain't fixin' shit here. Jobs can leave, but people still gotta eat. Most niggas ain't got no money to follow no job."

"Dang," Julius shook his head. "Left the place like a ghost town."

Travis led him down another walkway and they stopped at the back door to one of the buildings.

"What's this?" Julius asked.

"I told you," he said with a smile. "My spot."

Travis turned the knob and pushed the door open. Travis had turned out to be a cool guy, but Julius still had his reservations about him. He followed him carefully inside the huge building. It appeared to be some type of old warehouse with big empty white walls and large cement pillars scattered throughout.

"What is this place?"

"My home away from home," Travis answered as they journeyed to a corner in the back of the building where an old couch sat with a stack of pillows on it.

"You're not worried about the crackheads out there coming in here and messing around?"

"Hell nah, this my spot. They know I don't play. They know better than to come up in here, mucking around with my stuff."

Julius wandered around as he took in the massiveness of the rundown building. He surveyed the dingy floor that was riddled with newspapers and smatterings of two-by-fours, and he also studied the busted fixtures that hovered from the ceiling. After a short tour of the place, he found himself looking down at a crate full of spray cans.

"What's this doing here? You paint?"

"That's what I wanted to show you, nigga." He said as he stood beside him. "I got you these paints so you can hook my shit up in here."

"I've never used paints on a wall before," he picked up one of the cans and examined it.

"Dude, if you can draw on paper, you can paint on a fuckin' wall," he laughed as he patted Julius on his shoulder. "Get outta here with that foolishness."

Julius approached a barren space on the wall and looked over it. He didn't know where or how to begin. He closed his eyes and envisioned an idea and began applying the image in his mind onto the wall with the spray paint, just like he's always done with his drawing pad.

"Alright, don't breath none of that stuff in too much. I don't have any face masks."

"It's all good," Julius replied. "What do you do in here, anyway?"

Travis dove onto the couch. "I used to serve a lil' bit from here, but that cracka' ass cop that just passed us by back there always be in my shit now, so I stopped."

"Serve?"

"Yeah, nigga."

"You mean like sell drugs?"

"You mean like sell drugs?" he mocked him in a high pitch voice. "Yeah, nigga, I'll sell your ass if I could make some money off you," he giggled as he stretched out on the couch. "Just kidding, dude. I do what I gotta do, when I have to. I ain't never claimed to be no saint."

"You weren't scared to do that?"

Travis sat up and laughed. "Nigga, my momma's a crackhead. I ain't scared of shit."

"Oh. I can understand that."

"Anyway, I mostly bring broads up in here that ain't too scared to come down here, and I tackle there asses on this here couch."

Julius gazed at Travis from the side of his eye as he noticed the boy rolling up what he assumed to be marijuana.

"Do you smoke crack?"

"Nigga, do this look like crack?" He held up the blunt and gave Julius a mean stare.

"I don't know, man. I've never been around any drugs before. My bad."

"You're cool, Julius. You're cool. This ain't nothing but a lil' bit of weed, man. Nothin' to fear. Makes you smart. You want a hit?"

"Nah, man," Julius rapidly shook his head.

"Pussy!" he laughed.

"What?"

"You're a pussy, man. But it's all good. It just means more for me." He lit up the joint and took a hit.

"Whatever, man," Julius said as he dropped the paint can and approached him. He stood in front of Travis who was smirking at him as he moved around on the couch to get more comfortable. Julius didn't like the idea of Travis calling him a wimp for use of better words, and he wanted to prove to the older boy that he could do anything he could do. "Let me see that."

"This," he pulled the blunt from his mouth and held it up. "Get your ass on with that. That's the second time you turned me down. You don't want none of this. This here is for big boys. You still getting breast fed."

"Man, go 'head, I'm not scared to try it. I ain't no punk."

"Ah-ight, be careful with it, homeboy. That shit is as pure as you're gonna get it."

Julius snatched the blunt from him and stared at it. He never took any kind of drug before, and the smell of Vince's cigarettes and cigars made him want to gag. If he could take the previous few seconds back he would've, but his pride was working on all cylinders. He wanted Travis to see him as more than just some chump that gets picked on by everybody because of his looks. He wanted to show Travis that he wasn't afraid to take a hit, although he really was.

"Go'on, big dawg, take that hit. But be easy on them virgin lungs."

Julius looked at him and thought *what the hay?* It was a do or die moment for him, and he chose to do. He placed the blunt in his mouth and took a long hard hit, so hard he came up coughing profusely.

"Hey, nigga, hold on," Travis jumped up, snatched the joint and began patting Julius on his back. "Why you take it down like that, negro? You 'bout to be the first nigga to o.d. on a damn blunt."

"I'm good. I'm good," Julius claimed as he coughed with his bloodshot eyes.

He plunged onto the couch and Travis took a spot beside him. He slouched back in the chair as he slowly recovered and his body began to ease to the effect of the marijuana. Once Travis realized he was okay, he took another hit on the blunt and slumped onto the couch beside him.

"Feel better now, huh?" Travis asked.

"Yessssss," Julius nodded.

"Want another hit?"

"No."

"You better stop fooling up with me. I'll have your ass tore up with the quickness," he laughed. "So, what's this I hear about you getting peed on?"

Julius slowly rolled his head over to him, surprised by the fact that he brought up the incident between him and Ricky. "Damn, how'd you hear about that, and you never come to school?"

"I don't come to class! I be around. I'ma always know about what goes down at Washington. That's a fact."

Julius was about to give him the details, but he thought better of it. Besides, he felt like he was floating, and he didn't feel like wasting the last remaining brain cells he had left talking about Ricky Smith.

He didn't totally understand why, but he suddenly acquired the immediate urge to take a nap. He figured it had to be the weed as he turned opposite of his friend, and declared in slurred speech, "It's my business. I'll handle it."

"I don't know how you let somebody piss on you, dude, but you better handle that shit, for sho'. You let niggas disrespect you like that once, they'll never stop," Travis said. "Especially chumps like that punk ass Ricky Smith."

Although he couldn't feel most of his body, Julius cringed at hearing Ricky's name as he started to doze off. If he wasn't so high he would be mad, but the marijuana made him forget how to be mad. He just laid there as Travis talked.

"I used to kick his ass all the time back in the day. I know how soft he really is. He got y'all fooled, but not me. That chump still looks like he wanna piss his pants whenever he see me coming. If you need me to check that nigga for you, I will. Just say the word, Jules. Nigga like that will keep pushing you and pushing you. Don't know when to stop."

"Yeah, yeah," Julius mumbled as he began to drift off to sleep.

Travis looked over to him and smiled. "I'ma teach you how to fight for yourself, Jules. Don't you worry about that. When you roll with me, you ain't rolling with no lightweight. That's for sho'."

Chapter 9

As his pencil danced around the canvas of his art pad he carefully crafted his image in deep concentration. His latest masterpiece was nearly complete. All that was left for him to do was to put his final touches of shading onto his sketch of an elderly homeless man sleeping on the pavement while being draped in a pile of old newspapers. Over the past few days his mind was fluttered with images from the alleys he and Travis traveled down to get to their private hangout. With the stroke of his pencil, homeless people, neighborhood prostitutes and common drug dealers were all brought to life through his sketches. The only way for him to expel an image detained in his mind was to draw it and to start sketching the next one. When his eyes looked upon the people that dwelled in those rugged alleyways, he didn't see a lower class of people, he simply visualized living art–living art he somehow felt compelled to capture and release from his mind and onto his drawing pad.

His concentration was broken when he realized there was a shadow of a man standing before him. He looked up and there stood Mr. Bass holding a stack of papers in his hands. He sat them all down in front of him.

"What are these, Mr. Bass," Julius asked as he picked up the papers and began to thumb through them.

"College applications, son. There's one for the Art Institution of Atlanta, the Memphis College of Art, and the Savannah College of Art and Design. I have a few more applications coming in for you this week, but these are some of the best art schools out there. You'll have ample time to fill them all out before their application dates expire."

"Mr. Bass, I can't afford to go to no college." His eyes met the old teacher's eyes with a befuddled look.

"Julius with your talents, getting into a good art school will cost you little to no money at all. I'm going to help you get there, son. There are plenty of scholarships and grants out there for you to take full advantage of, and we'll look through them all. You're too darn talented to let those skills go to waste."

"But, Mr. Bass, I don't know about college, you know."

"You don't know about college? Well, what do you know about, son? Are you gonna sit around and let your God given talents go to waste?"

"I'm not trying to waste my skills or nothing like that, Mr. Bass," he sighed. "I just never thought about college, or anything after high school, to be honest with you."

"Well, son, now is the time. The world don't wait for nobody to sit around and think about what he or she wants to do with his or her life. The world keeps on moving, and by the time you think you have it all figured out, it may already be too late."

"Yeah, I know that, Mr. Bass."

"There's a lot of things being done with computers these days, Mr. Graves, and a good artist will always be in high demand. You have to learn how to use your gifts on all different types of platforms. Not just on the sides of buildings and sidewalks."

When Mr. Bass mentioned the sides of buildings, Julius immediately thought back to all the painting he was doing in the abandon building for Travis. The paintings were new and fun to him, but he didn't want to do that type of stuff for the rest of his life. Truth be told, he never really put much thought into anything professionally he could apply his skills to. It wasn't that he didn't want to have a career in art, it's just he never looked that far into tomorrow. Making it through the day without getting jumped on or picked at always sufficed for him. Besides, art had always been a way for him to escape from the real world that had always found a way to treat him cruelly because of how his face looked.

The bell sounded off, and the class began to pack out and leave for lunch. Unexpectedly, Trey approached Julius. Julius hadn't spoke the boy since the day he flipped on him at lunch with Ricky.

"Hey, Julius, I know you don't really say much to me man, but you should really listen to what Mr. Bass is telling you. I never seen anybody draw the way that you draw. I know you won't have any problems getting into a good art school," he said.

Julius nodded not knowing how to respond to him. He didn't hold any grudges against him, but he preferred not to have any dealings with him. After a brief awkward silence between the two, Trey walked away and went about his business.

As Julius headed for the door behind him, Mr. Bass said, "I expect you to fill out those applications, Mr. Graves. Your final grade for the class will depend on it."

"Say what, Mr. Bass?" Julius asked surprised.

"That's right, son. Completing those college applications is this week's assignment, and if you don't complete them, it will affect your final grade for my class."

"Mr. Bass, what do these have to with art?" he asked while waving the papers in the air.

"Everything!"

"Alright now, but when I was looking through these papers, man…" he said as he began to thumb through the applications again. "…a lot of these applications require money to be sent back with them. Money I don't have."

"You let me worry about that, Mr. Graves. All I'm asking you to do is to fill them all out."

Julius looked on and didn't respond. If Mr. Bass wanted to make him fill out the applications and spend his own money to send them all back, he was fine with it. Just because he was filling them out didn't mean they would accept him, and even if they did accept him it didn't mean that he'd have to leave, so he simmered down to the idea and headed for the door.

"Alright then, Mr. Bass," he said in leaving the classroom. As soon as he hit the door and entered the hallway he realized Travis was outside waiting for him.

"Man, who waits outside of the class they just got finished cutting?" Julius asked lightly.

"Man, Mr. Bass ain't gonna do nothing. He'll probably give me an A+ just for not coming," he laughed as he gave Julius a handshake.

"What are you doing here anyway?" Julius asked as they began to walk down the hall.

As they paced down the hallway, Mr. Bass walked outside of the classroom to close his door and was surprised to see Julius being accompanied by Travis. He shook his head as he observed the two boys. The idea of Julius hanging around with the young thug didn't sit well with the old art teacher, and he made a mental note to let Julius know about it whenever he got the chance to. Mr. Bass felt he had too much invested in Julius to let someone that didn't appear to care much at all about anything to ruin it.

"What are you doing after lunch?" Travis asked.

"Going to class," Julius answered.

"Class? Man, you need to roll with me today."

"Nah, man, I'm trying to pass and get out of school for good. I can't be missing no classes."

"Man, you can miss a half a day. They, like, let you miss ten days before you can even fail for the year. Cuttin' a half of day won't kill you."

"Nah, man, I'm not trying to piss my momma off neither. She never finished school because she got pregnant with me, and if she finds out I cut a class, I'll never hear the end of it."

"Who gonna tell her? You?"

"Man, they take roll and stuff."

"Man, they don't turn that shit in. Besides, I got a dime bag, and I was thinking we could head back to the spot and blaze the hell out."

"I can get with you after school lets out, but I can't go nowhere today. You should come in and get some lunch, though."

"I don't eat that shit," he laughed. "But I'll come in and chill out with you. Check and see what some of these lames been up to up here in Washington High School."

After entering the lunch room and grabbing his meal, the two sat at the table where Julius normally ate. Julius chowed down on his orange circle pizza and chocolate milk as Travis rambled on about his previous night of mischief. Julius enjoyed hearing Travis' adventures because it seemed he lived a life where there was never a dull moment.

"…And yo, the sister was like four hundred pounds, man. Talkin' about can you handle this? I said, hell yeah!"

"I know you didn't," Julius asked with his mouth packed with food.

"Boy, you know I like 'em big. I scooped them big ole' legs up over my shoulders and tore that big juicy thang up!" he laughed.

"Man, you're wild, Travis." Julius said, laughing.

"She got a sister and they having a party in a couple of weeks. We can tag team them broads then if you want to."

"Nah, man, I'll pass."

"What? You scared?"

"Nah, I'm just not into big girls, that's all."

Travis gave him a suspicious look. "Wait a minute, dude. You ever had any?"

"What man? What'ch you talkin' about?" Julius asked nervously. He didn't want to answer the question because the truth was embarrassing to him. He never had any type of intimacy with any female, not even a mere kiss. He had been ugly Julius for so long in his mind, he never even thought there would be a female on the planet that would even want to kiss him, let alone have sex with him.

"Ah shit, you ain't never had none! Daaaayuumn!"

"Man, go 'head now. Of course I had some before. I've had plenty!"

"From who, nigga?"

Julius rolled his eyes, frustrated by the conversation. He knew his answer was an emphatic zero, but Travis didn't need to know that. "Man, why are we even talking about this? This is my business."

"Oh we gonna get you a piece of ass, that's for sho. I can't be having no virgin rolling around with me. We gotta get your little Vienna sausage wet," he laughed. "Virgins get nervous about shit too fast. You might get us caught up in some shit at the wrong time."

"Ah, man, don't worry about me. I don't even…"

"Hey!" said a voice.

They both paused from their conversation and simultaneously looked up at Simone who was staring and smiling at Julius with her tray in her hand.

"Simone…" Julius nervously answered.

"Well, I'll be damned. It's the head cheerleader in the flesh." Travis uttered in shock. "Jules, you didn't tell me you were hanging out with the finest chick in the school. How do you do, mam?" Travis jumped out of his seat and did a playful bow to the girl.

She rolled her eyes and gave him a perturbed look, but only briefly because she heard many of the stories about Travis and his knack for being rude and obnoxious with females. "Former cheerleader, Travis."

"Everybody around here knows nobody can replace you with a face like that. Here, take my chair," he said as he signaled her to take his seat. "I was just about to head off to my next class," he laughed. "Like my main man, Jules."

She reluctantly took his chair as Julius looked on, not knowing how to respond. He could tell she was surprised to see him with Travis, and at the same time he feared Travis would say the wrong thing to her and make her mad at him.

"Jules, I'll check you out after school, homeboy," he said as he winked his eye and gave him a thumbs up. "We gonna talk about that thang we was just talking about, too."

"Alright, man," he answered. He was too relieved Travis was leaving.

As soon as Travis walked far enough away, Simone leaned over the table and whispered, "Julius, what are you doing with him?"

"What do you mean?"

"What do I mean? That boy, Travis. He's bad news, and he's always getting into something, when he comes to school, of course. And then he's older than everybody in the school except for the teachers."

"Travis is cool. He just likes doing his own thing."

"Well doing his own thing must be cutting class and acting like a jerk, but alright, Julius. Just don't let him get you into trouble," she nodded while pouring her dressing over her salad. "This is only my second year here at this school, but I've heard enough stories about him to last a lifetime."

"Yeah, well, everybody got something to say about somebody." From the corner of his eye he noticed Ricky entering the cafeteria with two of the guys that jumped him. His heart instantly started fluttering a mile a minute. "Ah, I gotta go."

"What? You're not even finished eating," she said staring at his plate. She recognized the sudden nervousness on his face and turned her attention to the area of the lunch room that appeared to have captured his interest. She quickly realized why he wanted to leave so fast. "Julius, you don't have to go anywhere. Are you gonna leave every time you see them?"

"Nah, it has nothing to do with them," he told her in a lie as he gathered his things. "I just forgot something in art class, that's all."

"Julius, stop. Don't leave because of them," she begged. "Julius…"

"Gotta go. I'll see you later on today," he said as he made a dash towards the exit.

Her eyes trailed him as he made his speedy exodus. She then turned her attention to Ricky, who was standing in the lunch line laughing it up with his buddies. She was furious by the sight of him. If she was a boy, she'd make him pay for what she'd heard he did to Julius.

As Julius fled from the cafeteria he noticed that Travis was still roaming the halls and hadn't left school grounds yet. He recognized the back of his head while walking towards the rear exit of the school, near the gym area. "Travis," he yelled as he began to sprint towards the boy.

"Jules!" he spun around smiled. "What happened? Did the cheerleader make you mad or something? Her stuck up ass."

"Nah, it's just…" he shook his head.

"You had a change of heart?"

"Yeah, that's it." he answered. "You sure a half day ain't gonna mess up nothin'?"

"Hell, no man," he snapped back. "You talkin' to the cut king! Now let's go to the spot and get blazed as hell," he said as he wrapped his arm around Julius' neck. They proceeded to the leave the school.

****

Felicia's stood over the tiny stove as she flipped over the last little bit of chicken she was frying in a sizzling pan of hot grease. Beads of sweat slid down her face because cooking anything in the small kitchen made the entire house feel like a sweltering hot sauna. Vince eased up behind her with an angry scowl on his face as he gazed over her shoulder.

"What's up with all this late eating lately? You normally have the food done almost two hours ago."

"It's almost done now," she answered, while spacing out the meat in the bubbly grease.

"I like to eat my food early," he complained as he reached around her and grabbed a drumstick from a bowl of cooked chicken. He bit into the meat as if he hadn't eaten in days.

She sighed and gave him a brief look as he took a seat at the table. She hated when he grabbed food before she was done cooking. "Did Julius get in yet?"

"I don't know. Ain't looking for him neither." he answered with chicken crumbs bouncing off his lips. "That boy comes in whenever he feels like, lately."

"Aren't you one to talk?"

"I'm a grown ass man. I can come in whenever I damn well please. You understand?"

Felicia shook her head while ignoring his question.

"Damn that. You over there with all that head shaking and shit. You do understand that I'm a grown ass man, goddamn it! Don't you?"

"Yes, Vince," she said while taking a deep breath and facing him. "No one is denying that you're a grown man and that you do whatever you feel like doing."

Each word leaving from her mouth infuriated him. His eyes were bloodshot. "Alright then, I don't know what the fuck kinda' comments need to be made about what I do. You need to be chastising that damn boy of yours and not my black ass."

"Vince, all I asked you was if you'd seen him…"

"And I told your smart fuckin' ass I didn't see his ashy black ass, didn't I?"

She didn't want to continue arguing with him so her focused went back to her cooking as she flipped off the stove and removed the grease from the stove eye. She had a quick thought running through her head to throw the grease on his grouchy behind, but she thought better of it.

Even when revenge became an understandable option for
her, she never carried an eye for an eye mentality. It was
that way when she was violated sexually by the man known
as Herman Joseph, and it remained true for her poor excuse
for a common law husband, Vincent. Her only alternative
for retaliation on anyone was if they hurt her son. And not
knowing the whereabouts of her son this late from school
was killing her.

"And fix my damn food, now. I ain't waiting on
nobody to come home. Ain't nobody the damn Huxtables
around here."

Julius eased into the house from the front.

"Julius!" his mother called out from the kitchen as
soon as she heard the door slam. "Is that you out there?"

"Yeah," he replied.

"Come on, then. Supper's ready."

"Okay," he answered as he sat his books down on
the edge of the sofa. He paused for a moment before
heading into the kitchen. He sniffed the back of his wrist,
and his shirt. The strong stench weed carried almost
skipped his mind. He didn't feel the smell was too strong,
but he thought it was strong enough to be noticeable.
Therefore, he slipped out of his hoodie, leaving only his
white tee shirt on.

"Julius, come on, now!" his mother yelled.

He trampled into the kitchen and the first thing he
laid eyes on was Vince, sitting at the table, digging into his
dinner. "Hey, Mom," he said as walked to her and gave her
a quick kiss on the cheek. He took a seat at the table beside
Vince and didn't make any eye contact with him at all.

"Vince is sitting there," Felicia said.

"What's up," he mumbled still not looking at the man.

Vince smiled as if he was slightly amused by Julius' half hearted greeting.

"Julius, school let out almost four hours ago. Why are you getting home so late?"

"I was at the library."

Vince slightly leaned over to Julius while looking dead in his face and took in a deep sniff of his sleeve. "Library, huh?" He let out a chuckle. Vince recognized the smell as soon as Julius hit the door.

"Yeah, the library," Julius gave Vince a nervous look.

"Maybe you should just say no to not having your momma worry about where your ass is gonna be at after school. The phone is back on, if you didn't know."

"The phones are on," she said as she sat a plate of food in front of Julius. "And you should let us know something if you're going to be coming home late. We're still new to this neighborhood. Verna Watts got robbed in the supermarket parking lot just last week."

"Sorry, Ma," he said as he grabbed a fork and began pouring into the food. He was nervous that Vince was going to say something about how he smelled. He looked up at Vince, and noticed the man staring right at him while chewing his food with a devilish grin.

143

Felicia sat her food in the chair across from Julius and claimed a spot at the table. "A girl called for you earlier."

"Really?" he asked as his heart raced. He knew it could only be Simone, but he never gave his phone number to her. He never had a reason to give his phone number out to anyone. "What did they say? Who was it?"

Vince chuckled. "How the fuck did you get a girlfriend? I bet she's just as ugly as your ass."

Julius dropped his fork. There was an awkward silence at the table as Felicia gazed at Vince, mad as hell. Vince looked at them both and continued to eat. Julius shook his head, and dashed out of the kitchen.

"You just don't care what you say to him, do you?"

"What?" Vince questioned. "What the hell I say wrong?"

"Don't you call him ugly again. If you can't treat him with respect and call him by his name, don't say nothing to him at all. Not one word."

"Ooh, you got me scared," he laughed. "What got your ass in a wad?"

She grunted and headed for the kitchen's exit. Before she could leave the room, Vince said, "When you get back, I'm gonna be gone. Ain't got no time for all this here sensitive shit."

"Good," she said as she continued out.

"Good?" he jumped up and yelled towards the door. "Hell, I won't ever come back, you keep talking like that. The hell you talkin' about, good!"

Felicia opened Julius' door and proceeded into his room. He was stretched out across his bed with his face buried into his pillow.

"I guess there's no better time than now to tell you," she said. "We're driving down to your Grandmother's place tomorrow."

Julius' head rose from the pillow as he let out a loud sigh. He didn't like being around his mother's people, and he couldn't believe she was planning a trip to see them. They all came off as uppity snobs. He worked just as hard to disassociate himself from them as they did to him and his mother.

"Why, Ma?" he asked. "Why in the world are we going there?"

"Kim and her husband are coming down to see Frank. He's hasn't been doing too well since the cancer has come back. Mom thought it would be a good idea for all of us to have a bit of a gathering."

"Awe, Ma," he sat up on the bed. "You know none of them people like me."

"Now that's not true, Julius."

"Yes it is, Ma, and you know it. You think I don't know they wanted you to get rid of me before I was born? It's the worst kept secret in anybody's family."

His words knocked the wind out of her because she knew there was much truth to them all. She didn't make a play to change how Julius felt about her family because she had always done her best to be straight up with her son, and she wasn't about to stop now. She simply yearned for a better relationship between Julius and her folks. To, at least, give him some type of relationship and feeling of family, even though they've both been outcasted for so long. All he had was her, and at times she just felt that wasn't enough.

"Julius we won't even stay long. We'll drop in, say hi, chat a little and come on back home."

He gave her a somber look with his nostrils flaring. "I guess I don't have much of a choice."

"No," she nodded. "You don't."

He laid flat on his back as his mother retreated towards the door.

"It'll be a nice little drive for you and I to catch up."

She left him idle on the bed, thinking about how much he didn't want to be around the family that gave him their butts to kiss before he even came into this world. It was one thing to be dissed by complete strangers every day in the school system, but getting clowned by your own flesh and blood was another thing. Although he didn't consider himself a part of his mother's family, it still hurt him to not be accepted by them. His trip to his grandmother's house was one journey he was definitely not looking forward to taking.

Chapter 10

A young Julius joyfully pushed a yellow Tonka trunk thru the well trimmed lawn of his grandmother's massive back yard all by his lonesome. From his knees, the seven year old boy had the metal truck loaded down with a pile of rocks and twigs he found throughout the edges of the yard. As he maneuvered the toy truck along the grass he caught a glimpse of another boy, his younger cousin Alvin, who was running towards him from the back porch. Julius reverted his attention back to the toy truck and his imaginary highway as he made buzzing truck noises while plowing through the lawn.

"Hey! What are you doing with my truck, ugly!" Alvin yelled.

Julius glanced back at the boy as he continued to push the toy along. He didn't know who the truck belonged to, he just knew it was there when him and his mother arrived earlier that morning, sitting and waiting for someone to play with it.

"Hey, fart face, I'm talking to you," said the boy as he shoved Julius to the ground. "My mommy says your mommy gets paid for doing the nasty. I don't want you to be touching my stuff with your cootie hands."

His cousin's attack was brisk, unexpected, and it completely knocked the wind out of him. Not only did he bang his knee on the metal truck from his tumble, but he slammed into the ground face first. His plunge onto the lawn probably wouldn't have been as severe if he was aware it was coming. He laid flat on his face as he spit out dirt and grass. His cousin hovered over him with an evil grin.

Alvin scooped up his truck and started walking back towards the house. Julius pulled himself up off the ground and all he could see was red when he laid eyes on his cousin again. The boy was still rambling on about Julius and the truck as he trekked back to the porch. Not only did Alvin call him out his name and viscously shove him to the ground, but he also talked about his momma–a cardinal sin on any playground, family or not. He ran up behind the boy in a fit of rage and tackled him to the ground with all his might. The Tonka truck went flying in one direction, and Alvin went crashing onto the ground in another.

"Don't you ever talk about my momma again," said Julius as he stood over the boy with tears fluttering down his face.

Alvin rolled over on his back with a busted lip as Julius peered down at him with his fist balled up. Julius' angry demeanor terrified him. "And you don't call me ugly, either!" Julius plunged onto the boy and mounted him, then commenced to pounding on his cousin's face. Alvin did his best to cover up with his scrawny arms, but Julius was on him like some fire ants scurrying over some stray breadcrumbs.

A few seconds went by and all Julius could hear was his mother and grandmother hollering and screaming for him to stop beating on his cousin as they rushed towards them.

"Julius," his mother screamed. "Julius, stop!"

Felicia dove on top of Julius to get him off the boy, and her momentum sent her and her son crashing to the ground. Louise ran to Alvin's aid and gently helped him to his feet. She began knocking off all the grass and dirt that had covered the boy's clothes. Everyone else that was inside the house began to file outside to investigate the commotion.

"He started it, momma. He pushed me first," Julius cried as he attempted to pull away from Felicia to get a little more of Alvin's hide.

"Oh, no you don't!" Louise shielded Alvin away from Julius by shoving him behind her, defending him from anymore harm. "You see Felicia, I told you not to have that... that creature. He's a savage. Just like his daddy. Just like I told you he'd be."

Julius froze. He looked up at his grandmother as she gazed down at him with her mouth balled up and her nose flaring. Even at his young age, Julius could feel her severe hatred towards him. Her hurtful words swooped him out of his anger towards his cousin and pierced through his heart like a flaming dagger. With more tears streaming down his face, he turned to his mother as she pulled herself up off the ground. He embraced her with a hug. She said nothing. She simply looked at her mother with a feeling of shock and disgust.

The old Cavalier roared down the barren wooded street as Julius sat in a daze as he rested his head on the passenger side window. Reminiscing about that day still made him want to burst into tears ten years later. The very last thing he ever wanted to do again was come back to the country to see his grandmother and his so called family.

From his understanding, a few years back they got an even bigger home built with even more things to brag and boast about, thanks to his step granddad's cashing out some stocks and bonds he had saved throughout the years shortly after his retirement. He was certain the snobby mentality they all exuded had expanded by leaps and bounds, and by no means was he in any rush to be around it.

He knew the family never liked him, and he honestly understood why. Therefore, he couldn't think of one good reason why he should've been forced to come along. He heard rumors about how they treated his mother just before bringing him into the world, so he couldn't think of one single reason for her to come either. With all the hell they put her through, he couldn't understand why she still cared. He didn't care if he ever saw any of them again and he was absolutely certain the feeling was mutual on their behalf.

Felicia glanced at her son with mixed feelings about making him come along. On one hand, she wanted him to feel as if he was a part of the family she once knew before she became a militant teenager that initiated the rift between the family because she always wanted to do things her way. On the other hand, she remembered the day Julius beat up Alvin. She knew her son wasn't stupid. She knew he hadn't forgotten the viscous words his grandmother spewed at him. It took her a long time to forgive her mother for that day. She feared Julius would never be able to do the same, and when she really thought about it, she figured *why should he?*

"What you thinking about over there?" she asked him.

He turned to her and smiled.

"What? Tell me." she asked with a smile of her own.

"You really wanna' know?"

"Wouldn't ask if I didn't."

"I was thinking about how long we were gonna have to stay before we head back home." He went back to staring out of the window.

"Julius, I know it's hard for you to tag along with me today, but I appreciate you for doing it. I know we can't change what's happened in the past, but as long as God blesses us with another day of living, we get another opportunity to stand strong."

Returning to the country to see his grandmother had him feeling uneasy and worrisome. He didn't want to be anywhere around his grandmother. Whenever he saw her, all he could think about was her cynical stare and those vicious words expelling from her lips, *He's a savage.* The words cut like a blade—a blade that had been lodged in his heart for over ten years with blood still leaking from it.

Truthfully, he didn't want to ever see anyone in his moms shady bloodline, especially his cousin Alvin with his narcissist attitude towards anyone that crossed his path. He only saw Alvin a handful of times since they were seven, and on every single occasion he wanted to whack him because of his constant bragging, and putting others down. The boy inherited the same snobbish attitude their grandmother possessed, and he couldn't stand it.

When they pulled into the driveway, Julius' anxiety grew stronger. He counted about twenty cars in the driveway and scattered along the front lawn. It surprised him to discover so many vehicles parked on the grass because his grandmother was known to always cause a fuss over things like that. He could just visualize her inside the house at that moment, having a hissy fit for people parking on her precious lawn.

"We're here," Felicia said as she turned the car off.

"Yup," he answered.

There was an awkward silence between the two. Neither wanted to get out of the car, neither wanted to be there for one reason or the other, but somehow they ended up there.

Julius observed the massive green lawns that each gigantic home rested on in the ritzy neighborhood. It made him think about how his yard only had small patches of grass that appeared to be tiny green islands in the middle of the dusty beige sandlot his home resided on. He was amazed by how his grandmother seemed to have so much, yet he and his mother had so little. He didn't fault his mother for not accepting hand outs from the family, however. He was actually very proud of her for it. If having tons of money made everybody act like his mom's people did, he surely didn't want any parts of it.

"You sure you want us to go up in there, Ma?"

"No, not really, but we made it this far. We may as well go in there and throw up our hands."

Julius let out a hard sigh, "Okay."

As they fled the car and walked across the lawn in unison, Julius was as nervous as a young child going to see the dentist for the first time. He kept fidgeting with his clothes, worried about if the hoodie and baggy jeans he was wearing made him look too much like a thug in front of all the snobby rich folk that resided on the other side of his grandmother's front door. He became accustomed to being picked on and talked about by his peers because of his facial features all of his life, but the idea of getting laughed at by a house full of snobs was an unfamiliar territory he wanted no parts of.

Felicia had her own set of worries. She didn't care to see her can't-do-wrong younger sister again also. She was almost certain this day would be the very last time she would ever see her step-father alive. Then the idea of being around her mother on her turf and in her element sunk in. Although the relationship she had with her mother was never a pleasant one, it was one that she sorely missed.

As they stood on the porch in front of the big white door, they gave each other a quick glance over. Felicia rang the doorbell.

After a few moments of silence Louise swung the door open and her face lit up like a jack-o-lantern, "Oh Felicia, I'm so glad you made it." Felicia, not nearly as excited, found her feet dragging onto the hardwood floor as her mother opened her arms and embraced her with a hug. Her mother's excitement stunned her. She was even more baffled when Louise released her and turned to her son and said, "Julius. It's really good to see you, grandson."

Grandson? He thought to himself with a baffled expression on his face. She approached him and gave him a hug he could only feel as being awkward. She barely embraced him with all of her body, and he didn't hug back. He just stood frozen and bewildered. She backed away with a smile.

"Okay," she said as she clasped her hands and rubbed them together.

"Hi," Julius answered, still shocked by her embrace.

"Most everyone is out in the back. There's a ton of barbeque chicken, ribs, steaks and a full buffet bar out there. Indulge in as much as you like and chalk it up with some of the younger folk out there. There's plenty to eat and plenty to do. You'll have a blast, Julius." She directed him to the back of the gigantic house.

Julius glanced over the stiff crowd of older folk that congregated in the den and noticed there appeared to be more people gathered through the window. He then issued his mother a stern look. He didn't want any part of the gathering, and he had no intentions on navigating through his grandmother's estate solo. His plan was to cling to Felicia as tightly as possible so they could dip as soon as she handled whatever business she needed to handle with her stepdad.

"Felicia, Frank's upstairs. He's not feeling well, but he really wants to see you," Louise said as she tugged on Felicia's arm, gently pulling her towards the spiral staircase.

"Oh…okay," she looked toward the stairs, then back to Julius. "Go on out back and grab a lil' something to eat, Julius. I'll be out there in a few minutes. I'm going up to see Frank with mother."

He was ticked. He feared if they separated she could easily lose track of time and have them spending more time there than either of them really wanted to spend. Feeling totally powerless, he watched his mother trail his grandmother up the stairs. He turned his attention to the back of the house as he noticed a larger gathering of people in the back yard over the heads of the crowd mingling and drinking in the dinning area. He reluctantly made his way through the crowd and towards the back of the house and exited through the big white double doors that led out into the patio area.

Outside, there was a DJ in a booth that hovered over the gathering, and he had some *Kool and the Gang*

spinning on his turntable. There was a good crowd of
people that appeared to be more loose than the people
standing in his grandmother's den. They were all bumping
and bobbing to the soulful sounds as they held their drinks,
laughed and talked. Overall, there was a nice sprinkle of
blacks and whites, some overdressed for such a casual
setting, and a few barely dressed.

It amazed him that a stuck up old lady like his
grandmother had so many friends. He was impressed by
the diversity of people at the party. He had expected to be
surrounded by a crowd full of old farts listening to some
opera music or something to that effect. The one thing he
liked most about the get-together was that he didn't
recognize nor know anyone there, and everybody there
appeared to be so caught up in their own thing that he
seemed nonexistent. No one even look his way.

As Julius pushed though the assembly, the savory
smells of the barbeque grazed his nose as he set his sights
on the huge buffet tables that resided off to the side,
accompanied by a group of caterers that were all dressed in
fancy white cooking attire. There was no doubt his
grandmother liked to go all out at her events, that was for
sure.

The food looked great, and he was certainly
prepared to dig in since he happened to be a bit famished
from the three hour drive through the country highways and
barren roads to get there. Suddenly, being at the snooty
engagement didn't seem that bad at all. He grabbed himself
a plate and piled all the food he possibly could on it. He
resided at a table in the back of the gathering all by his
lonesome.

As he sat and enjoyed the barbeque ribs, fried rice
and corn on the cob, digesting it like a homeless man that's

been starving for days, his mind began to wander away from the cookout. Simone's beautiful brown image emerged into his mind. Despite all the negative things that came his way thus far in the school year, she happened to be one of his rays of light. When she entered his mind, any anxiety generated from the negative and unnerving thoughts of Ricky Smith disappeared. Simone and art were the only things he had that kept him from fully cracking.

His calmness quickly dissipated when he heard someone yell out what sounded to be his name from the crowd. He looked up, and initially, he didn't see anything as his eyes scoured the mob of people. He soon noticed the crowd appearing to part for someone approaching his table.

"Julius," the voice repeated closer. A boy blossomed from the crowd wearing a white Tommy Hilfiger shirt and some baggy, black jeans. It was his second cousin, Raymond, and all Julius could do was shake his head at the sight of him.

He didn't hate Raymond, but he didn't care to be around him much either. He talked way too much for his liking, and he was an instant follower to anything he perceived to be cool.

"Man, I haven't seen you in ages. Nobody said you were coming."

"I know, Raymond," he rolled his eyes as the boy grabbed a chair and planted himself at the table.

****

When Felicia and Louise approached the master bedroom, Felicia's sister, Kim, was exiting the room and gently shut the door behind herself. At first glance, Felicia didn't know how to respond to seeing her sister since she hadn't seen her in so long. After so many years of purposely avoiding each other, seeing her again felt kind of strange. It was almost as if she'd seen a ghost.

"Kim," Felicia said. She wanted to say more, but that was the only thing that managed to slip out.

"Felicia," Kim answered, coldly with a slight nod.

She didn't stay to chat as she briskly made her way down the hallway. She didn't even make eye contact with her older sister. Felicia could only observe her sibling in passing as she didn't make any attempt to stop her. They were never close, and Frank was Kim's biological father, not hers. She always felt Kim and the rest of the family resented her since Kim got pregnant right behind her. The only difference was, Kim's pregnancy was from consensual relations, and hers was not. Despite her own teen pregnancy, Kim always remained the precious gem of the family.

None of it mattered to Felicia any longer. She was only there to do the respectable thing, and pay her due respect to the man that kept a roof over their heads when she was younger, not to resurrect lost relationships that were too long buried in the past to resuscitate.

Louise's only response to the awkward moment between her two children was opening the bedroom door and allowing Felicia to enter the bedroom. She never could find a way to make her daughters get along, and they were both too far gone to start now. Felicia slowly crept into the room as Louise slid back into the hall and gently shut the door closed.

Felicia took two steps into the bedroom and froze. The old man lying on the bed appeared to be asleep. As her eyes zoomed in closer, she realized the man resting on the bed looked totally unfamiliar to her, strange even. He was a far cry from the strong, healthy man she remembered as a teen. Once the tall, dark and handsome type, he looked so frail and weak it bothered her. He was always known to be well groomed and to sport a freshly cut temple fade, but the man on the bed had a graying, partially bald head and a rough, wrinkly, unshaven face.

She began to rethink saying anything at all and turning around, but before she could make her move towards the door, he spoke. "Fee."

"Yes, Frank," she replied with a hint of uncertainty in her voice.

"Is that you?" he asked as his head slowly rolled to its side in her direction. He laid on top of the sheets in a pair of light blue pajamas that appeared to be too big for him by several sizes, obviously from the weight loss. As she took another moment to survey his frail, lanky body, it suddenly dawned on her how little time we all have on this earth.

"Felicia," he mumbled. The smile that erupted on his face seemed as if it took every muscle in his body to formulate.

"Hey…Frank," she said timidly, as she slowly approached his bedside.

"I didn't think you were going to make it," he replied softly.

"No, I was coming," she said as she grabbed his hand and sat down on the edge of the chair that was on the side of his bed. "You doing ok?"

"Well, I'm still here. At least for now. I've seen better days though, dear."

"It's good to see you." Her face harbored a smile, but her mind had well over a million things running through it. She knew he didn't have much time left, and all the drama in the past seemed really small.

He was the only father she knew since her real dad ran out on her and her mother when she was only five. From what she could tell, he really never treated her any different than Kim, but she always rejected most of what he asked of her because in her mind, he wasn't her real daddy and he had no right to tell her what to do. Most of her childhood she believed that one day her real father was going to come back for her and take her to live with him, but that day never came. When her biological father passed away when she was thirteen years old, it set something off in her. Something that told her that she didn't have to listen to anyone anymore, not him, not her mother, not a single soul.

As she gazed into the weak eyes of the only real father she ever knew, she regretted all the grief she placed on him, making things so much harder than what they needed to be because of how she saw things, no matter how obviously blurred they appeared. If she could take all the bad things back she would try, but understanding how life worked, to live through those days again, she'd probably make the same mistakes better.

"Julius… did he come?" he asked.

"Yes, he's downstairs, eating… dad."

"Yeah, well…" he rolled his head up and stared at the ceiling. "I'm sorry"

"About what?"

"Fee, I know I'm not your real father, but I should've supported you better than I did. I regret allowing things to go the way that they did. I've regretted it for years. I hate that it's taken me this long to finally say it."

"Oh, dad, that's all in the past. It's nothing to be concerned with now, especially... especially when you're in here like this."

"You know, Felicia, I never told you this, but I'm proud of you." His eyes returned to her. "I'm proud of you for having him. It really takes a special kind of woman to do what you did under those circumstances, and I've always admired you for it." A tear slid down his face. "And I know it's late, but I owe you this apology. I do."

"Dad, you don't owe me anything," she said as her own set of tears began sliding down her cheeks.

"No, if I was any way near as strong as you, maybe this family wouldn't be the way it is now." He paused as he stared into her eyes. "Don't let anyone tell you different, you were right. You were always right."

She was lost for words and overrun with all different kinds of emotions. She jumped up and wrapped her arms around him. Her slow tears emerged into full cries, as they both lay there crying on each other.

****

When Alvin walked onto the patio and caught a glance of Raymond sitting at the back of the gathering talking Julius' ears off, he was ecstatic. He felt as if he won the lottery. There was nothing more fulfilling to him than belittling his cousin, Julius. The tall, handsome, athletic young man knew he was everything Julius wasn't, and he enjoyed making him aware of it every chance he got. Before him, another opportunity awaited.

Alvin moved through the congregation of people like he owned the place. His eyes were focused on Julius, and he couldn't wait to see the look on his cousin's face when he realized that he was in the building. Since that day him and Julius got into their scuffle over that toy truck, he had a vendetta against Julius. Julius had gotten the best of him that day, and it always burned him deeply under his skin. He's had an irrepressible urge to make his cousin's life a living hell because of it.

Julius sat annoyed with Raymond, barely paying any attention to anything that was coming out of his mouth while doing his best to finish off the ribs on his plate. He was hoping his mother wouldn't be much longer, so she could spare him another long winded speech from his second cousin about the latest video games released.

He looked up and almost instantly fell sick to his stomach when he saw Alvin approaching. Wearing his neatly pressed slacks and a polo shirt, he could spot his cousin's cocky smile a mile away, that arrogant smile he had grown to despise.

Alvin immediately noticed the distasteful expression on Julius' face, and it gave him a rush. He had already made ground at achieving part of his goal of getting on his cousin's nerves, and he had yet to utter a single word to him. He grabbed a chair at their table, turned it backwards and sat. "Fellas, what's going on?"

Julius dropped his rib on his plate, pushed back from his table and let out a sigh of frustration. He began wiping his hands with a napkin as Alvin's presence had made him lose his appetite.

He didn't answer Alvin, as the boy looked him up and down, with a grin plastered on his dark yellow face. If it's one thing they knew about each other, it was that they didn't like each other. Julius prepared himself for anything that would find itself outside of Alvin's mouth because he knew the boy couldn't resist keeping his big trap closed.

"Alvin," Raymond giggled. "Man, I didn't know you were going to be here."

"Yeah, me neither," he said with his eyes fixated on Julius. "So what's going on, Julius? I haven't seen you in a couple of years. We all thought you and Aunt Fee dropped off the face of the earth, or old Vince killed you and buried you somewhere."

"I've been around," Julius sat back and fiddled around in the back of his teeth with his tongue. He'd already given Alvin his first strike with his initial comment to him about Vince. He was prepared to see if the boy was going to completely strike out with his mouth.

"You've been around," he nodded his head with a demonic smile. "I see."

"Hey Julius, did you know Alvin has a Super Nintendo and a freakin' Sega Genesis, and he say he's gonna get that new console called the PlayStation this Christmas," said Raymond with an overload of excitement in his voice.

"Hells yeah," Alvin added. He and Julius had their eyes on each other like two angry gunslingers in the Old West. Each waiting for the other to make the wrong move.

"Are you gonna get one, Julius?" Raymond asked.

"Never heard of it," Julius replied.

"Of course he's never heard of it. He probably don't even have a TV set. They say their phone got cut off a couple weeks back. Didn't it, Julius?" Alvin asked.

"Man, whatever," Julius shook his head and removed himself from the impromptu stare down exchange. "If our phone or lights get cut off, it's our business. It's nobody else's business around here but ours." His eyes quickly shifted to the double doors leading back into the house. He hoped his mother would burst through them at any moment.

"Raymond, I bet you didn't know Julius' old man was a rapist, did ya?"

"Whoa! Really, Julius? Nobody ever told me about that," asked Raymond

"A poor family secret, I guess," Alvin added.

Julius gave Alvin a firm look. Alvin was out of line, and it was taking Julius every ounce of self control he had flowing though his body to refrain from jumping across the table and popping his cousin clean across his nose. Striking him would cause an uproar no doubt, but Alvin was begging for it. He always wondered why the boy loved to provoke him so much when he couldn't fight a lick.

"Man, what's up with you? Why every time we see each other you always acting like you gotta shine on me for some reason?"

"There's nothing wrong with me, Julius. I'm just being sociable. It's not like I'm sitting here lying. Aunt

163

Fee was raped by a serial rapist named Herman Joseph. Word is, she was his first victim."

"You need to check yourself, dude. That shit you puttin' out here right now ain't cool. It ain't cool at all," said Julius.

"But it's true, ain't it?" Alvin chuckled. "You never even met the dude. He got his in the big house when you were seven. Too bad Aunt Fee didn't have the guts to do what she should've done and dispose of the only thing he left behind when she had the chance."

Julius let out a chuckle. His hands began to tremble from the agitation of trying to restrain himself from attacking Alvin. He couldn't believe the boy was at it again with his slams. What appeared to be an okay outing at his grandmother's house was quickly becoming everything negative he had originally expected.

Raymond observed the expression on both cousin's faces, and the hostility of the conversation began to dawn on him. "Hey, hey, hey, guys. Let's chill out for a minute. We're all family." He said, in an attempt to play peacemaker.

"This ugly joker ain't no family of mine," Alvin frowned. "I don't have any relations to an offspring of a rapist."

"Man, whatever," Julius said as he slid away from the table and jumped up.

"Oooh, what you gonna do, Julius? Walk away and cry in the bathroom?" Alvin laughed. "I heard you're good at that."

Raymond didn't know what to say as he looked back and forth at both his cousins.

"Nope," Julius said as he passed by Raymond and was about to walk pass Alvin until he stopped in his tracks. "I'm gonna stay here and give you what you've been asking for."

In the blink of an eye Julius smashed Alvin so hard in the nose with his fist they both went crashing to the ground. The boys tussled across the patio floor as Raymond stood up, not sure if he should try to stop the squabble or let them continue to go at it.

Felicia was walking through the den to the back of the house as Louise silently followed her. She knew something wasn't right when she noticed the commotion through the windows of the double doors that led outside. All the partygoers in the back appeared to have all their attention focused in on something.

"Julius," she mumbled as she took off through the double doors. Louise quickly followed.

"You snobby son of a bitch," Julius cried as he smashed his cousin repeatedly in his bloody face. Alvin smiled with each punch as he looked up at Julius who was straddled on top of him. His taunts ignited Julius' rage even more as Julius continued to pounce on his face.

"Julius," Felicia screamed as she fought her way through the swarm of people.

Julius froze to the call of his name. His eyes searched through the sea of onlookers for his mother.

"What is going on out here," asked Louise. "Alvin!" she screamed at the sight of her bloody faced grandson as he laid trapped underneath Julius.

"Julius, what the hell is wrong with you?" Felicia asked.

Julius jumped up off of the boy and backed away from him as Louise dove to the ground to assist Alvin to his feet. Her immediate attention went to his lacerated nose, as she gently fondled with it to verify if it was broken or not.

"He started the mess. You can ask Raymond," Julius explained as he pointed to his second cousin who wore a puzzled look on his face. "As soon as he got here he started with his mouth and all. I wasn't even trying to say nothing to him, but he just kept going on and on."

"Alvin," Kim yelled out as she barreled through the guests to get to her son.

Felicia looked towards Raymond, who stood frozen with his eyes shot wide open. He was mumbling something, but he was obviously too frightened to take sides or even comment on that matter.

"Oh, who are we kidding here? He's just jealous, Felicia. Julius has always been jealous of Alvin every since they've been toddlers. Everyone knows it and I'm no longer going to bite my tongue about it," she said as she grabbed a stack of napkins from a table and handed them to Kim who began cleaning around Alvin's nose. "He's always attacking you." She said to Alvin, who went mum as he held his head in the air, but with the corner of his eyes on Julius as Kim tended to his nose.

"Yeah right, grandma. You're always there to take his wimpy side after he throws his rocks and hide his hand.

You don't even try to get the whole story before you start taking up for him." Julius said. "You know what, this is useless! I'm out." Julius began to stomp towards the woods in the back yard. "Nobody wanted to be around y'all uppity behind people anyway."

"Julius!" Felicia yelled. "Julius, come back here."

"Just let him go, Felicia. Don't let him continue to ruin our day. He's old enough to be on his own, anyway," Louise said as she grabbed her daughter's arm.

She snatched her arm away from her. "That's my son!" She was furious at her mother for her suggestion to let Julius go off on his own. With her mouth balled up and her eyes seeing red, she wanted to tell Louise a few choice words, but out of respect she said nothing and just shook her head at the bewildered old woman. She charged into the crowd and retreated through the double doors of the residence.

"Just let her go, Ma. I don't even know why you invited them in the first place," Kim said. "Some people just never change."

"You okay, baby?" Louise asked Alvin as she turned her attention back to him.

"I'm okay, grandma," Alvin nodded. "Just stings a little bit. He got me pretty good that time."

"Oh, don't worry about it, grandson. He'll get what's coming to him one day. We have to take you to the emergency room to make certain your nose isn't broken," she said while patting him on his back. "I can't believe he attacked you again."

The crowd of people began to clear out as Kim and Louise escorted Alvin back inside the house.

****

Julius trekked down the barren stretch of road with tears fluttering down the wells of his eyes. He knew all along it was a mistake to come. He knew his jerk of a cousin was going to do whatever he could to make him feel like an outcast. He was upset at his mother for even making him come at all. He knew they would never except him as family, Alvin said so himself. The only thing he wasn't mad about was smashing Alvin in his nose. He asked for it, and he got exactly what he asked for.

He could hear the familiar rattling sounds of his mother's car roaring down the street behind him. He knew it was her because the car needed a muffler change since about six months ago. He paid the approaching automobile no mind as he quickly wiped the tears from his eyes and kept walking.

"Julius," his mother screamed from out of her window as she slowly cruised up behind him. "Son, where are you going?"

He kept trekking, ignoring his mother.

"Julius, I'm talking to you!" she said as she eased on the side of him as he continued to walk.

He didn't feel good about not answering his mother, but he was so mad he didn't want to talk to anyone, especially to her. He just wanted to be left alone.

"Julius, damn it, answer me!"

"What, Ma? What?" he said as he stopped and held out his arms. He began to breath rapidly as he found it even harder to hold in the tears he had just wiped away. "You knew what was gonna happen. You knew it. They don't like me, Ma. When are you gonna figure that out? They don't see me how they see Alvin. All they see me as when I come around is the son of a rapist. That's all they ever gonna see when they see me. That ain't never gonna change, and you know it."

"Julius," she placed the car in park in the middle of the road. She felt solely responsible for what happened, and his hurt broke her heart. She wished she could immediately take his pain away. "Julius, I'm so..."

"No! Don't say nothing. You should've listened to them. You should've aborted me. That would've been better for the both of us."

The tears came pouring down his face even more rapidly as Felicia covered her mouth from his words. Her heart fell. She couldn't believe he felt the way that he did. She jumped out the car and rushed to grab him as he cried.

"No son, no, no, no." With tears now fluttering down her face, she wrapped her arms around his neck and rested her chin against the top of his head. "You don't feel that way, son. You don't. You can't."

"I'm tired, Ma," he muttered as he buried his face into her arms. "I'm so tired."

Chapter 11

As he placed the finishing touches on his latest creation on the last of the empty walls of the first floor of the abandoned building, his mind continued to deliberate on the altercation at his grandmother's house. When he was pounding on Alvin's cocky face it felt good, but after he had a few days to think about it, he began to regret attacking him altogether. He felt like a sucker for falling prey to Alvin's sick game, and after replaying the events in his head a few dozen times, he realized he gave the boy exactly what he wanted. He gave them all a reason to hate and despise him. He knew by him responding to Alvin the way that he did he had finally given them full validation for their feelings towards him.

The squabble with Alvin bothered him so much he hadn't returned to school since him and his mother returned to town. He knew his mom would flip her lid if she discovered he'd missed three straight days in a row, but with him fresh off of putting his foot in his cousin's pompous hide, he really didn't want to take the chance at bumping into Ricky Smith so soon for another possible clash. Although he wasn't really scared of the boy, he knew the boy fought dirty, and rarely did he fight alone. He felt the best way to prevent getting kicked out of school for simply defending himself, was not coming to school at all. Besides, working on his wall murals gave him peace and comfort. The only thing he missed about school anyway was not seeing Simone. The beautiful girl rummaged through his mind constantly. He couldn't wait to see her again, but not at the risk of getting into another fight. He was beyond tired of fighting.

"Damn, nigga, you been in here killin' it, I see," said Travis as he walked in with a crate full of spray cans and other supplies.

"Good, you got some more face masks," Julius said as he turned his attention to Travis and swiped off his old mask and tossed it to the dusty floor.

"What, you been in here all morning or something?" Travis asked as he handed Julius the crate.

"Yeah," he said while scanning through the cans to check out the paint colors his friend had brought him.

"No school?" he asked.

"Nah," Julius said as he took a seat on a stack of empty crates that were sitting in front of a pillar.

"I see that I'm rubbing off on you," he laughed. "I betcha' old one arm Bass is dead up looking for your ass." He slipped a blunt out of his pocket and began to light it up.

"I don't know why. There's nothing that I don't already know that he can teach me."

"You know them old geezers think they know every goddamn thang," he said as he took a hit of his weed and gazed at Julius' latest creation on the wall. "I had one of them old ass black power dudes down there on 2nd Ave tell me the other day that one day there's gonna be a black president, and I should get my shit together because it could be me."

"Word?" Julius said as Travis passed off the blunt to him.

"Yeah! I told his ass their ain't never gonna be no black president of the United States, and if the world ever did go crazy and put a brotha' in that White-ass-House it wouldn't be my crusty yellow ass. Them white folks ain't gonna try and kill my ass."

"It could happen," Julius said as he slowly exhaled the blunt with the back of his head rested against the pillar.

"Man there ain't never gonna be no damn black president. We're in America."

"It could happen. It just won't be your monkey ass," he teased.

"You got that right! I'll fuck around and turn it into the black house!" he chuckled.

"How did you even get into a conversation like that with dude, anyway?"

"Ah, it was this old cat that said he used to run with my old man back in the day. Said he used to be a stupid little nigga like me, until he found the church. Talkin' about I look just like my pops. Now ain't that some shit?"

Julius just shrugged.

"You got an old man, Jules? I ain't never heard you talk about the nigga."

The name of his criminal father quickly flashed through his mind, but he wasn't trying to get into that story with Travis, not after just having it thrown out the way that it was at his grandmother's gathering by Alvin. "Nah, nope!"

"I guess you're just the baby Jesus, huh," he laughed as he grabbed the blunt from Julius and took another pull. "That's cool, though. My old man dipped out on us when I was five. I barely even remember his ass. He wasn't shit, though. Used to beat the hell outta my momma. I think that's why she's the way she is now—all on crack and shit."

"Ain't nobody touching my momma."

"Hehehe... so you think you got a little bit of thug in ya', huh?"

"Nah, ain't nobody trying to be hard. Just ain't nobody gonna lay a finger on my mom, that's all."

"What if they got one of these pointed in your face, Jules?" he asked as he whipped out a pistol from the small of his back and pointed it at Julius' face. "You think a nigga can touch your momma then?"

Julius froze. He didn't know if the gun was real or fake because he'd never been that close to one, but he certainly didn't like the fact that Travis was pointing it at him, regardless. "Man, go 'head with that thing. Stop playing."

"Ain't no game, Jules." He lowered the weapon. "You see, Jules, when you got one of these, at the right place and at the right time, even the hardest nigga will turn bitch. Some beg. Some cry. It's only then that they realize that they really have no control over anything in their lives at all, and that's when all the control that they thought they had, belongs to you." He waved the gun in the air, "This here... this is power, Jules. And it's power belongs to whoever possesses it."

"That thing even real?"

"Talk shit and find out," he returned his aim to Julius.

"Man, go 'head now," Julius yelled as he held his hand up to shield his face as if his bare hand would stop a bullet.

Travis laughed, returned the pistol to the small of his back and took a seat on a stack of crates next Julius. "Shit's not loaded. I wouldn't do that to my boy."

"That's not even cool man,"

"Awe, stop being a pussy," he said. "So you don't have an old man? The nigga that bad you claiming immaculate conception?"

Julius shook his head. "Dude ain't even worth talking about. He was a rapist. My mom didn't even know his ass before he stalked her and raped her. For some reason she kept me when she found out she was pregnant, though."

"Damn." Travis didn't know what to say. He always had a joke for everything, but he didn't have anything prepared for what Julius had reluctantly revealed to him.

"Yeah, damn, is right," Julius replied. "I ain't never expected for nobody to love me because I wasn't born out of love. I was just some perverted nigga's nut."

"Man, fuck that! You here. Shoot, you know how many niggas end up on the abortion table every day? At least your momma had your ass. That's love enough. Ain't too many women out there doing that shit, that's for sho. Chicks ain't keeping kids they having from niggas they know," he laughed. "And look at my shit. My momma had my ass, but for what? If she could trade my ass in for a fat, juicy rock, she'd do it in a heartbeat. You may think your shit is bad, Jules, but the next nigga shit could be a whole lot worse than yours. You just gotta keep your head up, dawg."

"Yeah, I guess you're right."

"Hell yeah, I know I'm right."

Julius gazed at him while sadly shaking his head. The thoughts of always being the dark horse of the family were drilling inside him deeper than ever since the fight with Alvin. "It just gets rough sometimes. Sometimes you just wanna' give up, you know?"

He noticed the tears that were beginning to form in Julius' eyes and made a quick stride to change the mood. Travis hated being in a sensitive atmosphere and was never one to be someone's shoulder to cry on. "It's about time for you to get another cut, ain't it?"

"Man, I don't have time for that drama." Julius immediately knew where Travis was going when he said the word cut, and he wasn't about the unnecessary beef, even if it was beyond time for him to get another haircut.

"There ain't gonna be no drama. We just gonna stop by your boy Flip's spot and get you a much needed cut. This chick I bang from time to time is gonna be throwing a house party next week, and I can't have you rolling with me with your shit all jacked up. You know my shit's gonna be straight 'cause it always is. I just gotta look out for you and your upkeep."

"Man, I don't do house parties," Julius said.

"Man, stop being scared of every damn thing. If somebody say something to you, I got your back. You think somebody really gonna step to you about anything when you're rolling with me? Niggas know I don't play."

Julius frowned, still begrudging the idea of going to a party. "Man, I just don't like being around a bunch people I don't know in some tiny ass house. And then you talking about going up in this dude barbershop to get a cut when he done shut me down from getting one twice already."

"You're not even about to have any problems from this dude when we get down there."

"Why won't we? What you gonna do, Travis?"

"You don't worry about it. I'll handle this cat." Travis proclaimed. "How many times I gotta tell you?"

"Man, dang!" Julius gripped.

"And stop shooting down everything before you even try it. The chick throwing the party is mad cool, but we'll talk about all that when the time comes. Right now, you need to get that wool chopped off your head, so you won't keep walking around town looking like a damn sharecropper," Travis joked, in attempt to change the tone of the conversation.

"And why you can't cut me?" Julius asked.

"Cuz, my barbershop closed. I'm done cuttin' nappy headed niggas," Travis laughed. "Now are we rolling or what?"

Julius stared at him with a smile, but he was frustrated on the inside. He didn't care for the idea of making another trip down to Flip's barbershop, but he knew he would never hear the end of it from Travis if he didn't, so he folded. "Alright, man. I don't have no time for the drama, though."

"Ain't gonna be no drama. I already told you that me and my cousin used to run all over that nigga, Flip. He gonna just give you this cut, and that's gonna be the end of it. I promise."

****

"Nigga, B.I.G. can't mess with Pac, what the hell is you saying?" Tadpole proclaimed while pointing his clippers at the customer sitting directly across from him, waiting next to get a cut.

"All I'm saying is if you listen to my nigga Biggie a couple of times, you'll know he's killing it like nobody else in the game right now," The customer replied. "East coast is strong, my nigga."

"You saw how Suge Knight called them cats out at the Source Awards a few months back, didn't ya'?" Flip's customer chipped in as Flip kept his complete focus on trimming the top of the older patron's head. "The west coast ain't playing, neither. Suge Knight looked like he was 'bout ready to cut some ass."

"Man, them niggas need to stop following behind all these dumb ass radio station djs and record producers, and cut out all this beefin' before somebody gets killed," Tadpole countered.

"How much is any of y'all cats getting paid for keeping tabs on any of them fools?" Flip broke away from his customer's head and asked. "This is all y'all niggas talk about whenever you all get together up in here."

The barbershop went quiet as they all exchanged stares at each other. Flip had just spoiled another intense conversation between the last stragglers in the barbershop, and no one had anything to counter Flip with but blank stares.

"Exactly," Flip added. He let out a chuckle and commenced to finishing his customer's haircut. "Y'all niggas on these niggas jock like some hungry bitches, and y'all ain't seeing one red cent."

The bells above the entrance suddenly chirped as the door slammed closed. Everyone's attention focused in on the two figures standing at the door–Travis and Julius.

Tadpole looked over to Flip and smirked as he rolled his customer around in his chair to turn his back to the door and the new customers. He knew all too well of the past beefs between Travis and Flip, and he wanted no parts of it.

As soon as Flip realized Travis had entered his shop with Julius, he knew nothing good was about to happen. Flip quickly realized he had been badgering the wrong person, and it was about to come back and bite him on his behind.

"Flip, what's happen, bruh?" Travis asked with a huge smirk.

"Travis," Flip replied as he pulled the tape from around his customer's neck and snatched the barber cape from over his body. His customer whipped out a ten dollar bill and stuffed it in Flip's hand. The lone customer waiting, jumped up and headed towards Flip's barber chair.

"Whoa, whoa, whoa, homeboy," Travis said as he stepped up and extended his arm to block the customer from jumping into the barber seat. "My man Jules got next."

"What?" the patron frowned.

Travis quickly flipped up the front of his shirt to reveal the butt of the pistol he had stuffed above his waist. "I said, my man Jules got next. You got a problem with that?"

The man caught a glance at the pistol and quickly backtracked. "Oh, my bad. No problem. No problem at all," he said as he began to cower back to his seat.

Flip and Julius stood frozen by the brief altercation. Tadpole turned around for a second and quickly focused back on his customer. He was a bit ticked at Flip for hatin' earlier, but he didn't want to see him get killed. However, him and Flip wasn't tight enough for him to put his name on Travis' crap list, so he opted to mind his own.

"Alright, Jules," Travis signaled Julius to get into Flip's chair.

"Yo, Travis, dude right there was next," Flip said.

"What nigga?" Travis asked with an angry scowl as he reached for his piece.

"Nothing, man," Flip rebutted as he brushed the hair out of the chair with the barber cape. "Come on, dude."

Julius still hadn't moved an inch because he feared how far things would go with Travis and his temper. It was like Travis had multiple personalities that switched from cool to maniac hot at any given moment. Julius thought that a haircut wasn't worth all drama it was beginning to cause. He also was nervous about not really knowing Travis well enough to know if he would actually shoot somebody over a haircut.

"Yo, Jules, what you waiting on?" Travis asked. "The nigga waiting on you to take a seat."

Julius looked at Flip then the chair. Flip rolled his eyes toward the ceiling. Julius slowly walked to the chair and hopped in.

Travis slid behind the chair and took a spot next to Flip. "My man here need a temple fade, on the house."

"On the house?" Flip quickly asked.

"Yeah, nigga, on the house. You hard of hearing?"

"Nah, I heard you."

"I'm glad you did, because I don't feel like repeating myself, like I had to do for my man sitting over there," he chuckled. "I heard your customer service ain't what it used to be up in here so I decided to come in and check on it for myself. How soon niggas seem to forget."

Flip didn't respond because he knew Travis and his antics well. If Travis felt disrespected by how he responded to anything he said to him or if he felt like he was being given some type of shade, he knew things would get physical.

As soon as Flip realized Travis came through the door, his mind flashed back to the old days when Travis, and his older, crazier cousin Merc used to push him around and bum haircuts off of him. He thought those days were long gone when he heard Merc was shot and killed, and he couldn't honestly say that he wasn't happy to hear that he had finally got his. Merc was a true O.G. and it was only a matter of time before somebody ended up putting him in the ground. After Merc got wasted, he had no worries because Travis never stepped foot in his shop since, and he only saw him every now and then from afar, slanging his dope up and down the neighborhood streets.

Travis took the chair next to the customer he denied the next cut to. He then pulled out his pistol and sat it on his lap and began tapping his finger on the trigger. That action managed to catch the attention of everyone in the barbershop and had them all asking the same question in the back of their minds, *what is this crazy dude about to do with his heat?*

"Tadpole! You can't speak, nigga?" Travis yelled.

"Nah, nah, what's up Travis," Tadpole answered timidly.

"Shit," Travis shrugged. "Why aren't you over there cracking any of your corny ass jokes?"

"No reason. No reason at all." He answered.

After about thirty minutes of the most intense haircutting of his entire life, Flip placed the final touches on Julius' fade. His normal cuts took a little longer, but with Travis' pistol catching the corner of his eye every time he turned Julius around in the chair, he knew he had to get the two out of his building as fast as he could. He knew the faster he could get Julius out of his chair, the sooner he could get his heart from racing a hundred miles a second. If he had only known Julius had ties to a nutcase like Travis Nelson, he would've treated him with a whole lot more respect and not given him such a hard time. But as his mouth and arrogant tactics had done so many times in the past, it managed to get him in a spot where he had to look into the face of one neighborhood thug no one wanted to have anything to do with.

"Damn, Flip, boy you can cut! You really did a good job on my boy," Travis said as he tucked his piece back under his shirt, returned to Flip's barber's station and observed the back of Julius head.

Flip nodded and said, "We good?"

"Almost," Travis said as Julius hopped out of the chair and brushed himself off. "Since you did such a good job and your customer service game is back up to where it used to be, I know you got my man here, Jules, on the house every two weeks for the rest of the school year."

"Every two weeks!"

"Yeah," he said as he slid up his shirt and flashed his pistol. "You got a problem with that, homey?"

Flip's eyes focused in on Travis' waist as he shook his head, "Nah, I don't have a problem with it. I got 'em."

"Cool," Travis chuckled. "Well, we thank you. I hope I don't have to come see you again. It won't be good if I have to come back. It won't be good at all."

"I said I got him, Travis." Flip answered fretfully.

"I sure hope so," Travis added.

Julius stood astonished by how rapidly the arrogant barber had become so wimpy in Travis' presence. He remembered how conceited and nasty he was on all his previous visits. How he treated him like a piece of trash and denied him service. As he stood before Travis, he could see the fear in Flip's eyes as he recalled the trembling he felt from his knuckles up against the back of his head during the entire cut. Julius never wanted anyone to feel that way because he knew the feeling himself, but if anyone deserved to go through those type of emotions, he thought, Flip certainly did.

"Come on, Jules," Travis waved Julius to the door.

Julius gave Flip one last stare as the man's eyes quickly angled towards the floor. He couldn't even look Julius in his eyes, and Julius thought it was simply amazing. He quickly trailed Travis out of the shop.

"Yo, that was off the chain!" Julius said as the two walked down the sidewalk.

"It wasn't nothing," Travis said nonchalantly. "Cats like Flip have to be put in their place from time to time. If nobody comes around and check a fool like that, he'll lose his damn mind and get his self killed with that mouth he got on him. You won't have no problems out of him no more, that's for sure."

"I mean he went from being a straight up ass to becoming a little sissy. I know his boys in there are like, man…" Julius said, still excited from seeing Flip get his just deserts.

"I told you, Jules, when you're holding this heat," he said as he tapped on the spot on his waist the butt of his gun resided. "…even the hardest niggas turn bitch. Now let's get something to eat. All this intimidation done made a nigga hungry."

****

Julius slowly eased the front door shut behind himself after entering the dark house. As he made an earnest effort to tip toe his way through the living room, unbeknownst to him his mother had her eyes zeroed in on him as she sat quietly on the couch.

"Why are you coming in here this late? This is a school night," she asked.

Julius froze in his tracks. His mother flipped on the lamp beside the sofa as he turned around to face her.

"School don't give a fuck where I'm at, Ma," he answered as he turned and began to make his way down the hall.

Felicia jumped out of the chair and snatched him by his arm. "Boy, what the hell is wrong with you? You don't leave when I'm talking to you!"

Julius ceased moving as he whipped back around and rolled his eyes. "What, Ma? What?"

"Don't you *what Ma* me! And who in the world do you think you're talking too? One of the hooligans out there on the street? You don't curse in my house. I pay the bills here."

"My bad, Ma, but I don't know if you noticed but the cycle has beyond started again. Everybody is ganging up on your hideous little Julius just like every other place you put me in. It's just a matter of time before they kick my ass out for being ugly again."

"I'm not going to say this again, you watch your mouth in this house, boy," she demanded while pointing her finger. "Now I didn't raise no quitter. How you look is how you look. Nobody can change that, Julius. But what you can change is what's inside. That's all that matters. What's inside of you. It don't matter how you look on the outside."

"Yeah, that's easy for you to say, Ma. You ain't gotta walk around with this," he said as he pointed at his face.

"Mr. Bass called here today."

"What did he want?"

"He told me you've been acting differently and skipping class. Said you've been hanging out with this thug that has nothing going for him."

He laughed. "Nothing going for him, ha! I don't have nothing going for me." His bond with Travis had gotten so tight, any jab at his friend felt like a jab at him.

"Go to school, Julius. There's nothing out there in those streets, son. If anybody knows that, it's me."

"Yeah, well, maybe the apple don't fall too far away from the tree, Ma."

"And what does that suppose to mean, boy?"

"It just means what it means."

"Look, Julius…"

A loud crash sounded off from the back of the house. They exchanged baffled stares at each other, then they both looked towards the kitchen door. They both zipped into the kitchen. Felicia flipped the back porch light on and peaked through the door curtain.

"Who is it," Julius asked his mother.

She swung the door open as they both observed Vince spread out across the garbage dumpster and all the trash that was once in it. He was completely covered in garbage as he continued to waddle through it, unable to get to his feet.

"Fee… Fee, help a nigga up," he cried. He was sloppy drunk and she could smell the stench of alcohol from the door.

Felicia folded her arms and shook her head in disgust. Julius let out a chuckle as she stepped backwards into the house and slammed the door shut.

"Felicia," he yelled in a slur. "Felicia! Don't leave me like this!"

"You're so worried about my whereabouts, maybe you better worry about his," Julius added as he rushed out of the kitchen.

"You just take your tail to that school when you're supposed to be there!" she barked back. "I mean it, boy!"

She didn't know if she should throw something or just scream, she was so furious. She opted do neither and simply took a seat at the table and swiped both of her hands over her face. She felt things between her and Julius were beginning to spiral out of control, and her deadbeat common law husband was only adding more stress to the situation.

Chapter 12

Julius stood outside of the library and peaked in through the small window at the door. He scanned the library floor the best he could as his eyes quickly zeroed in on exactly who he was looking for–Simone. It had been nearly a week since he last saw the girl, and his heart raced at the very sight of her. Unfortunately, through his observations he also caught a glimpse of one of the girls she was often with that always had a nasty frown to dish out to him whenever she saw him. He debated if he should even walk in and talk to the girl with her around. He knew the first thing Simone would want to know is of his whereabouts the last few days. A question he had no sensible answer for.

"Girl, this Chemistry is not for me," said Raven as she slammed her book closed.

"How do you plan on becoming a biology major without it?" Simone asked as she removed her eyes from her own textbook.

"Sleeping with the professor!" she laughed.

"You probably would," Simone grinned.

"I'm just kidding, girl," she said with a devious smile. "I mean, I may…if he's fine."

"That's not even cute, Raven"

"You gotta evaluate the situation, and do what's necessary to stay on top, girl. Damn struggling."

"But sleeping with the professor? Really?"

"Hey, don't judge me, girl. Some of the most powerful business transactions in the world have been brokered right between the sheets."

"Oh, my gosh," Simone chuckled. "You are too much." Simone's eyes fell back into her book as she decided not to entertain anymore of Raven's silliness.

"Simone," Julius called out nervously as he slowly approached the table the girls were sitting at. He felt as if he was walking in slow motion as his heart was pounding so hard he thought it was going to burst out through his chest.

Raven snapped around to Julius and a frown quickly spread onto her face. "Speaking of not cute," she said under her breath.

"Julius," Simone answered, shocked by the sight of him.

"This is where you guys are having the study group, right?" he asked. He heard Raven's insult, but paid it no mind. He was more consumed with Simone's beauty yet overrun with nervousness at the same time.

"It was," said Raven as she quickly gathered her books and jumped up out of her chair. "About an hour ago."

"It is, Julius," Simone intervened while squinting her eyes at her rude friend. "Where have you been?"

"Well, I for one, really don't want to know the answer to that, so I will let you two have at it," Raven continued. "Simone, don't forget we'll be picking you up around five tomorrow, so please be ready, girl."

"I will, Raven," she nodded.

"Mr. Julius," Raven said to Julius in passing.

"Julius, where have you been?" Simone asked again. "I thought you dropped out of school or something. I called your house but no one ever answers."

"I had to deal with some things," he said as he dropped his books on the table and took the seat across from her.

"What kind of things are more important than school, Julius? This is your senior year. I mean, this is it. I hope you didn't stop coming because of Ricky."

"No..no, I'm not even sweatin' that dude," he quickly lied. "Just some family issues. It's all taken care of now."

"I hope so, Julius. When you're trying to get into a good college, they take attendance very seriously. It's not always about the grades, you know?"

Julius shied away when she mentioned college. The last time he thought about college was when Mr. Bass brought it up, and it hadn't ran through his mind since.

"You are planning on going to college, right?"

"I thought about it once or twice. I never put too much thought in it, though."

"Julius, with your gifts, the possibilities you have are limitless. I'm sure you can get into a good art school with no problems at all. With your artwork, you could probably even get a full scholarship. I thought we talked about this before."

"Yeah, I don't know. College just seems like a good way to spend a bunch of money on a whole lot of nothing. I draw because that's what I do. I ain't never thought it could take me anywhere except out of reality. My own place. That's it."

"Maybe you should think about it taking you to other places, Julius—in this world. The world should see your wonderful gift," she smiled. She slid out the picture he drew of her from her notebook, looked at it for a moment and flipped it around for him to see. "I mean, I love your work, Julius. I really think you need to consider doing more with it. College deadlines are just around the corner. It's not too late."

He gazed at the picture and then back at her. He was amazed by how she looked at him, and even more astonished by her words about his work. It made him feel really good that she appreciated his work, and it really surprised him that she kept the picture he sketched of her. He still had his reservations about college, but her words of encouragement made him feel more compelled to look into it.

"I'll try to see what's up."

"I hope you do more than see what's up," she sighed.

"I will, I will," he said.

"Okay. Well, anyway, I do have to leave now, Julius." She began gathering her books.

"It's time to go already?" he asked as a feeling of sadness crept in as he watched her pack up her things.

"Yup," she answered. "Although Raven was kinda blunt about it, we have been here for quite some time. You just happened to miss the rest of the group leaving, before you came in. I know my Mom is out there waiting on me by now."

"That's cool, that's cool," he said as he eased out of his chair when she did.

"You know, tomorrow night we're going to the fair," she said. "Have you gone yet?"

"Oh no," he said while shaking his head. "I haven't been to a fair since I was little."

"Well, I'm going to be there with the girls tomorrow night, so if you decide to go, we can hang out some, if you like."

He thought his ears had deceived him. She actually wanted to be around him without books, or a teacher in front of them giving out lectures. "But you'll be with those girls, won't you?"

"Only if I don't see you. I mean, how much bougie talk can one plain ole' girl be around in one night?"

He laughed, "You are not plain. Far from it."

"I'm glad you think so, Julius," she smiled. "I hope to see you there."

"I'll see what's up."

"Yeah," she chuckled. "I know."

He nodded as she walked away. His eyes trailed her to the door and he continued to stare at the door once she passed through it. He couldn't believe she asked him out on somewhat of a date.

****

191

The smell of cotton candy and a scrumptious blend of fried foods consumed the cool autumn breeze. Simone silently took in the colorful flashing lights and festive sounds of the fair as her and the group of girls maneuvered through the blanket of people that occupied the fairgrounds. As the other girls talked and joked amongst themselves, Simone remained somber, wondering if Julius was going to take her up on her offer and meet with her at some point during the night. She and the girls had already blazed through the fairgrounds twice, and there was no sign of Julius anywhere. She figured he probably wouldn't come, but she remained hopeful.

"Girl, why you so quiet?" Tammy asked her with a gentle nudge.

"No reason," Simone answered with a petite smile.

"We came here to have fun and you're out here trying to drag us down, looking all sad and mess. You barely even rode on anything, girl," Tammy pointed out. "You on your period?"

"No," Simone answered, slightly perturbed.

"Hell, I know if I was on my period, the way that thing gets to running sometimes, I wouldn't be out here at no damn state fair," one of the girls added.

"I'm okay. I'm just enjoying the moment." She looked towards the other girls and explained, "And I'm not on my period, either."

"Well, come and get on this Sonic Boom ride with us. The line is nowhere as long as it was the first time we came around," Tammy asked while looking up at the massive roller coaster as they all walked towards it.

"No, you guys go and get on. I'll watch. I don't really have the stomach for all of that twisting and turning right now."

"Come on, Simone," Raven begged. "It'll be fun."

"Seriously, you guys get on. I'll wait."

"Girl, it's her period," said Tammy as she laughed and grabbed Raven by her arm.

"Uhm hmm," Raven added with a smirk.

Simone simply rolled her eyes as Raven and Tammy led the other two girls in the group to the back of the rollercoaster line. Simone then wandered towards one of the many gaming areas and observed all the happy fairgoers scattered around her, playing and enjoying the different array of games.

Julius walked through the crowd with his eyes bouncing everywhere in search of Simone. He couldn't believe he actually found himself off of that grungy city bus to come out. The idea of seeing Simone away from school made him feel jittery, and somewhat exposed. As much as he wanted to see her, part of him just didn't want her to be there. He feared he wouldn't even know how to act around her if they were to hook up. He'd never been on any type of a date, nor anything that resembled one.

From the moment she asked him to accompany her there he couldn't help but wonder what in the world would make her want to be around him. What did she even see in him that the rest of the world couldn't seem to visualize? He asked himself those questions so many times his head started to hurt. He couldn't contemplate any explanation that made any sense to him. His appearance always seemed to be a problem for so many people that he couldn't fathom why it never appeared to be a problem for her.

The more he searched through the sea of unfamiliar faces, the more he believed she wasn't even there. He just knew she couldn't be serious about hanging out with him, but that's when his heart almost fell right out of his body. Over by the Whack A Mole games she stood sporting an oversized Jordan jersey and some dark blue jeans, staring so beautifully at two kids trying their earnest to smash the head in of an artificial mole.

His entire body went limp. She appeared utterly angelic in her stance to him. As he admired her in awe, doubt and fear swiftly overcame his body. His eyes drifted to multiple reflections of himself in the carnival mirrors that were just behind her. His face, he thought to himself, *Why would she want to be around someone with a face like mine?* He slid his hood over his head and began to back away and walked in the opposite direction, but at that moment she looked up and realized he was standing there. He stood frozen like a deer in shining headlights. After her smile came the call of his name, "Julius... Julius,' she said.

He removed the hood from over his head as she ran towards him. She greeted him with a tight and surprising hug. Her embrace caught him off guard. He just held his arms out, as he was too nervous to hug her back. Everything was happening so fast, his mind felt like putty. The first clear thought to materialize in his mind was the whereabouts of her friends. *Where were they? Were they looking?*

"You made it," she said.

"Yeah," he said as he backed away.

"I almost thought you weren't coming. It's gotten so late."

"No, I was coming. I just had some errands to run for my mom." It was a little white lie he made up quickly. He actually sat at the bus stop for two whole hours and let it pass him by four times before he finally decided to hop on.

"Uh uh," said Raven as she approached the couple with the gang of girls. "Simone, what's this?"

"Julius," she said as she hastily whipped around to face the girls and positioned herself in front of Julius.

"I know who he is," she replied while nodding. She tilted her head to gaze around her and at Julius with a hateful frown plastered on her face. "What's he doing out here?"

Julius didn't know how to answer the girl since he felt the question was geared towards him. He felt a bit intimidated by the angry scowls facing him from the four girls, not one friendly look in sight. For his sake, he didn't have to worry about giving any response because Simone was quick to answer. "I just bumped into him, and I told him I'd get on a few rides with him."

"So you can get on rides with him but you leave your girls hangin'," Tammy added, as she made an attempt to register the absurd gesture in her mind.

"Come on, Tammy, it's not like that," Simone pleaded.

"I guess her stomach feeling better now," Raven said.

Julius stood quietly on the sidelines of the crossfire as Simone's friends candidly expressed their displeasure of her attempting to bail on them to be with him. With every snide remark and attempt to find out what could possibly wrong with her and if she was serious or not, Simone held her own.

As the exchange of words grew more animated between the girls, he couldn't help but feel responsible for ruining everyone's night. He wished he could just disappear from the scene so all peace could be restored. Besides, his stomach was already churning in knots because he knew he didn't have enough money to get on any rides. He barely had enough cash to get on the bus and pay admission to get into the fairgrounds. His mindset was just on getting there and possibly seeing Simone, he failed to consider anything beyond that.

"Well, we're about to leave," Raven snapped while rolling her eyes at Julius.

"That's fine, Tammy. I'll be okay," Simone answered. "Julius will be taking me home."

"I am?" he blurted out with a puzzled look on his face.

"Yup," she said as she placed her hand in his.

Tammy and the other girls all had blank and confused looks registered on their faces. Not only did they feel royally betrayed by Simone for leaving them to be with Julius, but none of them could understand why. They all felt he was harshly unattractive and completely beneath them. They thought Simone had lost her mind for even wanting to be seen in public with the boy.

"Okay, whatever, girl," Raven hissed. "You know you're foul for what you pulled. I *will* be calling you about this."

"That's fine, Raven," Simone answered. She couldn't believe her so called friends were making such a stink about her spending the rest of her time with Julius. There wasn't one girl out of the group that never left her stranded to be with guys they barely even knew on several occasions. Simone simply took their behavior as a grain of salt and hoped they'd find a way to be alright. "You girls have a goodnight."

Raven cut her eyes at Julius one last time. "Let's go, ladies," she said as she pulled Tammy's arm and led the girls in the other direction.

"Come on, Julius," said Simone as she led Julius down the row of rides in the opposite direction.

"Hey, Simone," Julius said nervously, glancing back at her previous companions as they stormed off. "You sure you wanna let them leave? I didn't drive here. I don't even have a car."

She stopped in her tracks. "Well how did you get here?"

"I caught the city bus."

"I can ride the bus."

"I'm not certain you want to do that, either. The city bus can be off the chain at night. There's all kind of nuts on the route out here. Especially with this fair traffic."

"Well, you're getting on it."

"I know, but I'm a dude."

197

"Okay, and what's that suppose to mean," she dropped his hand and rolled her arms up.

"No, no, no, it's not like that," Julius tried to explain. He knew he stepped in a pile of dog mess with his remark, and he didn't have enough experience with the opposite sex to concoct the right words fast enough to backtrack.

"Yeah, I bet, Julius."

"My bad," he threw his hands up, knowing good and well there was no fixing what he said.

"Do I look like I'm scared, Julius? I live in Westmont Heights. I think my days of being afraid to be in rough areas have long disappeared since my parents were forced to move us there."

"You live in Westmont?"

"I sure do."

"Oh," Julius uttered. He was surprised she lived so close, in a neighborhood he understood wasn't much better than his own. "That's not too far from where I stay. Several blocks actually."

"See," she said. "And you thought I was a lightweight."

"I didn't say that."

"You insinuated it," she squinted her eyes while pointing at him. "I got you, though, Mr. Julius. Don't let the cute face fool you. I can handle myself just fine."

"I won't," he smiled.

"So are we gonna stand here and talk about the city bus all night or are we going to get on some rides before this place shuts down?"

"But.."

"And, don't worry, Julius," she stopped him while pulling out a stack of tickets. "I have plenty of tickets for the both of us."

When she revealed the batch of tickets, it gave him an enormous sigh of relief. She had thought of everything. He didn't know why she liked him, or even what she wanted from him, but for some reason she was there with him. And for once, he stopped worrying about it. He decided to just let the night take him wherever it was going to lead him as they began their stroll through the illuminated lights of the carnival.

"Want to get on the Ferris Wheel?" she asked.

He looked up at the ride. "Sure."

She led the way to the ride, and they cuddled in one of the pods once the ride operator cleared them to hop on. Julius was still nervous by the girl's company and feared that the night was all a wonderful dream that he just didn't want to wake up from. He never really cared much for amusement park rides, but somehow his feet guided him mindlessly into whatever direction Simone would lead him. Her sweet flowery scent placed him under a spell he couldn't snap out of, nor did he want he want to come out of it.

As the ride slowly began to take off she placed her arm inside his. His eyes fell on their connecting arms, as he sat psyched by her soft touch. He then raised his eyes to hers. She gave him a smile and he returned with one of his own.

The carnival ride elevated them even higher into the calm night skies as the ride operator started the ride up after the last of the couples loaded in. The higher they rose, the more beautiful the sea of lights that sprinkled throughout the carnival below took their breaths away.

"You okay?" she asked.

He nodded with a smile. She then moved her face into his and bestowed him a slow, soft kiss. His eyes shut and the rapid beat of his heart slowed. She had placed him in an area he'd never ventured. She pulled away, gave him another look and an enchanting smile. He didn't know what to say or do, but he knew how he felt–amazed. He didn't want the moment to ever end. She placed her head on his shoulder and wrapped her arms around his waist as they continued on the relaxing twirl of the Ferris Wheel.

Their time at the fairgrounds together was short but filled with excitement. They journeyed on every ride they could before they found their way outside of the closing doors of the fairgrounds to the crowded bus stop on the other side of the entrance gates. Hand and hand, they stuck together like a couple in love. They sat in the back of the bus, and observed all the ruckus Julius had earlier predicted, but the wild late night bus crowd paid the two no mind. That didn't stop Julius from tightly clasping her hand, posturing on high alert in preparedness to protect his female companion. He was determined to defend her if something was to go down, but it didn't.

The bus dropped them off just up the block from her home as they rounded out the final phase to their night with a trek to her abode. Julius wasn't worried about getting home because the walk from her house to his was only a hop, skip and jump away. Besides, he knew he could handle himself. It was only his duty to get the lady home as smoothly and safely as possible.

"I had a great time tonight, Julius."

"I did too."

"I'm glad you came. At first I thought you weren't going to make it."

"I thought I wasn't going to make it either. I don't really go out a lot," he said while looking towards the ground.

"I'm sorry about how Tammy and the girls acted."

"It's all good," he shrugged. "I'm use to it."

"They're my girls and all, but they see things like they see them," she explained.

"I know."

"I hope we get to see more of each other, Julius."

"I hope so too, Simone."

They strolled onto the large wooden porch, which was completely dark as was the rest of the house. The overhang was dressed with dark outlines of potted plants hanging on the outer boundaries from the porch. The only light was that of the moon that snuck in streaks of moonlight through the branches of the trees that hovered over the house.

"I guess this is goodnight," said Julius as he stood before her.

"Yeah," she said. "I guess it is."

He was hopeful for another kiss and that's exactly what he received as she slowly moved her tender lips into his. Suddenly, the porch light flickered on above them. They both moved a step back from each other as they noticed someone was at the front door unlocking it.

"Simone, where on earth have you been?" asked the middle aged woman with her arms wrapped up in a thick, furry night coat. There was no denying she was Simone's mother as she appeared as an older version of the girl. Julius remembered getting only a glance of her from the mall that day. "I called the girls and they've all returned to their homes hours ago. Where were you?"

Simone was lost for words as she had no idea how to explain to her mother she ditched her girlfriends to hang out with Julius. It appeared she had every element of the night planned expect that.

"Simone, who is this boy?" her mother asked. "Is that the boy from the mall?"

A tall, muscular man with a bald head and a thick, graying goatee emerged from behind Simone's mother and issued Julius a stern look as soon as he saw him.

"This is my friend, Julius, from school. I was with him, Ma."

"And how did you end up doing that," the woman asked. She then issued Julius a weird look with her mouth wide open. It certainly felt like his cue to leave.

"Hey, I'll see you Monday, Simone." Julius said.

"Julius, wait," Simone yelled as he began his stride off the porch.

"You got a lot of explaining to do, young lady," the man said with his deep voice. "Now get in there with your mother and get ready for bed. We'll talk about this in the morning."

"Yes sir," Simone answered.

Simone's dad jogged off of the porch and down the walkway behind Julius, "Whoa, whoa, whoa. Hold on there, son."

"Dad, don't," Simone begged.

"It's all good, baby girl. I got this," he whispered back to her with a smile. "Now go on in there with your mother."

Julius whipped around and noticed the man approaching him from behind. He knew the man trailing him couldn't be a good thing, but against his better judgment, he yielded and waited for the man's approach.

"How you getting home son?" the man asked.

"I just live a few blocks down the way. I was gonna walk."

"Walk?" he laughed. "Come on, son, I'll take you home."

"It's okay, Mr. Wilson."

"You take my daughter out on a night of fun, without me knowing anything about it, it's the least you can do, son. I promise I won't bite."

Julius looked down the street in the direction of where he was about to walk and then back at Simone's father. He was reluctant to go anywhere with the man because it was a no brainer that men are always protective of their daughters. He felt in his gut he should turn the man's offer down, but he got the impression the gentleman wasn't going to take no for an answer.

"Okay sir," Julius said.

"Come on, young man. This is my pickup," he said as he directed Julius to the old blue Toyota truck parked on the curb. "It's unlocked. Ain't got nothing in it that nobody wanna steal." He chuckled as they hopped into the vehicle.

Julius closed the door and his eyes quickly did a double take towards the man when he noticed the guy sitting at the wheel just staring at him. "So your name is, Julius, huh?"

"Yes sir," he answered.

"Nice to meet you, Julius," the man said as he held out his hand for a hand shake. Julius shook his hand. "Alright. Where to, young man?" asked Simone's father as he started the truck and eased onto the street.

"I live three blocks down from the Food Mart on Grayson Blvd." Julius explained. "Just off the corner of the bus stop."

"Okay, yeah, I know that area," the man said.

Julius nodded as his eyes peered down the road. Comforting thoughts of Simone flashed through his mind, but those images that danced around in his mind were greatly overshadow by being alone in the presence of the middle age brute he recently discovered to be her father.

The first few minutes of the ride was met with dead silence until the man asked, "You ever heard of Franklin Yards, Julius?"

"Yeah, I've heard a little something about it. Neighborhood across town."

"Yeah. Rough place."

"Yes sir, that's what they say."

"I grew up in that spot. Hated it. Hated every minute of it."

Julius noticed the man's driving speed had drastically reduced as he continued talking. He glanced over to the speedometer, but not for too long because he didn't want the man to notice him staring.

"I really had to do some fighting to get out of that crazy ass place, Julius," the old man chuckled. "Boy, was it rough in the Yards. When I got older and came into my own, and started making a family, I did all I could to make sure my family would never have to see the likes of a place like that. You know what I mean?"

"Yes sir."

"But sometimes it seems like no matter how hard a black man try, the world just keeps pushing down on him as hard as it can. Clinton nor none of them politicians really give a damn about nobody. All they care about is lining their own damn pockets. Making laws to suit the highest bidder, while we're all out here suffering and shit. All that politics stuff is fixed to keep the rich richer and the poor poorer. You know that, don't you?"

"Yes, sir," Julius nodded.

"Hell, I bled and slaved at Williams Trucking for over fifteen years of my life, and do you think any of them assholes did anything to stop them greedy suits from moving my job to some sweat factory overseas? Hell no!"

Julius just nodded in agreement to everything the old man said. Although he was taken back a bit by the man's use of language and his openness, he couldn't help but wonder why he was sharing his feelings with him.

"I was clearing over eighty grand a year, Julius. Did you know that?"

"No sir," he answered as he pointed down the street to the direction of his house. "Down that street, Mr. Wilson."

"I see ya'," the man said as he made the next turn. "I never intended on having any of my babies nor my wife in any place that put me in the mind of Franklin Yards, Julius. But what can you do when there's no jobs out here that wanna' pay you anything above minimum wage? Huh?"

"I don't know, sir."

"I guess what I'm trying to say in so many words, Julius, is why don't you go out and find yourself one of these little fast tail ghetto chicks out here and date one of them."

Julius looked over to the man with his mouth wide open. The man's remarks came out of nowhere, "Sir?"

"You know what I'm saying," the man looked at him with a grin. "I think they're more your speed. I was young once. A young dude. I know how it is. I just need for you to ease up off of my baby. My little girl got goals.

Things she wants to accomplish out of life. And if it's the last thing I do, I'm gonna see to it that she has the best opportunities to reach them goals. You feel me on this, Julius?"

Julius just nodded in agreement as he pointed to his house, "Right here."

"It's nothing personal, Julius," Simone's father explained. "I just can't let my baby girl get accustomed to this type of living. I can go through it, but not my kids."

Julius grabbed the door handle. Before he could step foot outside of the truck the man grabbed him by his arm.

"Julius, I will do whatever it takes to protect my little girl. You understand, right?"

Julius glanced down at the man's firm grip, then back in his face. The old man offered a stern look as the silence grew with the intensity of his grasp. "Yes sir," he said.

"Cool," the man said as he released his hold. "That's what I wanted to hear, son" he said. "You're a good man, Julius."

Julius hopped out of the truck and slammed the door shut. He watched the vehicle pull off and disappear into the night. He felt as if his heart was ripped right out of him, right when he finally got the chance to feel a different element. He could tell Simone's father would do what he had to do to protect her, and he didn't want to deal with anymore drama than he was already dealing with. His mind quickly second guessed the whole night as he thought through everything that happened. What would a pretty girl do with such a horrid looking dude like him anyway, he asked himself. He knew it was all too good to be true.

Chapter 13

Julius laid spread out across his bed as his pen did its crafting on a sketch of Michael Jordan dunking over the behemoth of a basketball player, Patrick Ewing. It was an image that was glued in his head ever since he first saw it live on his television set from a game he caught a glimpse of earlier in the week. He was never a follower of basketball or any professional sport, but Simone's admiration for Jordan's game peaked his interest, and in doing so, he too became a fan.

His concentration was swiftly broken by what sounded like pebbles being thrown against his window. His head sprung up as he rose up off of the bed. When he glanced out of the window he was stunned to see Travis standing outside, decked out in all black attire, frantically swaying his arms to get his attention. Julius rushed to his door, peeked out of it, down the hall to see the back of Vince's peasy head positioned in a way he knew to mean he was sleeping. He eased his door shut, returned to the window and slid it up.

"What are you doing out here," Julius asked as he dropped to his knees and leaned out of the window.

"Waiting for your black ass," Travis said as he moved closer to the house. "We 'bout to go."

"Go where?"

"To the party I've been telling you about, fool."

"Man, how many times I gotta tell you that partying ain't my thing?"

"Bruh, what is your thing? It's Friday night. You ain't got shit to do but sit up in your room and draw like some nerd. You do that crap all week. Come on and have some fun for a change. Take your mind off ole' girl."

When Travis mentioned Simone, the incident with her father quickly flashed through his mind. A few days had already passed since he told Travis the whole story, and him bringing it up so casually, reminded him exactly why he didn't want to tell him about it in the first place. He was so torn up about the whole situation he felt the need to tell somebody. Travis was the closest thing he had to what could be considered a friend, despite his obnoxious personality at times.

"Man, I'm good."

"Come on here, negro! Put some gear on and quit playing. This party is gonna be bumpin', and I promise you we're gonna' have a good time."

"Travis, I'm good, man. I'm just not feeling it tonight."

"Come on, Jules. Have a good time for once."

From the look on his friend's face he could tell he wasn't leaving without him. Dressed down in an oversized Black Orlando Magic jersey and some baggy Fubu jeans, bottomed out with a fresh pair of red and black Jordans, Travis was ready to get the party started.

As Travis continued his rant from below about why he needed to tag alone, Julius' feelings about going to the house party started to change. He was growing tired of sitting in the room, moping around, being sad about Simone and all the other irritating altercations he'd experienced thus far in the school year. One thing was for certain, anytime he rolled with Travis he was guaranteed some kind of excitement. He was suddenly overwhelmed by a desire to just let loose and say hell with it.

"Alright," said Julius. "Give me a minute."

"That's what I'm talking about," said Travis as he backed away from the window and made his way towards the front of the house.

Julius shut the window and immediately turned his attention to his closet. He'd never ventured off to any type of house party before and he didn't have a clue as to what to wear. He didn't own any of the flashy clothes that Travis consumed, nor did any of the popular gear that everyone else wore appealed to him. He was content with simply equipping himself with his routine attire–black hoodie, blue jeans and some Timberland boots.

After getting himself together, the hard steps from his boots echoed throughout the house as he journeyed down the hall. He was surprised to see Vince's grungy face as he sat in his favorite recliner, staring dead at him as he entered the living room. He had hoped the old grouch would still be sleeping before he left.

"Where do you think you're going?" Vince asked while raking his belly over his dingy wife-beater.

"Out." Julius answered without haste as he grabbed the doorknob.

"Don't be coming back in my house all late at night smelling like no goddamn reefer. You come back here smelling like weed and your ass is gonna' be sleeping in the weeds. And your momma ain't gonna be able to do shit about it, neither."

"Man, whatever," said Julius as he brushed off the warning. He could hear Vince's chuckle from behind him as he slammed the door closed. He met Travis at the edge of the porch.

"Damn, nigga, you ain't got nothing else to wear?" Travis asked. He couldn't believe Julius was not only wearing the same clothes he wore daily to school, but also around the hood.

"What?" said Julius giving himself a self observation. "What's wrong with this?"

Travis shook his head and decided not to even bother. "Nothing man, let's just go," he said as they started their hike down the sidewalk. "We need to make a stop at the Food Mart too. Gotta get us some Blacks. Gotta get right before we even step foot in that mutha."

"That's cool."

"So how long were you planning to sit up in that room moping about old girl?"

"Who said I was moping?"

"Shiiiit," Travis laughed. "You was moping, nigga. I could tell pops burst all the air outta' your bubble when you first told me about what happened. You can't blame a nigga for trying to keep tabs on his daughter, though. As fine as that hoe is, I'd most definitely tag that ass if I had the chance."

"Well, she ain't no hoe, man."

"Hehehe, you really do have feelings for her, huh?" He decided to ease up a bit once he realized Julius was clearly pissed by his gesture. "My bad, Jules. I know the cheerleader is a good girl and all. It's just a figure of speech. I didn't mean to offend you, being that you all in love with her and shit."

"Man, nobody said they was in love with nobody. Besides, I'm good."

"Sure you are," he laughed as he grabbed Julius around his neck and playfully jerked him towards him. "Your ass is gonna be good by the end of the night, though, my nigga. I'ma see to that."

They strolled into the corner store and wandered off in separate directions. Travis took a spot in line at the register as Julius walked to the back of the store to get a drink. When he returned to the front, Travis was next to get to the register.

"Who's that?" Julius asked, as he noticed there was a young white guy he'd never seen before behind the counter.

"Hell, if I know," Travis answered as he signaled Julius to place his drink on the counter. "Yo, my man, where's Savit?"

"Oh dude, he went back home to Harlem. His mother isn't doing too well," said the tall, lanky, brown haired Caucasian man. "I'm just filling in for him for the next couple of weeks. Things kind of serious with his mother's condition and all."

"Damn, that's messed up. Let me get two things of Blacks, too," Travis said while pointing at the smoking items positioned behind the young clerk.

The clerk grabbed two packs of the cigars without looking behind himself and sat them on the counter. "See some ID," he said.

"Nah, I don't do ID." Travis shook his head.

The cashier paused for a moment. He took a second to look over both boys, then shrugged his shoulders. "Alright," he rung Travis up on the register as the boy placed his money on the counter.

"Keep the change," Travis said as he grabbed his items and exited the store with Julius trailing behind him. "Did you see how nerdy that cat was back there?"

"Who?"

"The clerk. That white boy."

"Yeah, what about him?"

"With Savit out of town like he is, I bet we could knock that mother fucker over and get a fat stack."

"Knock over?"

"Nigga, you know what I mean," he said brandishing his piece by flipping up his shirt. "Wouldn't be nothing to it, neither. Just in and out. Who would stop us? Not his geeky ass."

"Man, I ain't robbing nobody," Julius said.

"You ain't gotta do nothin'. Just stand your ass outside and be my look out. I'll handle the rest."

"Travis, shut up, man. You're talking crazy."

He took a look at Julius and grinned. "Yeah, maybe I am, crazy, but how in the hell you ever gonna' expect to pull a dime like the cheerleader and you don't ever have no cash flow?"

"Man, girls don't look at me," said Julius. "I know how I look. I just try not to worry about it."

"That's the thing, Jules, it don't matter how the hell you look. As long as you got this in your pocket, the chicks will always come running," said Travis as he pulled out a thick roll of hundred dollar bills from his pocket and waved it in Julius' face. "Always."

"I hear you, but I'm not trying to rob nobody to get it, though."

"You roll with me long enough, I'll show you how to get it in plenty of ways. You just gotta trust me."

Julius' eyes followed Travis' hand as he stuffed the cash back into his pocket. Travis always seemed to be loaded with money and never appeared to have a worry in the world. The way his friend was always strutting around with loads of money appealed to him, but he wasn't sure he had what it took to do the things he figured Travis did to get it.

He knew if he had that kind of cash his mother wouldn't have to work as hard. Life would be a tad bit easier for her, since Vince had her carrying all her weight and his load too. With all the drama he was finding himself getting into at school, he was contemplating quitting school altogether and just getting a job to help with the bills. He knew his mother would never allow it, but it was something he was strongly considering. He knew if his mom wouldn't approve of him dropping out of school in efforts to get an honest job, she sure as hell wouldn't approve of him knocking over corner stores for cash.

The duo arrived at the party after they hit a few blunts at their hang out spot to take the edge off. The little house was packed with a whole bunch of faces that Julius had never seen before. There was only a handful of the people he could easily recall from his high school, everybody else looked older and all foreign to him.

He and Travis took up post against a wall in the back of the living room. With bloodshot eyes and reeking of marijuana, they sat back and observed the other partygoers as they drank, danced and celebrated the moment. Travis pointed out all the people he recognized to Julius with a joke or a wisecrack. Julius was so blazed and the music was so loud, he couldn't make out half of what Travis was talking about. However, he did think it was quite funny how everyone had blue neon lit eyes from the black lights that illuminated from different areas of the house. He thought they looked rather evil, and it made him laugh. He knew the bud made it all seem funnier than it probably really was.

An obese girl accompanied with a much thinner female companion approached them. Both girls wore skimpy, snugly fitted outfits that didn't do any justice for either ladies. The chubby girl stood directly in front of Travis with her hand on her hip.

"Hey, nigga, you gonna stand on that wall all night or you gonna give me that dance you promised me," said the plump girl as she slid between them and wrapped her arm around Travis' waist. Travis lifted his arm with his blunt hanging from his fingers as she leaned against his chest.

"Damn, girl, you know you twice my size, shit," said Travis.

The skinny female that accompanied her appeared as if she absolutely didn't want to be there. She constantly

looked back towards the crowd of people behind her and on
the side of her with a repulsive look on her face.

"Uh-uh, why you gotta act like that," the chunky
girl said as she backed away from Travis. "You know good
and well you were the first person I invited here tonight.
Don't be trippin', nigga."

"Girl, you know I'm just playing with your fat ass,"
Travis said as he pulled her closer to him. "Come on here
and keep daddy warm." He yelled over to Julius, "More
cushion for the pushin', baby."

Julius expected the stocky female to be turned off
by Travis' comments, but from the smile on her face, along
with the way her fingers danced around his shirt,
everything appeared to be all good. It looked as if she
could, she would rip Travis' clothes off of him right then
and there.

Travis looked at her friend and said, "Hey, Keita,
take my boy, here, out there on the floor and grind it out
with 'em for a little bit. He good people."

She looked over Julius once and grimaced. "I ain't
dancing with that ugly nigga! Do I look like some type of
charity provider to you?"

Julius, still a little buzzed, looked at both of them,
trying to figure out how he got elected to dance with a
female he didn't know and had no interests in whatsoever.

"Bitch, you better dance with my nigga, before I…"
he looked downwards to the big girl. "Shawna, tell your
girl to dance with my boy before I put my foot in her ass."

Shawna said while caressing Travis' abdomen, "Kieta, just dance with the nigga—shit! That's why nobody wanna' deal with your ass now."

"But, Shawna," she said.

"Just do it, girl," she demanded. "Can't you see I'm trying to get my groove on? Stop acting like you all that and shit."

"Come on," she pouted, while squinting her eyes at Julius. The girl stomped out onto the dance floor.

Julius looked over to Travis as he was relishing the way Shawna was grinding against his crotch with her behind. "Go 'head. She ain't gonna bite," he laughed.

He met Kieta on the dance floor as 'Freak Me' by Silk played from the stereo. The girl walked up to him and wrapped her arms around his neck and began slow dancing with him. She looked in his face for a moment but briskly turned her head the other way to avoid any eye contact with him.

He could barely keep up with her because he never danced with anyone before. He looked over to some of the other partygoers to check out their dance moves. No one appeared to have anything too stunning in their dancing repertoire, so he mimicked what appeared to be the most common male dance at the gathering—the two step.

Caught up in the music, she looked into his face again but quickly shook her head. "Oh, hell no," she said as she turned around and pushed her buttocks up against his crotch and began to grind on him. She flipped one arm above her head and gripped the back of his neck as she rotated against his manhood. Even though he found her just as unattractive as he knew he was to her, it didn't stop his manhood from rising to the occasion. Her moves easily broke the consistency of his two step.

Once the music stopped, she refrained from her erotic performance with him and quickly abandoned him. As she disappeared into the crowd, his eyes trailed over to the entrance. To his surprise, he caught a glimpse of Ricky Smith walking into the party with a group of guys behind him. His heart raced. He immediately looked over to the wall where he left Travis with his molester, but there was no sign of him or Shawna.

As soon as he began to make his way over to his original post in hopes of Travis returning, he felt a sharp pain from his neck jerking as he tumbled face first onto the floor. He knew immediately he was pushed. He rolled over on his side and looked up to the neon outline of a group of guys standing over him. The music stopped and the crowd above him began to gather around the commotion.

"Yeah, chump, I pushed your punk ass," said Ricky as he hovered directly over him, pounding his fist into his hand.

Julius eyes scanned over towards the crew that was standing behind Ricky and he realized he was greatly outnumbered again. He recognized each of Ricky's boys from him getting jumped in the bathroom and quickly figured they wanted another round.

He felt fear and anger at the same time. He didn't know if he should just get up and try to run or jump up and get one good lick across Ricky's nose before they whooped his ass again. He reckoned one good swipe at Ricky might've been just worth the brutality he was guaranteed to receive.

"Whoa, whoa, whoa! Do we have a motha' fucking problem up in here tonight?" asked Travis as he stormed through the crowd.

When Ricky laid eyes on Travis, it was as if he'd seen a ghost. He wasn't the only one noticeably shaken, his whole crew appeared to be rattled also.

"You got a problem keeping your hands to your fuckin' self? What the fuck, nigga?" Travis shoved Ricky into his crew. They did their best to keep Ricky from falling and held him up to his feet. "Get your ass up, Jules," said Travis as he pulled Julius up from the floor.

"Travis, you ain't got nothin' to do with this," said Ricky.

"What, nigga, you addressing me now?" Travis said.

"Ain't nobody got any beef with you, man. Just let this buster right here handle his own battles."

"Homeboy, if you got a beef with this dude right here, then you got a beef with me," Travis explained.

Ricky glanced at his crew and noticed a few of his boys had fallen back a few feet, somewhat distancing themselves from him. The only one that stuck to him closely was Ice. Ice was his general. He knew no matter what, Ice would always have his back. With the added comfort of his number one guy standing firm behind him, he said, "I told you I don't have no beef with you, Travis. This is between me and the monster boy. You making things a whole lot more than what they need to be."

"Nigga, everybody know you don't fight by yourself. You always gotta have your little bitches helping you out. Unlike myself, I handle all my shit solo, and if my bitch ever wanna help," he said as he pulled up his shirt and revealed the butt of his pistol, "She can join in on the fun if she feels the urge. Any of y'all niggas wanna meet my bitch tonight?"

"Man, go 'head," said one of Ricky's boys. "I'm not about all this, Rick, I'm out." The boy rushed for the front door as some in the crowd began to chuckle. Ricky barely even cut his eye at the cowardly boy, although his desertion infuriated him.

"I recommend you fall back with 'em, Rick," said Travis. "Before things start getting to more than what they need to be."

Ricky looked over to Ice as he stood a bit antsy with both his fists balled up and his eyes peering directly on Travis. He knew Ice to be just as wild as Travis, but he wouldn't put his money on him against Travis. He was fool, but not as fool as they all knew Travis to be.

"And, Ice, oh nigga, you know what's up. I don't even know why you mean-mugging me like that for. You know how I get down, nigga," said Travis. "You know."

"I done told you it don't even have to be like this, Travis," said Ricky.

"Then bounce, ball boy. Nobody sent for you. All of you herbs need to bounce before y'all piss me the fuck off."

Julius gazed at Ricky in pure anger in disgust. He had no problems taking Ricky on one on one. If he got beat down, he got beat down, but at least it would be a fair fight.

Ricky and his crew stood firm, and all wore the nastiest scowls they could compose, however, none of them said one word out of the way to Travis. Ricky observed the straight faces of the crowd as they all had eyes on him and his crew, as they eagerly awaited their next move. For a house party full of people, it was so quiet, you could almost hear a mouse fart.

"Did I stutter, nigga?" Travis asked.

Ricky, with all he had inside himself, wanted to say something really foul towards him, but a fight with the notorious thug was an altercation he just didn't want to deal with. Travis' reputation of being a scrappy fighter brought fear to many, and Ricky was no different. In one last ditch effort to prove he was still the badass he wanted the world to believe he was, he issued Julius the meanest look he could muster.

"Let's roll," Ricky told Ice. In an instant they all trailed behind Ricky through the crowd and exited the house.

Julius looked on with a smile. He enjoyed seeing Ricky getting punked for a change. He only wished he was able to do it himself.

"Punk asses," Travis said to himself. "You good?"

"Yup," answered Julius.

"Let's get the fuck outta' here. These niggas done messed up my damn high."

"Cool."

They walked through the back of the house as the music started back up, and all the partygoers began to mingle amongst each other since all the ruckus finally appeared to be over with.

"You know I had it, right?" Julius said to Travis as they brushed through the kitchen.

"You looked like you had it."

"Nobody scared of dude. He just got all that mouth when he with his boys."

"Chumps like Ricky got mouth with or without his boys. You gotta put niggas like that on their ass one good time to shut 'em up. He'll only get the message then. He's seen me put niggas down before, all of 'em have. That's why they shake in their boots when they see me coming. They know my résumé."

The screen door rattled shut as they made their way out of the house and down the back porch steps. Travis stopped halfway down the steps and lit a cigarette.

"You're gonna have to put him on his ass one day, Jules," Travis explained as he took a hit from the cancer stick. "That's the only way he'll stop. You gotta beat his ass and beat it good. Niggas like that don't get the point otherwise."

Julius looked up at Travis as he hovered from the steps. He figured Travis was right. Ricky wasn't going to stop until he finally fought him and won. He was just so tired of fighting all the time. He just wanted a break from all the beef for a change and be left alone.

"Um, excuse me," said Shawna as she poked her head out from behind the raggedy screen door. "Where do you think you're going? I thought you was gonna hook a sista' up."

Travis turned to her with a chuckle. "Damn, my bad, ma."

"Yeah, I bet it's your bad," she said. "You so busy tryin' to fight these corny niggas out here, you forgot all about my ass."

"Nah, nah, nah, Ma. It ain't even like that," said Travis. "Give a nigga a few minutes with my ace out here. I'm coming."

"Alright, I ain't got all night," she said. "I gotta start clearing these people outta' here before my sister gets off work. I don't wanna hear her mouth yappin' about me still having this party going on. She know she gets on my nerves."

"I got ya. I got ya," he said. "Gone and take your fat ass upstairs and get ready for me. I'll just be a minute."

"It better," she said as she rolled her eyes and shut the door closed.

Travis trampled down the stairs and said, "Boy, I tell you...them big girls know they love some good pipe."

"So I guess you're staying?" asked Julius.

"Yeah, I'm gonna break her off a lil' somethin', somethin'," Travis nodded. "She maybe chunky, but good gracious..."

"That's cool."

"But hey," Travis said as he flicked his cigarette away. "I got something for you."

"What?"

"This," Travis said as he whipped out his pistol and handed it to him. Julius grabbed it without thinking about it.

"I want you to take this."

"What do I need with this?" Julius asked, almost dropping it.

"Hold it tight, nigga. Damn! It's loaded," said Travis. "You need some protection, homeboy. You never know when a bitch nigga will try to graduate into something more than he really is. I was gonna give it to you a while back, when those niggas pissed on your ass, but I was still checking you out. Now I know what you're about, so everything's all good."

"And what about you? What are you gonna flash around whenever you got a point to stress?"

"Hehehe, boy you're real funny," Travis laughed. "For your information, they don't call me the rifle man for nothing. I got plenty more where that came from."

"I appreciate the offer and all," he said while attempting to hand the weapon back to Travis. "But, I'm good. I don't really need this."

"Boy, take that shit and put it up."

Julius gazed down at the gun. He knew Travis wasn't going to take no for answer, so he stuffed the gun in the small of his back and covered it with his shirt.

"You gonna be straight getting back to your crib?"

"Yeah, I'm good."

"Cool then," said Travis. "Let me go see what big girl is in there talking about then." He gave Julius dap. "I'll holla."

Julius stood frozen as his eyes trailed Travis up the steps and into the house. He felt conflicted about holding on to the firearm. On one hand he was nervous as hell about the idea of walking around with a loaded gun, but on the other hand, he felt a strong sense of security by having the piece handy.

****

The soothing sounds of Marvin Gaye's 'Let's Get It On," blasted from the record player and throughout the house as Vince relaxed on his recliner, horribly reciting the words to the song in between guzzling down a forty ounce bottle of Old English liquor.

Felicia was in the bedroom with a clothes basket tucked under her arm as she scooped up Vince's dirty pants from off the floor. Every article of his clothing she picked up infuriated her. It made no sense to her for a grown man at Vince's age to just sling his clothes off to whatever part of the floor he felt like and leave them there for her to pick up. Julius was just entering into adulthood, and he didn't even do the trifling things she allowed Vince to do and get away with.

When she walked through the living room with the basket full of his clothing, Vince sat his drink on the floor. He rushed to grab her by her arm and said, "Hey, hey, you know it's been six months. It ain't good for a man to do without."

She snatched her arm away from him and said, "I'm sure you've been getting by."

"Well hell, gone and be like that then," he growled as he plunged back down in his chair. He picked up his bottle and took a swig when she darted through the kitchen door. "Trifling ass woman."

She dropped the basket in front the washing machine that resided next to the back door, then took a moment to gather herself. She hated when Vince touched her. His pathetic ways made her detest him and she knew eventually something was going to have to change. There wasn't a day that went by over the past several years that she didn't think about leaving, but she was old enough to know the difference between thinking and doing. Even though he provided very little to help her at this point in their relationship, at her age she carried the fear of starting over, and being without someone to grow old. However, as much as she worked and he stayed out drinking and partying, she already felt like she was alone. She was just too reluctant to place their separation in a more official capacity. Honestly, she really carried the hope that he would just get up and leave one day.

She flipped up the top to the washing machine and began tossing his dirty jeans into it after shaking them out thoroughly. Vince was good for leaving liquor store receipts and tissue in his pockets that wound up getting all over his clothes. She hated pulling the little particles of paper off of his clothing. He made such a fuss about it when it happened, she often wondered why he never thought to empty out his own pockets before flinging his clothes all over the floor.

When she shook out the last pair of his pants before dumping them into the washer, she thought her eyes deceived her when she noticed a small plastic baggie fall out. She got down on one knee and carefully picked it up.

She knew exactly what it was, but she just couldn't believe where it came from.

Al Green's 'I Can't Get Next To You' was now extruding from Vince's stereo as he danced in his chair with his arms swaying in the air. He was feeling good and there was no denying it. Felicia returned to the living room and marched to the record player. The needle made a loud screeching sound when she flipped the record off of the turntable and onto the floor. The music ceased.

"Hey! What the fuck is wrong with you?" Vince yelled. "You done scratched my damn record."

Felicia marched in front of him and said, "I will not have any drug addicts in my house."

"Woman, what the hell are you talking about?"

"I'm talking about this," She held up the crack baggie and threw it up against his forehead.

Vince tried to block it from hitting him in the face as his eyes trailed the baggie onto his lap. When he realized what he left in his pocket, he couldn't do anything but chuckle about it.

"So what? You trying to call me a crackhead or something?"

"Well, it's crack, ain't it?"

"Man, everybody does a little dope. I ain't gotta answer to you. Even that damn platypus mouth boy of yours does it. Look at how black his lips have been getting."

"Not in my house."

"You know what woman…just like I just said, I ain't gotta answer to you. What the hell you questioning me for? You don't ask me no questions. I'm the damn man of this house."

"Well, as long as I'm the only one working up in here and my name is on the lease, I'm the man of the house! And I don't want no drugs in it!"

"Oh, it's like that?"

"Yeah, Vince, it's like that. And you need to start looking for another job, too." She stormed back into the kitchen.

Vince picked up the baggie, looked at it and then started laughing hysterically. "This bitch right here." After a few moments, his laughter swiftly evolved into anger. He began to breathe heavily, and his nose began to flare. He got angrier and angrier the more he thought about what had just transpired. "You know what—fuck this!"

Felicia stood over the table with tears running down her cheeks. It was bad enough he wasn't working, but now he's a druggie, she thought. She knew without a doubt they'd reached the twilight of their relationship.

In a brash of anger, Vince stormed through the kitchen door and grabbed her by her hair. "Ain't no woman gonna try to run me. Not in my house," he declared as he smashed her face first into the table.

The force of the collision made her lose her footing and she fell backwards. She slid along the sink cabinet with the back of her head crashing onto the hard wood.

She looked up at him as he hovered over her. Her vision was blurry and the room was spinning. Her face ached like hell. She couldn't believe after all the years they'd been together he would actually put his hands on her. He made plenty of threats in the past, but he never acted out on any of them, ever.

"You need a lesson in knowing your damn role," he said.

Blood began trickling from the side of her face as she crawled backwards on her elbows. She realized he was approaching her. He wore a deranged, evil look on his face. She didn't recognize the man in front of her, and there was no telling what he would do next.

"I gotta teach you what it means to be a woman. Trying to tell me what to do." He began unfastening his belt. "Yeah, this is how old Herman Joseph took it. He had the right damn thing in mind. Maybe this will teach you some fuckin' respect."

"Vince, whatever you're thinking about doing, you need to rethink it right now," she cried.

"Oh, I don't need to rethink nothing," he said as he kicked at her leg. "You should've re-thought messing with me when I was in a good fuckin' mood. You should've re-thought giving a nigga a piece of ass, after going damn near the whole year without any. Your ass is the one that needs to do all the rethinking. Not me!"

"Vince stop," she screamed. "Just stop."

"Shut the hell up," he said as he dove on top of her. He grabbed a fist full of her hair, pressed his lips closely to her ear and said, "You think you're so goddamn high and mighty just like that sadity ass momma of yours. Talking about you're the man of the house. You and that damn boy of yours talking to me like I ain't nothin' every day. You think I don't get tired of that shit? I'm 'bout to straighten this shit out real quick." His hand ran up her dress as he went pulling for her panties.

"Vince stop. Stop it," she screamed as she did her best to fight him off. All the elbowing and poking him in his face did nothing to push him back from his drunken rage.

He ripped her panties from her legs and said, "I'm gonna enjoy this shit." He used one arm to fight off her jabs as he used his other hand to work his pants down.

"Someone help," she screamed. "Somebody help me, please." In one final attempt to force him off of her, she took her fingers and dug them into his eye. It was enough to force him backwards.

"You bitch," he yelled while covering his eye.

Bloody and sore, she began crawling away from him on all fours. Before she could get too far, he scurried to his feet and drove his fist into the back her head while plunging all of his body weight on top of her. The force of the blow was enough to knock her out momentarily.

"Try that again, bitch." He rolled her wilted body over and ripped her blouse open, exposing her bra. "Now, where was I?" he asked himself. "I'ma teach your ass something now."

He pushed down his drawers and hopped on top of her. The weight of his sweaty, smelly body was enough to revive her as she immediately began swinging at his face again. He was too strong, but just as he was about to penetrate her, a loud bang erupted in the kitchen. It was a gunshot. It froze them both.

"You better get the hell off my momma."

Vince looked towards the door, and to his surprise, Julius was standing in front of him with a pistol pointed dead in his face. Small particles of debris fell from the ceiling between them from the first shot.

"Julius," Felicia huffed. She was shocked to see him carrying a handgun, but at the same time relieved he had come to her rescue.

"Felicia, this little motherfucker got a gun," said Vince. He was too afraid to move as Felicia began to scoot from under him.

"Julius, Julius, it's okay," she said as she hurried to her feet.

"Nah, Ma, it ain't okay. I know what he was trying to do you."

"Just put the gun away baby." she asked with her hand out in an attempt to cool Julius down.

"I'ma kill this motherfucker right now, Momma. He putting his hands on you. You got blood on you. He been hittin' all on you."

"Baby, there's a lot of things not worth losing your life over in this world, and he is one of 'em. Give me the gun, son."

"You need to listen to your momma, boy," Vince said easing to his feet while sliding his pants up on him. "You need to put that thing away before somebody gets hurt."

"Shut the fuck up!" Julius yelled.

"Give me the damn gun, Julius," Felicia begged. "Give it to me."

Tears began to form in the wells of Julius' eyes as he trembled in anger. He knew if he pulled the trigger he and his mother would never have to deal with the lazy bastard again. It was so simple, yet so hard. He lowered the pistol and burst into tears. Felicia grabbed him and embraced him with a hug.

Vince stared at both of them, still too scared to make a move, but not nearly scared enough to keep his mouth shut. "I knew you ain't had the balls to shoot," he laughed.

Felicia pulled herself away from Julius and grabbed a cast iron pan from the stove. She swiftly struck Vince across his face with it with enough force to send him tumbling to the floor.

"Now you get the hell out of my house!" she yelled standing over him.

****

Julius sat in an old lawn chair on the front porch beside his mom as she had the pistol hanging from her hand with her arms folded. They both watched as Vince stumbled down the steps with a huge bandage plastered over his forehead and a box full of the last items he had remaining in the house.

Flex stood in the driveway beside his old Chevy truck as he waited for Vince. Vince's old recliner, the record player, garbage bags full of his clothing and all of his belongings was tied up on the back of the rusty white Cheyenne. When Vince made it halfway to the truck, he turned around and faced Felicia with his sad swollen face.

"Don't you say a word," said Felicia. "I swear if you say one thing to me or my son, that might be enough for me to take this here gun and shoot you myself."

He could tell by the look on her face, she was serious. He thought better than to say whatever parting words he originally thought to be okay to release from his lips and joined Flex in his truck.

Felicia watched the pickup truck pull out of the yard. Once the vehicle disappeared down the street, she immediately felt as if a huge burden had been lifted from her. He was finally gone.

She turned her attention to Julius. "Son, I don't know who you got this thing from, but it's in your best interest to get it back to them." She handed him the gun.

He looked up at his mother and didn't know what to say. Everything had happened so fast, he didn't know what to say or how to even respond. He just nodded, "Okay."

She took a deep breath. "I'm sorry about all of this, Julius. I really am," she said, attempting to hold back her tears. She resigned into the house.

Julius bowed his head while simply staring at the pistol. He knew that his mother meant business about him getting rid of it, but he wasn't ready to. The cold, hard metal made him feel a way he never felt before–protected. It was a feeling he wasn't ready to relinquish.

Chapter 14

A few days had passed since he and his mother banned Vince from the premises, but the altercation was still fresh on his mind. He was so relieved to have the old bum out of the house he decided to take a few days off from school to enjoy the house to himself, without his mother's knowledge of course. He decided to make his way to school this day, because he figured he was getting awful close to the maximum amount of days he could miss school before he wouldn't be allowed to graduate. The thought of spending another year in high school was enough motivation for him to get dressed and hustle down to the school grounds despite the constant aggravation from some of his peers, namely Ricky Smith.

He eased out of the house and started making his way down the sidewalk.

"Julius," a familiar voice called from behind him.

He whipped around to see Travis jogging towards him. He stopped and waited for his friend to catch up. Seeing Travis this early caught him totally by surprise since the earliest he'd ever seen him was around ten in the morning. He honestly didn't think the boy woke up this early.

"Wow, you coming to school this morning?" Julius asked.

"Hell nah," he huffed as he stopped and kneeled over before him. "I gotta quit smoking so damn much. A nigga can barely breathe."

"You ain't lying about that," Julius added. "You look like you're struggling."

After a few deep breaths from Travis, they started walking down the sidewalk.

"So where you been hiding, Jules? I haven't heard from you since the party. Them chumps didn't put you into hiding, did they?"

"Nah," Julius answered. "Just been home, chilling."

"Still got that cheerleader on your mind, huh?"

"Nah, just keeping a low profile, that's all," he lied. The only thing that occupied his mind more than the recent episode with Vince was his frequent thoughts of Simone. Thoughts of her hadn't ceased rummaging through his mind since he last saw her at the fair. She was the only constant in his mind.

"So did you get a chance to think about what we discussed?"

"Think about what?"

"Robbing that white dude at the corner store?"

"What? Were you serious about that?"

"Hells yeah! Man, the past few days I've been watching that spot like a hawk, taking notes and shit. I figured out the perfect time we could go in there and get that money. Won't take more than five minutes, tops!"

"Travis, I'm not robbing that place with you, man. I'm not trying to be held up in nobody's jail."

"Nigga, you ain't going to no jail. Besides, I'll be the one doing all the work. All you gotta do is be my look out man."

Julius couldn't believe Travis was still thinking about robbing the place. Travis may have talked him into going to the house party, but he swore to himself there was no way in hell he was getting him to help rob a corner store.

They stopped on the curb across from the school yard.

"I hear what you're saying, Travis, but I can't roll with you on this one, man. Cats be getting twenty plus years for robbing stores and mess. I see it on the news all the time."

"Twenty years? Nigga, are you for real? Nobody give a shit about that rusty ass corner store. Besides, we ain't gonna get caught. I told you I got it all planned out."

Julius just shook his head, solid with his decision, "Man…"

"Look, just think about it, Jules. We can make some heavy cheddar knocking over that joint, and I'm gonna need you, just like you needed me at that party. Have *my* back for a change. That's all a nigga asking."

Travis walked away as his parting remarks left Julius speechless. He didn't expect him to throw the party up in his face in such a way. He appreciated Travis for standing up for him like he did and he was glad that he did, but trading an ass whooping for possible prison time just didn't make sense to him.

He didn't doubt the robbery would be quick and seamless, but the thought of ending up behind bars like his sperm donor, rapist dad was just too much for him. It would give his mother's side of the family the perfect opportunity to say, *I told you so.*

****

Julius' mind was a mess. Normally, he would spend his fifty minutes in the art class so involved with his work, the whole sitting would feel like a mere ten minutes, leaving him yearning for more. From missing Simone, to his altercation with Vince, and now the peer pressure of robbing Savit's corner store with Travis, he felt as if his life was spiraling out of control. On top of everything else that was going on, he knew he had to watch his back from Ricky and his crew. With the way Ricky was embarrassed by Travis at the party, he knew the boy would eventually come looking for blood.

The bell rang and Julius quickly packed up his things and headed for the door.

"Hey, Mr. Graves let me speak to you for a few minutes," said Mr. Bass as he stopped Julius at the door.

"I do something wrong?" asked Julius.

"You guilty of something?"

"No."

"Alright then. Let me talk to you for a few minutes," he said as he shut the door closed behind the last student to leave the class. Julius reluctantly waddled to the first desk in the class and sat on it.

Mr. Bass eased to the edge of his desk and leaned on it, positioning himself directly in front of Julius.

"Mr. Graves, so how are we today?"

"I'm cool. I'm a little hungry, though."

"Don't worry, son, this will only take a few moments of your time," he said. "I haven't seen you as often as I've been accustomed to seeing you. Is everything fine at home?"

"Yeah, yeah, everything's fine at home, Mr. Bass. Really I was just a little under the weather the past few days."

"I see," he nodded. "Did you get an opportunity to fill out any of those college applications I gave you while you were out?"

"Uhm, I think I did one," Julius said, lying.

"Oh, just one. I see," said Mr. Bass. He took his glasses off and laid them gently on his desk behind him. Then he said, "When I was around your age, my father once told me, 'Son, never try to bullshit a bullshitter.'"

"Sir," said Julius. The teacher's choice of words caught him off guard but it gained his complete attention.

"Oh, Mr. Graves I'm sure you've heard worse out there in those halls on the other side of that door. I just want take a moment to find out what's going on with you, son."

"Like I said, Mr. Bass, I'm cool. Nothing to worry about."

"Don't tell me that, son," said Mr. Bass. "You've got more talent than any student I've seen come through here in the past twenty-five years, Mr. Graves, and I'm afraid you're about to throw it all away."

Julius turned his head away from Mr. Bass as his eyes pierced through him. He could feel the teacher's eyes on him as he wished he had just kept on walking out of the class and pretended as if he didn't even hear his request for him to stay behind.

"You know, Mr. Graves, I lost my arm in a car accident. This guy, after having a wild night out with his pals, decided to jump behind the wheel, drunk as hell, and crashed into me head on," he said as he pushed his glasses further along the desk and positioned himself more comfortably on the edge of his desk. "This guy, with his carelessness, hurt me badly, costing me an arm, but the crash also killed my fiancée."

When Mr. Bass mentioned the loss his fiancée in the same accident where he lost his arm, Julius couldn't help but turn around and face him as he told his story. He felt the old man deserved at least that much respect.

"Yes, Julius, I lost my arm, but my love, the only one I've ever come to love, she lost her life. We had plans, oh we had some plans. Plans that would never come to pass."

"I'm sorry to hear that, Mr. Bass," Julius said.

Mr. Bass nodded and said, "The only reason I'm telling you all of this, son, is because since then, people have always looked at me differently. They point, they make jokes, laugh–you name it. I've seen it or I've heard it. The crazy old man with the one arm, they say. But it's okay, Mr. Graves, because looks aren't everything. People are going to talk, they're going to say things that you may not like, they may even want to harm you, but through it all, the only thing that ever really matters is what you feel about yourself. Do you hear what I'm saying, Mr. Graves?"

"Yeah, I hear you," Julius answered.

"If I could give the only arm I have left to get my Clarissa back, I would chop it off and hand it away myself. You see, Mr. Graves, it's her memory that keeps me. It kept me going when I didn't want to go on anymore. When the crying, the pointing and the laughing became too overwhelming, it was her that kept me," he said with watery eyes. "Mr. Graves, never let how other folk think you look determine who you are. Life is bigger than someone else's opinion. You have to find what matters most to you in this world, and you have to make it mean something to you, son. Life ain't fair, but this is your moment in time. Don't let someone else cheat you from it. Because if you allow life to do it, it will swallow you up. A strong mind will always persevere. You remember that."

"Yes sir, I will." Mr. Bass' words sunk deep in his mind. He never thought that with his one arm, the old teacher could actually relate to what he had been going through his entire life, but he did. The art teacher's words allowed him to see the man in a completely different light... A light that revealed the old art teacher to be an ally.

"I expect you to get those college applications completed and in to me tomorrow, Mr. Graves."

"Tomorrow?"

"Yes, tomorrow. And I also expect to see you in class every day for the rest of the school year."

"Oh you don't have to worry about that, Mr. Bass," said Julius as he began walking to the door.

"I know I don't, but you should," he laughed. "Have a good one, Mr. Graves."

"You too, Mr. Bass," said Julius. He swung the door open and to his surprise Simone was standing in the hall with her arms wrapped around her textbooks.

"Simone, what are you doing here," he asked.

"Waiting for you. I saw you walking to school this morning with that boy," she said.

"You did?"

"Yes, I did," she replied. "I knew this would be the one class you would show up to, so I decided to come seek you out myself since you're obviously avoiding me."

Seeing Simone's gorgeous face surprised him. He was ecstatic to see her, but in the same instant, he wasn't sure about how to handle talking to her again. The last thing he needed was her father breathing down his neck, badgering him about why he decided to disobey his wishes and continuing communications with his baby girl.

"Look, Simone…"

"Why haven't I heard from you since the fair, Julius? You don't even answer the phone when I call you," she said. "Did my father say something to you?"

"Look, I don't even wanna' talk about it." he said.

"Talk about what? He did say something to you, didn't he? He chased you off, didn't he?"

"Nah, I'm not saying all that. It's just…"

"It's just what, Julius? What is it?"

She was eager for answers as to why he was distancing himself from her, answers he wasn't willing to provide her with.

"Look, let's just be straight up with each other. We're from two completely different places," he said. "You live in your world, and I live in mine."

"Julius, what are you talking about? Why are you even acting like this? When we were together at the carnival, I thought we...we..."

"You thought what?" he asked. "You thought we could be together? Come on, look at me and look at you. Seriously! Not only are we complete opposites, but you come from a whole different side of the tracks than I come from. You don't really wanna be a part of my world, Simone. My world is sooooo much different than what you can imagine. It's not what you think, and it's not what you really want. You don't want to be in my world and have people look at you the way they look at me. I don't think nobody wants that."

"Julius, this don't even sound like you," she said. "Why are you being so standoffish?"

"Man, just stop trying to make me your charity case and step off. Please," he said. He couldn't even look her in her eyes. The helpless expression written all over her face made him feel like utter garbage. Before she could even gather her words together for a quality response to him, he rushed down the hall, not even giving her a second look.

"Julius, wait!" she yelled, nearly in tears. "Julius!"

****

243

He hated shunning her away, but he knew it had to be done. Her father made it clear to him he wasn't going to allow them to see each other, so he decided it was best to just leave well enough alone. He figured he already had enough on his plate, and he didn't want to burden the girl with his problems, let alone, create new ones for the both of them by not adhering to her father's warning. Being with Simone was a pleasant fantasy to him, but that's exactly what it was–a fantasy. To him, there was no way in the world a girl so beautiful could possibly want to be with someone that looked as horrible as him. It just wasn't possible.

As he peeped through the classroom window at her, he was careful not to let anyone see him. While staring at her, he couldn't help but wonder what things would be like if he were someone else. Someone handsome and confident, someone so classy, if her father was to see him with her, he couldn't help but be pleased. Someone that was a complete opposite of him.

Gazing at her only depressed him, so he retreated down the hallway and eased into the stairwell. He took a seat on the top step and pulled out a cigarette. The smoke was from a pack that Vince had left behind, and he figured he wouldn't have the nerve to come back to the house to claim it so he figured he may as well help himself to it. Whether it was weed or nicotine, smoking seemed to help him take the edge off, and being on edge was a feeling he was definitely getting acquainted to frequently.

"What the fuck," yelled out a voice from the bottom of the steps. It only took a few moments for Julius to recognize the voice, as he peered down the stairs in hopes that his ears had deceived him. Unfortunately, his hearing was right on point and Ricky, accompanied by one of his goons, Tim, was indeed standing at the bottom of the stairs below.

"Your ass," Ricky said with a face full of rage and anger.

"Shit," Julius said to himself. He quickly jumped up and dashed through the door.

Ricky and his companion immediately gave chase as they hauled up the stairs behind him. Julius wasn't a full two feet out of the door when he crashed into another student trying to get down the stairs. As he attempted to gather his books that went scattering across the floor, he soon realized the student that he'd managed to bump into was another one of Ricky's homeboys, the one called Jermaine.

"Ah, shit, why?" Julius said under his breath, while scooping up his books.

"You again," said Jermaine.

"Grab his ass," Ricky screamed rushing from the door. "Don't let that punk get away."

Julius tried to make a dash for it, but Jermaine lunged at him from behind and clipped him up, sending him sliding face first onto the floor.

"Dang it," Julius moaned while clutching his chin.

"Now...," said Ricky as he approached Julius. "I'm 'bout to fuck you up!"

"Your partner ain't here to save your ass this time," Tim laughed from behind Ricky.

Julius rolled over on his back and drove his foot into Ricky's leg, sending the boy tumbling to the floor on one knee.

"Son of a bitch," Ricky squealed in pain.

Julius hopped up and took his thick History book and slammed it across Ricky's face, sending him backwards onto his back.

"Get his ass," Ricky yelled to his homeboys while clutching the side of his face.

Tim fronted Julius with his arms open as if he was waiting for the right moment to grab him. Julius began swinging the book wildly as the boy hopped backwards with each sway.

"Leave me the hell alone!" yelled Julius.

Jermaine regained his footing, grabbed Julius from behind, and slammed him against the lockers. Somehow Julius was able to keep a firm grip on his book and smashed Jermaine across the bridge of his nose with it. Jermaine went plummeting to the floor while gripping his nose in agony. Tim swung a haymaker at Julius and missed. Julius then cracked the book over the back of Tim's head, knocking him head first into the wall of lockers.

Just before Julius could clock Tim across his head once more, they all froze to the sound of a familiar voice screaming out from the other end of the hall. "Gentlemen! Gentlemen!" yelled Mr. Benson as he briskly stomped down the hall.

No one moved an inch. Julius kept his eyes on Tim as he violently huffed and puffed, completely out of breath with his clothes all mangled and torn. He would cease combat per the principal's abrupt wishes, but if they started swinging again, he was prepared to happily follow suit.

"Just what in the hell do you people think you're doing out here?" Mr. Benson asked angrily.

"This dude right here, he just started attacking us with his book, Mr. Benson. We didn't do a thing to him," said Ricky.

"That's a damn lie!" Julius barked back.

"Son, you do realize this is a school that you're talking like that in?" Mr. Benson asked.

"Yeah, I know, but he's lying and…"

"I don't care," Mr. Benson said. "This is supposed to be a learning institution, not some bunkhouse brawl. I also thought I made myself quite clear to you earlier in the school year of what my expectations were of you, Mr. Graves. Did I not?"

"Yes sir, but…"

"I don't want to hear it," said Mr. Benson.

Julius could tell by the way the man was speaking to him that he was going to be the one to take all the blame again. Instead of trying to explain himself to the principal, he just allowed him to talk.

"Ricky, you and the others, I want you all to go ahead and report to Coach Dyson. I will speak with you all later," Mr. Benson said while pointing. "You, you, Mr. Graves, you come with me to my office, now."

"That's all? What about them? They started the whole thing. What about them, man?" Julius cried. "I was just minding my own business."

"Mr. Graves, that's enough!" Principal Benson said sternly. "I'm the authority figure here, and you will do as I say. All of you, for that matter."

Ricky had a small smirk on his face but was careful not to let the principal see it as he climbed back to his feet with his buddies' assistance.

"Oh man, this is bullshit!" Julius screamed.

"Mr. Graves, you watch your mouth in my presence. You may speak with such a foul tongue out there in those streets, but you will not talk in that manner when you're within these school walls. Now you're coming with me, and that's all there is to say about it. Now, let's go."

Julius looked over at the boys, in uncontrollable anger as they just gazed back at him. Although they all wore straight faces, he could tell they were enjoying the show and that they all wanted to burst into laughter. Somehow, they managed to win again. Feeling defeated, he started making his way down the hall.

"Coach Dyson's office," Mr. Benson said to the boys again, still pointing. "I mean it."

"Yes sir," said Ricky, as he limped behind his crew as they made their way down the opposite end of the hall.

****

Felicia pushed the laundry cart into the hands of the lone worker of the laundry room for the night, Clarence. He eagerly greeted her with a smile.

"Alright now, Fee, I see you. Looking good there," he said.

"Thanks, Clarence," she said, smiling back at him. Clarence wasn't really her type, but it made her feel good to be turning heads again. Since Vince left the house, she took a few extra minutes before she left for work to make herself up. She had no intentions on hooking anyone, but looking good always had a way of making her feel better about herself. At some point while just going through the motions with Vince, she stopped caring about how she looked at all.

Even though she was only confined to wearing the skimpy grey and white housekeeping skirt, the compliments and smiles felt good coming in again. To some women, the tiny skirt would be a bit demeaning as a requirement to work in, but she always reverted back to the long nights she spent as a dancer where she wore very little or nothing at all. She was never proud of the life she led back in those days, but she held no regrets because she only did what she felt she had to do to keep her child fed and a roof over their heads.

"Felicia, what are you still doing here?" Barbara asked while waddling towards her. "I thought you would've been at the school, by now."

"At the school for what?"

"You mean that old slew-footed Lance didn't tell you?"

"Lance didn't tell me what, Barb?" she asked. As soon as she heard the word school, she immediately thought of her son and a quick chill rushed throughout her body. Whenever Julius got into trouble, she always feared the worst.

"It's your son. I thinks he's gotten into a little bit of trouble at the school, darlin'. The school secretary called here just over an hour ago, trying to reach you. Lance said he was gonna deliver the message to you himself."

"He didn't tell me a damn thing," she said furiously.

"Well that sounds like his sorry ass," Barbara said while shaking her head. "Don't make no sense."

"Okay, people, you don't get paid for standing around, chittering and chattering," said Lance as he approached them while looking over his clipboard. "Time is money when you're here on my clock."

All Felicia could see was red as Lance drew closer. "Where the hell do you get off?"

"Excuse me, Ms. Graves?" he asked with a surprised look on his face. "Are you referring to me?"

"You knew the school called me about my son. Why didn't you tell me or send one of the girls upstairs to come get me?"

"Well, you were busy," he replied nonchalantly. "And if you don't mind, I would prefer to have this conversation in my office."

"I do mind, and I need to find out what's going on with my son at the school."

"If you leave this building, Ms. Graves, you don't have to worry about coming back," said Lance. "I've been more than nice to you on more than a few occasions by allowing you to keep your job, but if you abandon me while I'm shorthanded tonight… well, let's just say, there's no amount of groveling you could do to save your spot this time."

"Do you really think this place is more important to me than my son?"

"Hey, it's a paycheck, and one of which a lot of young ladies outside these walls would love to have a chance to get their hands on," he smiled.

She yearned to smack him across his lips one good time, and if she was a man she probably would've, but he wasn't worth the time nor the guaranteed night in jail. She couldn't stand not knowing what the situation with Julius was any longer so she simply walked away. "Keep your money," she said.

"What?" He stood flabbergasted and somewhat embarrassed, as the other workers began to huddle next to him. "Felicia Graves, where do you think you're going?"

"To see what's going on with my son."

He scanned over the nosey faces behind him as they all seemed amused that Felicia was walking out on him. It made him feel the need to get some sort of last word. "I'm serious, Felicia, you leave this building and you don't have to worry about coming back!"

She didn't give him a second look as she stopped at the time clock and punched out. She then continued down the hall to the back exit.

"Felicia…Felicia, you get back here right now! I'm gonna hold your check back for two weeks, so don't think you're getting paid on Monday!" His other staff members began laughing and made comments amongst themselves. He hated being shown up by anyone. "Alright, people the shows over. Get back to work or she won't be the only one out the door."

****

"How is it that you find yourself in so much trouble, Mr. Graves?" Principal Benson asked Julius. He sat behind his desk shuffling through the boy's school records as Julius sat silently in a chair opposite of him. "Your file is full of fights and all kinds of mischief on school grounds. I'm amazed that you were even allowed to get into any school in the district with a record like yours."

"What does that have to do with anything?" asked Julius. He was still hot about being the only one that had to report to the office for the altercation. This wasn't the first time he had been singled out, he was just tired of it. "I didn't start the fight, they did. I was just minding my own business."

"Minding your own business in the halls while you should've been in Mr. Rawls' classroom. A class you haven't reported to in over a week."

"Yeah, well, it's the same class your prized basketball player hasn't been in either for about a month or two."

"Mr. Smith's absences are excused, unlike your own," said Mr. Benson. "And why would he even want to waste his time bothering you? That young man has the world at his fingertips, and he's placed this school on his shoulders with his talents. He's managed to get a positive light on Washington High for a change."

"So what the hell... does that make him untouchable?"

"You watch your mouth in my office, young man. I'm not going to continue to ask you to watch your language," he said while repositioning himself in his plush leather chair. "You know, Mr. Graves, jealously is a horrible trait to possess."

"Jealousy?" said Julius. "Man, this is a joke."

"This maybe a joke to you sir, but when your mother gets here…"

"You called my mom?"

"Oh yes, this is serious business, Mr. Graves. I warned you. I don't play games in my school. Right now you're looking at expulsion, son."

"For a fight?"

"Oh, not just a fight, Mr. Graves, but cutting class, the repetitive tardiness to your classrooms, when you actually decide to make appearances, and also missing entire days. You see, I've been watching you. Ever since your last episode we chatted about, I've been keeping close tabs on you."

Julius fell hopeless. He knew with the latest altercation and all Mr. Benson was putting up against him, his high school days were most likely over. The last thing he wanted to do was be forced in to night school to get his GED. He also couldn't help thinking about how disappointed his mother was going to be once he's officially kicked out of the school.

"I actually assumed your mother would be here by now," he said while glancing over the clock that rested on the wall behind Julius.

"Well, she does work nights this week, so you might as well just let me go home, like you let those other dudes go. Unless you're planning on having us wait here all night."

"Oh, no, Mr. Graves, it's not that simple. You're in some serious trouble."

"Well, we're gonna end up being in here all night then," Julius explained.

"Well, it's just your luck that I don't have anything else better to do tonight," said Mr. Benson.

There was a knock at the door.

"Please come in," said Principal Benson.

Julius didn't dare look back at the door behind him. He could sense it was mother, and he knew if she had to leave off work early she was going to be pissed.

The secretary, Gladys, escorted Felicia into the office. The first thing that caught Mr. Benson's eye about Felicia was her beauty. She was so beautiful, he couldn't put her to actually being Julius's mother. "Ms. Graves?" he asked somewhat bewildered as he stood up.

"Yes," Felicia nodded as she crept into the office.

"Great, great, great," he smiled. "Okay, Gladys, I got it from here. You can leave now. I'll make certain everything is locked down appropriately."

"Thanks," the secretary replied as she eased the door closed.

"Ms. Graves, please have a seat," he said as he directed her to the seat next to her son.

"Please excuse how I'm dressed," she said bashfully. "I was in the middle of my shift when I got word that Julius had gotten into something." She gave Julius a bit of a side eye as Julius didn't even look her way.

Mr. Benson was quick to let her know she looked well enough for his eyes. "No, no, you look fine. Uh, you're fine." He said with a greasy smile.

The sight of the man falling all over his mother sickened Julius to his stomach and surprised him at the same time. He'd seen plenty men in the past grovel over his mother throughout the years, so it wasn't anything new to him, it was just who it was coming from this time–a man that had just got finished talking to him like he was a dead man walking. He knew all along Benson was full of shit with his Joe Clark routine. He was just another greasy old man at the sight of a pretty woman.

"Well, the reason why I called you here tonight, Ms. Graves, is because I caught Julius attacking some boys out in the hall when he should've been in class," said Mr. Benson.

"Oh, you did," she said as she issued Julius quick, angry stare.

"Yes mam, and this hasn't been the only incident that Julius has been in since he's been here at Washington."

"Really?" she asked.

As the principal went on talking about Julius, he was finding it increasingly difficult to keep his eyes off of Felicia's cleavage area. The way her skirt curved under her neck revealed a smooth, flawless complexion he just wasn't used to seeing on a daily basis. All the while, he wondered how the hell she spit out Julius.

Felicia sat outraged by the things Mr. Benson was telling her about her son's behavior, but at the same time, she found it peculiar that the man couldn't keep his eyes off her body.

"So, Mr. Benson, what kind of punishment are we looking at here for Julius," she said cutting him off. She couldn't take any more details about Julius' behavior.

"Well…Ms. Graves, he's looking at expulsion," he said reluctantly, but not without looking at her breasts one last time.

Felicia shook her head and looked over to Julius. He looked straight ahead as he had been doing the whole time since the principal started talking about all the things he was doing wrong. Some things were completely off base, but not worth the hassle of defending himself since most of it was all true. Bad stuff always seemed to look worse when it was all packaged in together.

"Julius, go outside," said Felicia.

"What?" he asked. It was the first time he looked her in the face.

"I said go outside," she said. "I need to talk to your principal alone."

Mr. Benson perked up in his chair as he looked almost as surprised by the woman's request for Julius to leave as he was. Julius cut his eyes at the principal and begrudgingly headed for the door.

He shut the door behind himself and left the administrative office to sit out on a bench just outside the door. Something told him not to even come to school, but he did so anyway, and it turned out to be more trouble than it was worth. He knew his mother was going to be mad as hell on the way home, and he hated the fact that Ricky and his crew were going to get off scot-free. The thing that bugged him most of all was how his mother abruptly asked him to leave. He didn't like how Mr. Benson was looking at her, and he preferred to stay and hear all the details of his fate.

Suddenly his mother stomped out of the office. "Come on, boy."

He looked up and noticed her skirt was a bit twisted on her, and not quite the same as it looked when she first entered the office. He immediately became suspicious. "What you do in there?"

"I said come on," she said as she flew right by him.

"You heard your mother," the principal walked out of the office and stood in the doorway. Julius' mind went haywire when he noticed the man's zipper was halfway up.

"Whatever man," Julius said as he began trailing his mother. "You screwed him. You screwed him, didn't you?"

She didn't answer as Julius increased his speed and was now directly behind her.

"You fucked him!" he yelled.

She froze. She turned around and slapped the daylights out of him. "Don't you question me. You don't question a thing I do for you. You hear me? Do you hear me?"

Julius nodded while rubbing his face. "Yeah. Yes mam."

She gave him a good look over and started making her way back towards the exit.

He did all he could to hold back his tears as he watched his mother stomp down the hall. Instead of breaking down, he simply chose to run away. He swiftly dashed down the opposite end of the hall.

Her instinct whipped her around and as soon as she realized her son was running off in the opposite direction she yelled, "Julius… Julius, you come back here!" She didn't even bother to try to follow him. She knew she was now the last person he wanted to be around. She cut her eyes at Principal Benson, who remained standing outside of the office with his arms rolled up, and then continued out of the building.

****

Simone hopped out of the car and ran to the back yard where her father was under the hood of his pickup truck.

"What did you say to him?" she asked him.

"Say to who, baby girl?" her father asked as he grabbed a towel on the side of his truck and began wiping his hands.

"You know who, dad. Julius!"

"Ohhhh," he said with a slight frown. As soon as he heard the boys name, he knew what it was all about. He thought it would've been brought back on him sooner, but he expected to hear about it eventually. "Awe, baby girl, I just told the young man that you're trying to focus on your studies, that's all."

"Really, dad? It wasn't even your place to say that. Besides, I know that you said more than that to him. You ran him off."

"Baby girl, it's for the best. I know characters like Julius. They sit around the 'hood doing nothing all day. If they're not reclining on the porch all day, shucking and jiving, getting drunk or getting high, they're out here breaking into somebody's house or selling drugs on the block. I can't have that for you. I know you can do so much better than him."

"I bet you do, dad," she said with tears streaming down his face. "You didn't even give him a chance."

"I was only trying to protect my baby girl." He eased towards her with his arms held out.

She stepped back quickly and said, "Just like grandma tried to protect mom from you, right?"

He was held speechless as she stormed off into the house. He ran his fingers through his head as she disappeared off into the house through the back door.

****

Travis' uncle pounded fiercely on the room door as the loud music coming from the other side of the wall made an average knock nearly impossible to hear.

"Man, what the fuck you knocking on my door like that for? What the hell is wrong with you, nigga," asked Travis as he swung the door open. His eyes were as red as a pomegranate as the weed smoke oozed from the sides of his door.

His uncle quickly stepped back and said, "It's the door. Somebody out there for you. You would've heard me calling you up front if you would cut that goddamn music down."

Travis had a suspicious look on his face as he took a step out of the room and looked down the hall, towards the living room. He wasn't expecting any visitors, and he wasn't sure if he could trust his uncle to tell him if the cops were outside for something. "Who the hell is it?" he asked.

"Go out there and find out," his uncle said as he started making his way into his own room.

He stared his uncle down as he crept into his own room and slammed his door shut behind himself. Travis took a step backwards into his room and grabbed a 9mm he had laying on his dresser beside his door. He stuffed it down the small of his back and proceeded to make his way down the hall. He eased into the front room and looked over to the sofa where his mother sat, spaced out as usual. All he could do was shake his head at the very sight of her.

He crept over to the thick, wooly curtain covering the window beside the front door and carefully peaked out of it. He then hurried to the door and swung it open. "Jules," he said. "What the hell are you doing out here?"

"So you say all I gotta do is be the look out?" Julius asked.

A huge smile sprung on Travis' face. Julius' words were music to his ears. "My nigga." He wrapped his arm around Julius' neck. "Come on. Let's take a walk." They both eased down the steps and towards the sidewalk.

Chapter 15

He was dressed in all black–black hoodie, black jeans and black boots. The pistol his friend had given him was laid out in the center of the bed. He sat at his desk in a trance with the intimidating weapon. He had the gun hidden in the bottom of his closet since the night he forced Vince off of his mother with it. His mom told him she wanted him to give it back to whomever he had gotten it from, but he just couldn't. The cold, hard, metal gave him a feeling of safety that he just wasn't used to, and he enjoyed it. Now it was giving him another feeling–the feeling of fear. Fear of the trouble he knew awaited him if he grabbed it and walked outside his mother's house with it.

His eyes scanned up and across the wall where he had an ensemble of different sketches he'd created throughout the years. His wall was consumed with so many wondrous images that were derivative from a gift he was blessed with having but never truly understood what to do with, besides making a hobby out of it. The largest and his most cherished creation on his wall was the drawing adjacent to his widow–a sketch of Simone smiling on the Ferris Wheel. It was an image that rested in the back of his mind since the night he lived it.

His eyes hopelessly fell back onto the metal coldness that sat at the center of his bed. He raked his face with his fists a few times. His mind was still muddled with confusion and trepidation. His anger towards his mother for the deal he believed she made with her body with his sleazy principal was also still burning inside him. It was a deal that kept him away from home the past few days and sleeping on the couch at the place he and his only friend in the world referred to as the spot. A deal that was the tipping point to all the bullshit he had to go through this school year and all the others. A deal that pushed him out of his chair to grab that cold hard metal that was about to change everything.

Travis stood at the bottom of the porch steps with a cigarette hanging out of the corner of his mouth and both his hands stuffed down his pants pockets. He too, was dressed in all black, the same as Julius. He was trying to remain calm and collected, but he couldn't shake the nagging feeling that someone was watching him, so he couldn't help but look left to right every few seconds as he waited for Julius to return.

Despite his edginess, committing crimes for money was nothing new to Travis. When his cousin, Merc, was alive, they did tons of dirt together on a nightly basis–from robbing dope boys for their cash and drugs to shoplifting cds and clothes at the local malls. They did it all. However, since the time Merc was murdered he remained confined to offenses he considered petty like selling a little weed from time to time or moving stolen goods he got off the neighborhood crackheads.

In a way, he felt like robbing the corner store would be his rite of passage. Not only would it be a nice lick for him and Julius to rake in, but it would also make him feel as if he was on the same level as his cousin, Merc, whom he considered to be a ridah in the purist form.

He looked towards the front door when he heard Julius stepping out. "Damn nigga, I thought you were worried about your mom getting back here before you could grab your gat, but you're up in there taking all night long. I hope you washed your ass while you were up in there," said Travis. "You smell like shit."

"Man, whatever," Julius replied.

"So, did you get it?"

"Yeah, right here," Julius answered as he tapped his waist at the spot he stuffed his gun.

"I don't know why the hell you didn't keep it on you in the first place," he said. "You knew them chumps were gonna come at you again. Herbs ain't gonna do crap when they see me around, but the minute they catch you by yourself, they man up and wanna fight."

They started walking down the sidewalk.

It angered Julius all over again to think about his last encounter with Ricky and his crew. He said, "It was probably good for their sake that I didn't have it on me, anyway."

Travis chuckled, "You ain't got the heart to smoke nobody. Quit playing."

"How you figure that?"

"You just don't," he said. "You're not made that way. A nigga like me, if I got to, I'm blasting. And I'm not knocking you, but you're just not built that way, Jules. I just gave you that piece to flash it at them pussies if they ever came around talking that smack or wanting to jump you. I knew good and well you'd never use it, but I thought your ass would at least keep it on you."

"What you think I'm scared to blast on one of them clowns if I had to?"

"Shit, I hope so," Travis laughed. "I know I'm not, but that's what separates us, Jules."

Julius wanted to convince Travis otherwise, but he knew Travis was one of those see it to believe it types. Talking went but so far with dudes like him. He felt as if he could've shot Vince easily if he didn't get off of his mother when he confronted him, but he wasn't sure if he could have lived with himself if he had shot and killed him.

Julius always feared the world looking at him as if he was his father. Most people's greatest fear was death. His was simply being compared to Herman Joseph, the monster that had folk dancing in the streets when word got out that his cellmate took it upon himself to issue out retribution and shanked him to death while he was sleeping. A punishment that allowed his young eyes to see laughter and tears at the same time on his mother's face when she received the news. A punishment he grew to appreciate once he was old enough to understand the type of maniac that had a part in birthing him. Travis may have owned the belief that their past actions were what separated them, but Julius knew he had blood running through his veins from an evil far greater than either one of them could ever imagine. If there was anything at all, that's what truly separated them.

They took up post on the side of an abandoned building that was positioned directly across the street from the corner store. Barely visible, they tucked themselves closely to the dark side of the wall. In the shadows, they calmly observed the barren convenience store.

"I told you this was the best time to do this shit," Travis whispered. "It looks like a ghost town over there."

Julius' nerves were running rampant as he could barely peel himself from the wall long enough to get a good look at the shop. He had yet to break a single law, but he was already feeling like he was a fugitive.

"You sure this place is gonna have enough money in it to make this junk even worth it?" he asked nervously. "It's not like this is the first of the month when everybody in the hood is up in there, spending all their cash."

"Of course it is. My man Shawn used to work up in that spot a few summers back before Savit got paranoid and let his ass go. He got nervous after Shawn walked in on him while he was stuffing a ton of loot in a hidden safe in his office. A safe different than the one he had for the cash tills."

"Really?"

"Yeah, and he swore up and down Shawn was gonna set his ass up and get some of his rough neck cousins to come in and rob the place. He didn't have to worry about nothing, though. Shawn was a square. He wasn't about setting nobody up like that, but he did go around telling folk there was an ass of money up in there. I always figured he wanted somebody to get back at Savit for firing his ass for nothing.

"How do you know that white boy even got access to the secret safe or even the regular safe?"

"I don't, but where else is he gonna put all that money? His ass surely ain't taking the chance of walking the shit out of that store and into this hood with it," he said as he whipped out his gun from the small of his back and stuff a full clip in it. "Savit may not trust one of our black asses with that safe, but he'll give that geeky white boy full reign, even if it's only to what he's earned since he's been covering for him. Besides, with Savit being gone that long, I know he gotta be keeping that money in one of them bad boys. If we can get square off that secret one with that load of loot, that'll just be a bonus."

Watching Travis load the pistol made the situation too real for him to grasp. He was just moments away from being an accomplice to an armed robbery. He couldn't stop his hands from trembling as the back of his throat began to dry. Part of him wanted to just turn around and run back home, but a bigger part of him didn't want to let Travis down. He wanted to prove to his friend that he had his back even though he was scared as hell.

Travis looked at him and noticed his nervous demeanor. "What? You still scared?"

"No," Julius said as he took a deep breath and tried to play off his nervousness. "Well, yeah, a little. I mean, I ain't never did nothing like this before, man. How do you expect me to be?"

"Man, just calm the fuck down. You ain't even gotta do shit but stand right near the entrance," he said while pointing towards the store. "And just like I told you before, if you see somebody coming, all you gotta do is holla at me through the door that somebody's coming and you haul ass back to the spot just like we originally planned. That's it. You got that?"

Julius took another deep breath and nodded. It all sounded a lot easier than it really was. Travis took another look at his friend. In the back of his mind, he was hoping Julius could just keep it together long enough for him to get into the store, grab the cash and get the hell out of dodge.

"Alright," said Travis as his attention returned to the store. He then moved slightly away from the edge of the building and scanned both ends of the empty street. "Now we need to get over there looking cool and normal. Once we cross the street we're gonna hang to the back of the store, alright?"

"Yeah, we good," Julius assured him.

They flipped their hoodies up and calmly strolled across the street to the back of the corner store. The swift walk across the street took only a few moments but it seemed like a lifetime to Julius. He felt as if the entire world was looking in on them.

They gathered themselves in the shadows near the back of the store. Travis got down on one knee and slipped out a balaclava from his back pocket.

"What's that?" Julius curiously asked.

"I gotta cover up my face?"

"Why don't I have one?"

"Nigga, you're wearing your hoodie up," Travis said slightly irritated. "I'm the only one going up in there. Besides, don't you think that shit will scream out robbery if your ass is standing out here with one on?"

"Well… yeah, yeah, okay," Julius nodded.

"Well, alright then," said Travis. "Remember, you stand near the entrance. If you see somebody coming, you just yell in through the door and haul ass."

"Okay," said Julius.

"Don't bitch out on me, Jules," said Travis. "I need you on this."

"Cool, I got you," Julius reassured him.

Travis flipped his hoodie up and slid on the balaclava. He then recovered his head with the hoodie.

"Don't bitch out on me, Jules. You see something, you warn me."

"I will. I told you I got you," said Julius.

Travis slid out his 9mm from his pocket and swiftly crept towards the front of the store. Julius' heart was beating a thousand beats per second the closer his friend got to the entrance, and it darn near stopped thumping when he saw him walk in.

"Alright, put your hands up," Travis barked as he ran in and pointed his gun towards the register. To his surprise no one was standing behind the front counter. The store appeared to be empty. "What the fuck?" he said as he ran up to the register and jumped halfway over the counter to see if anyone was hiding on the floor.

He then heard a toilet flush from the back of the store. A few seconds later he heard the door to the restroom swing open. He whipped around and said, "Alright, motherfucker, this is a robbery!"

Travis almost dropped his gun when he realized the man exiting the restroom from the back was Savit. The magazine Savit had stuffed under his arm immediately fell onto the floor as he quickly raised his hands up.

"Anybody else up in here with your ass?"

"No, brotha, it's just me," said Savit. "Just me."

"Where's that snowflake you had running shit up in here the last couple of weeks? He back there, too?"

"No brother, no. He's gone. I relieved him of his duties earlier this morning."

"Well, he better not be hiding up in here, nowhere, because if he is I'm blasting the both of you fools!" Travis scanned his surroundings as much as he could as he remained cautious that someone else could be hiding in the store secretly.

"Oh brotha, brotha, brotha, please don't shoot," Savit begged. "I have a wife and two kids. Twins."

Seeing Savit standing there nervous and rambling with his hands in the air made him feel like not robbing the store at all. Holding up the place with someone other than Savit at the helm would've made things so much easier.

Although most of Savit's store items were gravely overpriced because he had little to no competition in the hood and everyone often griped about it, he still felt some type of bond with him. Savit often allowed him to pay for items later and even given him small breaks on prices in the past.

Even though Travis harbored mixed feelings about going through with the robbery since it would mean he'd be robbing Savit instead of the goofy white kid he had prepared for, he knew he'd already reached the point of no return. With Savit being there, he understood he would have access to even more money.

"I want all your money."

"What?" Savit asked.

"You heard me. I want all your money, goddamnit!" He ran up to Savit and grabbed him by the collar of his pleated shirt. "Get your ass back there and open up that damn register."

"Okay, okay, I'll do whatever you want. Just be calm, brotha," Savit said.

"Don't tell me to be calm. Just open that fucking register up."

"Okay, brotha, okay," Savit said nervously as Travis shoved him behind the register counter.

With a few keystrokes on the register the machine popped right open. Travis eyes lit up like a pair of flood lights at the sight of the till full of cash.

"Here, take it. Take it all," Savit begged. "Take it and leave. I don't want any trouble."

Travis swiped a paper bag from the counter and handed it to the man. "Stuff it all in this bag and don't try no funny shit."

Savit briskly emptied all the money from the cash drawer and into the bag. He quickly handed the bag of cash to Travis. "Here, take it" he said. "Now, please go."

"Nah, not so fast," Travis said while shaking his head. He shoved the bag of money into Savit's chest. "Now, I want you to take me to the real shit."

"I beg your pardon?" Savit asked.

"The safe motherfucker," he yelled as he cracked Savit across the shoulder with the butt of the pistol. "You know what the hell I'm talking about."

"Travis?" Savit said as he suddenly recognized the forceful voice underneath the mask.

"Shut the fuck up," Travis yelled as he jerked the man by his collar and shoved the gun against the back of his neck, guiding him towards the office on the other side of the store.

Julius stood near the back of the store trembling like crazy. He almost choked a lung when he realized a black Crown Victoria was approaching the lot from the main road. He immediately lowered his head as far as he could while still trying to verify if the car was an unmarked cop car or not.

"Hey, little nigga, the store closed?" asked a raspy voice from within the car.

Julius raised his head slightly and breathe a sigh of relief when he realized the car was sitting on a set of twenty inch rims. He didn't make any eye contact with the driver of the car and only answered, "Nah, they closed."

"Alright then," said the driver.

As the car cruised on down the street, Julius raised his head and let out another deep breath. If that had turned out to be a cop, he knew he would've pissed his pants. He gazed towards the store. In the back of his mind he prayed Travis would hurry the hell up.

Travis kicked open the door to the small office. He could see the rugged metal safe underneath one of the office desks as soon as they walked in. "I want all the cash you got tucked in your safe!"

"Okay, okay. I'll do whatever you want," the man said as he scurried over to the safe and dropped to his knees.

"Nah, not so fast, my nigga," Travis said. "Not that safe. I want the loot in the real safe."

"What?" said Savit as he perked up and looked back up to Travis.

"Oh, you know what the fuck I'm talking about," Travis said as he picked up his foot and stomped Savit in his back. The old Indian man's head smashed into the edge of the safe and blood immediately began to ooze from it. "Don't play with me, nigga. I want the cash from your main safe. Now where is it?"

"Okay, okay, brotha. Just be careful with that thing ," he said. Savit took a quick glance at a file cabinet behind Travis. He kept his 38 magnum in a custom holster bolted to the side of it. He knew if he could get to it he could put an end to the situation.

Beside the rugged grey safe was what appeared to be solid wood, but that wasn't the case at all. Savit slid the wood off to the side of the wall and behind it was a state-of-the-art stainless steel pushbutton safe.

Travis was wooed by the site of it. He knew he'd struck it big this time. "Oh shit," he said to himself. "Open it. Open it now," he demanded.

"Okay, okay, brother," Savit answered nervously. He quickly entered the combination and the safe popped opened. He pulled the door open and looked back at his robber, unsure what he wanted him to do next.

"Move," said Travis, flinging the gun at him to get out of his way. Travis walked closer to get a better look at all the stacks of money and cash bags that filled the safe. He was mesmerized by it all. He had never seen so much money in his life.

Savit slowly eased towards his file cabinet. Travis' gun remained pointed towards him but the boy wasn't paying nearly enough attention to the man to notice his slick movements. Travis began grabbing stacks of money and dropping it into the paper bag below the safe with one hand while he had his other hand holding the gun, erratically pointing it towards Savit. His attention flipped back and forth from Savit and the money. Savit was only waiting for the right time to lunge to the file cabinet and grab his gun. He could see the holster from where he was positioned on the floor.

When Travis dug a little deeper into the safe to retrieve the money further in the back of it, that's when Savit saw his opportunity to make his move. He briskly leaped over to the cabinet and grabbed his gun.

Travis noticed the movement from the corner of his eye and quickly spun around with his gun angled at the store owner's chest, but as soon as he turned around Savit shot him, grazing his arm.

"Damn it," Travis screamed in pain as he let off a shot of his own, barely missing Savit's shoulder as he dove to the floor.

"You mut'a fucka," Savit yelled letting off two more shots without looking as he scrambled through the office door.

Travis danced around the small office dodging the gunfire as he grabbed his arm. He examined it for a moment, and although the blood was drenching heavily through his sleeve, he realized the bullet had only grazed him. Now, overrun with anger, Travis darted through the door, leaving the bag of money on the floor behind him.

When he ran out of the office another shot pierced into the wall behind him causing him to hunch downward. Travis then pointed his gun at Savit to let off a couple of shots of his own, one hitting Savit in his leg. The man fell to the floor and let out a scream that could be easily mistaken for a woman experiencing harsh labor pains. As the man grabbed at his wounded leg, he crawled down the aisle towards the back of the store.

Travis could hear the man panting and sliding down the aisle as he stooped down directly across the exit. He knew the police would be there at any moment, so he made a dash towards the door. Halfway near the door, he realized he'd left the money in the office. He looked back towards the short hall that led to the office, then down the blood soaked aisle where Savit had retreated. He knew it would be all for nothing if he left the money. Unfortunately, the wounded leg was not enough to keep Savit down as he hopped up from behind a shelf in the back of the store and began letting off shots again. The first shot narrowly missed the back of Travis' head as the bullet pierced through and shattered the glass door to the front exit.

Julius quickly realized things had gone array when shards of glass burst from the door and sprinkled the ground around him. He thought he'd heard faint pops coming from inside but thought they were just warning shots by Travis in an attempt to scare the store clerk. As he moved closer to the front door to get a look inside to see if his friend was coming, Travis burst from the door breathing heaving and clutching a bloody arm.

"Run," Travis yelled. "Get the fuck going. Get the fuck going, man."

"What?" Julius frantically blurted out.

"This nigga shooting at me. Go!" Travis screamed.

They both took off in different direction, but with one destination in mind–the spot. The journey back to the hangout was a frantic one for Julius. He had no idea what happened, and he didn't see anything in Travis' hands running out of the store but a bloody gun.

He arrived at the spot first, and couldn't stop himself from pacing back and forth. He couldn't help but wonder where the hell Travis was and what was taking him so long to get there.

When he heard someone coming into the building, he quickly grabbed an empty paint can and turned it upside down to swing, not knowing if it was Travis or the police coming. He didn't want to pull out the gun and accidentally fire or get fired on, but he knew he had to protect himself somehow. He dropped the paint can and became at ease when he realized it was just Travis hobbling in.

"Travis, what the fuck did you do?" He asked hysterically while running towards him. "I heard gunshots, man. And you got blood all over you. Nobody was suppose to get hurt."

"I didn't shoot first," Travis said while clutching his arm. "He did."

"Is he dead?"

"No. I shot him in the leg, but he was shooting at my ass to kill."

"What do you expect?"

"I didn't expect, Savit. That's what."

"Savit?"

"Yeah, the white boy had already left this morning or something."

"I thought you cased the spot out this morning, man."

"I mean, I walked around. Shit, the white boy was there all this week. How was I suppose to know Savit would be in there tonight? Damn!"

"Because you was suppose to check the place out! That's what you said you were doing the whole time," said Julius as he kicked a small stack of crates near him. "I bet he knew who you were."

"Nah, there's no way," he lied. As soon as Julius brought it up, he thought back to Savit recognizing his voice. He knew if he let Julius know about that he'd have a nervous breakdown right on the spot.

"Is he dead?"

"Hell no, he ain't dead. I told you that already! You didn't see me dodging them damn bullets on the way out?"

They both stood silent for a moment as they could hear multiple police sirens screeching from the main street. It sounded like total chaos beyond the walls.

"Oh shit, man, we're going to jail," Julius said as he raked his face. "I knew it. I knew it."

"Jules, just calm the fuck down. I told you he didn't know who I was. I'm gonna burn this damn face mask and ditch the gun. We can't be traced, homey."

Julius just stared at him. His words did little to convince him everything was going to turn out favorably for them. "What about your arm, man? You look like you need to see a doctor."

"It's just a flesh wound, Jules. It looks worse than it really is," he said while moving his arm into a ray of moonlight that beamed in from the window above them. "See."

"And where's the money?"

A frustrated look appeared on his face as he just bowed his head.

"Awe, man, all this for nothing. Travis, what happened to the money?"

"Man, I left it behind when all the shooting started. I freaked out when I realized I was shot. I tried to go back, but Savit went Rambo on a nigga."

"Damn, man, all this crap for nothing," Julius said to himself. "We're about to go to prison for nothing."

"Man, shut the hell up," he said as he shoved Julius with his good arm. "I told you we ain't going to no goddamn prison."

"Why aren't we, Travis? Why aren't we?" he asked. "They're out there looking for us now."

"Looking for who?"

"Huh?"

"Exactly! They don't know who did what. Stop being so damn paranoid. Just walk home and act normal. If anybody ask you, you were chilling at the mall all day."

"What about you?"

"I'm gonna stay here and ditch all the shit that can attach us to the robbery. Then get this arm to stop bleeding," said Travis.

"You sure it's just a flesh wound," Julius asked.

"Yeah, the bullet just grazed me. Stings like hell, but I'll be alright," Travis explained. "Just get home, Jules. I made the mess. I'll clean it up."

"You gonna be alright?"

"Yeah, just go, dude. Try not to look like you just got finished robbing a corner store while you're at it," he laughed.

Julius didn't laugh because he felt nothing about the night was a laughing matter. He took another glance at his friend's arm, and although he was apprehensive about leaving him behind, he slowly exited the building.

Travis' eyes trailed him out of the door until he could see his partner no more. He knew he was screwed. He was all but certain Savit had recognized him by his voice, and Savit could be spilling the beans to the cops about who he thought robbed him right at that very moment. He knew if he told Julius about Savit speaking his name he would be more of a train wreck than he already was. All he could do was hope and pray Savit wouldn't believe that the voice he heard was actually him.

****

He rushed into the house, slammed the front door shut and backed into it with his eyes closed. The half mile walk home felt like an eternity to him. Breathing profusely, for the moment, he finally felt safe. When his eyes parted he was shocked to see his mother frozen before him, standing at the door that led to the kitchen.

She remained motionless with a glass of milk and a slice of red velvet cake she had placed on a small saucer. She wanted to say something to him because she could tell he was in trouble, but she didn't have a clue as to what to say. She knew he would never look at her the same after she did what she did, but she only did it to prevent him from getting kicked out of school. She knew he would never understand her reasons, though.

Just like his mother, he didn't know what to say. He was still extremely angry with her for doing whatever she did with Benson, but he knew a simple hug from her would ease all the pain he was feeling inside. She was always the only one in his corner when he was in trouble, but now that bond was broken. Instead of making an attempt to reconcile, he just rushed down the hall to his room without saying a word, and she let him. The fact that he was finally home was good enough for her, for the moment, anyway.

He rushed to his closet and stuffed his gun under a stack of clothes. His mind was barraged with a thousand thoughts a second. *Did somebody see me? Did somebody see Travis? Is Savit dead? Are the police coming for us?* The questions wouldn't stop dancing around in his head. He frightfully looked out of his window, and his eyes scanned all he could see out of it. He then briskly shut the curtains and sat on his bed while rubbing his hands together. He couldn't shake the feeling that the police were nearby and coming for him, and that they were coming soon.

Chapter 16

He sat in a daze with the empty wall across the room. His pencil was clinging to his hands but it wasn't moving. Julius couldn't stop reliving the events of the previous night in his head. The entire situation was so overwhelming for him. He just couldn't get the harsh thoughts of getting rounded up and locked away for life out of his mind.

The rare instances he wasn't dreading about potential jail time was when questions about Travis overtook his thinking. *Where was Travis, and why hadn't he heard from him? Were his injuries worse than the flesh wound he claimed to have had? Did the police get him? Did he ditch the gun and his bloody clothing? Or even worse, did he leave any evidence behind?*

No matter how hard he tried to create something artistic on the blank sheet of paper, he just couldn't do it. The feeling was strange to him since art was always his escape from reality. Now his reality was flooded by his nightmares of being incarcerated. The fear of being his father's son had finally set. Like criminal father, like criminal son.

"You okay over there, Mr. Graves?" The teacher asked from his chair at the front of the classroom while staring straight at him. The question spurred the interest of his other classmates, who had all eyes on him also.

"Yeah," he said while nodding his head, somewhat mystified in his response. "I'm good."

All of the students went back to their work as Mr. Bass kept his eyes on Julius. Julius didn't want to get into a staring match nor did he want to trigger anymore questions from the teacher, so he proceeded to aimlessly doodle on his paper.

The door swung open, and all eyes quickly beamed in on Travis Nelson. He paused with one foot in the door and appeared somewhat appalled by all the interest his arrival had acquired. He was an unexpected sight for everyone in the classroom since he hadn't reported to class in weeks. His arrival was even more of a surprise for Julius. The boy couldn't fathom what in God's green earth his troublesome friend was thinking by coming into class when there was a possibility the police was looking for the both of them.

"Mr. Nelson," Mr. Bass said as he glanced at the clock that hovered over the door. "How nice of you to join us again."

Travis proceeded to walk in and appeared to gingerly move his arm. He was wearing a thick jacket, obviously in an attempt to cloak any bandages he may have been wearing underneath, but there was clearly something wrong with him. Observing Travis' movement placed Julius even more on edge.

"Umm, son, what's wrong with your arm?" asked Mr. Bass.

"Nothing really, just banged it on the court," Travis answered.

"I thought an O.G. like yourself was too cool to be out there on the court playing basketball," Mr. Bass joked.

"Well, you know, Mr. Bass, I gotta go out there and drop in on them younger cats every now and then and show 'em how it's really done," Travis laughed.

"Ahh, I see. And, Mr. Nelson, is that a book in your hand?" Mr. Bass asked astonished.

"Mr. Bass, you always got them jokes," he said as he eased into his seat. He noticed Julius staring dead at him. He gave his friend a brief nod. He then pulled out his notepad and immediately began sketching.

Julius' mind was bombarded with questions on why Travis even bothered coming. Travis had missed so many classes he looked strange by just sitting there. Julius suspected everyone in the small class had to have been suspicious of his return, also. He looked to the front of the class and noticed Mr. Bass staring at him again. He could tell the old man knew something was up, and Travis' presence enhanced his paranoia.

There was a double knock at the door right before it swung open. Mr. Benson walked in, and he had company. A slender Caucasian man with a thick bushy mustache, wearing a cheap brown suit walked in with two fully uniformed police officers. Julius nearly passed out at the sight of them.

"There he is, right there," Mr. Benson pointed in Travis' direction to the officers. The two uniformed cops immediately headed Travis' way, as his head popped up. His mouth nearly hit the floor.

"Principal Benson, what's this all about?" Mr. Bass questioned while jumping out of his chair.

"Easy there, Mr. Bass," said Principal Benson. "The officers here just want to take Mr. Nelson downtown for questioning."

"It couldn't wait until after class?" asked Mr. Bass.

"No, It couldn't," Principal Benson said bluntly.

Julius' heart was pounding so hard through his chest his ears started to thump. He immediately expected the policemen to come his way and take him away also. One of the officers tapped Travis on his shoulder to motion him to get up. He jumped up without saying a word as they guided him towards the door. He proceeded to the exit with his eyes set on Julius.

Mr. Benson walked to Travis' desk and grabbed his things. He gave Julius a brief stare with somewhat of a smirk on his face. The students in class exchanged blank stares with each other while keeping their comments amongst themselves. No one knew what was going on but Julius, Travis and possibly the police.

The way the door was cracked open, Julius could see the officers handcuffing Travis out in the hall. There was no doubt in his mind they knew Travis was the one responsible for the robbery, and he suspected there would be only a matter of time before they would be taking him in right behind him. Maybe not during class, but definitely soon.

A few minutes had passed since the officers and Principal Benson barged in and escorted Travis out of the room. Mr. Bass made an earnest attempt to smooth things over with the class by advising them the situation with Travis probably wasn't anything serious at all. With the track record Travis had garnered, they all knew better and they weren't buying it one bit. Only Julius knew the whole truth. They were taking his friend in for the botched robbery they both attempted the previous night, and his fear of going to prison was getting too real for him to handle.

When the bell rang Julius gathered his things immediately and rushed for the door behind the other students. The way his peers dashed through the doors ahead of him, he knew they were all eager to spread the word about Travis getting taken away by the cops around the school grounds.

"Mr. Graves," said Mr. Bass as he cut Julius off at the door. "Would you like to tell me what's going on?"

"I don't know what you're talking about, Mr. Bass."

Frustrated, Mr. Bass shook his head and said, "I pray, for your sake, son, that whatever trouble Mr. Nelson has gotten himself involved in, that it doesn't include you."

Julius didn't respond. He simply walked around Mr. Bass and exited the classroom.

****

Felicia sat at the kitchen table in a deep trance with the two piles of job applications sitting before her. She spent the better part of the day filling out each application as accurately and complete as she could. Since she walked out on her job at the hotel, she had been on an urgent blitz to find another hotel for work with no luck. Work at the temp agency was helpful but the odd jobs weren't supplying her with nearly enough money to help her stay afloat with the rent before her savings would be completely exhausted.

The knock at the door brought her out of her trance. She quickly jumped up and fled through the living room to answer it. She was in such deep thought, she wasn't sure how long the person on the other side of the door had been out there knocking. When she swung the door open she was surprised to see her mother standing before her. With the somber look and the streaks of mascara running down the sides of her face, the old woman didn't have to open her mouth for Felicia to know why she was there.

"Mom... oh, Mom, I'm sorry," she said as she embraced her with a hug.

"I'm gonna be alright, Fee," her mother said, trying her earnest to fight back the tears. She shut her teary eyes while welcoming the embrace by her daughter.

Felicia grabbed her hand and guided her into the house after taking a quick peak outside to see if anyone was accompanying her. She took a seat right next to her mother on the edge of the sofa and held her hands in hers.

"He passed away in his sleep. He went peacefully, though," she said. "No more suffering in this here world."

"Oh, Ma," she said before giving her another hug. She had no words to ease her mother's pain. Her relationship with her stepfather was always rocky to say the least, but she still loved him. She wanted to feel a lot worse than she did, but she was so far removed from the family she couldn't shed a single tear. Despite the lack of tears, she still felt extremely sad about her stepfather's passing. If not completely for her own reasons, at least for her mother. She had lost a man she had spent nearly half of her entire life being with and loving.

"Knowing the things we knew about his health, it prepared me for this day. But it doesn't ease the pain, Felicia. It doesn't stop it, not one bit." She slipped out some tissue from her purse and began wiping her eyes.

Felicia squeezed her hand and caressed her shoulder. Despite all the turmoil they suffered between each other in the past, it still pained her to see her mother so devastated.

"I know I shouldn't be in here crying like I am to you. The things we did. The things I did," she said. "He loved you, Felicia. No different than Kim, like you were his own. I know it's hard to believe it, but he really did."

"Ma, I'm not worried about any of that right now. What's in the past is in the past," she said. "My only concern is you and how you're holding up."

"For a long time I blamed myself for you getting violated by that… that monster. A huge part of me was happy that you ran off on your own like you did, so I wouldn't see in you how bad of a mother I was," she bowed her head. "I failed you in so many ways, Fee. So many ways."

"Ma, come on," she said. "All that's in the past. Nobody's even thinking about that right now. All I wanna do is help you get through this."

The old woman looked into her forgiving daughter's eyes and smiled. "Where's Julius?"

"He's at school, Ma," she said.

"Is he doing okay?"

"Yes and no, Ma."

"What's going on."

"I don't know," she answered while shaking her head. Her own eyes began to water when her son came to mind. "I don't want the streets to have my baby, but what more can I do to stop it? He's not listening anymore. He won't listen to me," she sighed. "And why should he?

What kind of an example have I been? Lord knows, I tried."

"Things will get better between you and him," Louise said. "You two have always had that special bond."

"I don't know, Ma. I don't know about this time. I just don't know."

The old woman dug into her purse and pulled out an envelope. "Maybe, this will help," she said.

Felicia took the envelope with her nickname 'Fee Fee' written in cursive on it. It was what her stepfather often called her when she was a little girl. When she first met him and he called her that name, she hated it. She felt not only was he trying to replace her daddy at the time, but he was trying to rename her on the sly, also. All she could do was stare at the envelope. Seeing her nickname in his handwriting was enough to bring her drought of tears to an end.

"Frank wanted me to give you this, just before he passed. There's a check in there with enough on it for you and Julius to move to anywhere you want, and not have to worry about slaving on nobody's job ever again."

"I don't know what to say, Ma."

"You don't have to anything, baby," she said. "He wanted to make sure you got that from him, himself. The handlers of the estate will be contacting you for some other things, but this was directly from him. For you and for Julius."

As the tears rolled down her face, she knew she should've felt happy that the dark cloud from her lack of finances was finally letting up, but she knew it would take more than money to fix her family's problems, but for the moment, it appeared as if everything was about to be alright.

****

The interrogation room was cold and uncomfortable. Travis sat at the desk, slouched down in his chair, biting his fingernails as he awaited the return of the detective that brought him in for questioning. He'd never met Detective Rogers before, the officer that brought him in, but he was very familiar with Detective Ramsey–the renowned bad cop in the investigation. He'd had plenty of run ins with Ramsey in the past, and the officer actually vowed to lock him up for a long time the next time he got into trouble. He knew Ramsey couldn't wait to make good on his promise.

Detective Rogers tried his best to get him to just confess to the robbery, barking about possibly having his prints at the scene of the crime and that Savit recognized his voice. His fears about Savit recognizing his voice overwhelmed him the moment it occurred, but leaving his fingerprints at the store was something he neglected to consider. Before going through with the robbery, he thought through every aspect of the crime except bringing something as simple as gloves along. He felt like an idiot for not wearing any.

He knew if they could pull his fingerprints from anything in that store, he was done for. He realized if they had that much evidence against him, the only reason Ramsey was questioning was to get him to own up to the robbery. Travis understood the legal system well enough to know that they always preferred a confession first, even if they had a crap-load of evidence against you.

Detective Ramsey walked into the room with a smirk on his face. Travis knew if the prick was smiling about anything, it was all bad for him.

Travis sucked his teeth and let out a huge sigh, "Oh, it's you."

"Yup," he said as he slammed the door shut and strolled in. "It's me, you little shit."

"Are we done yet?" Travis asked. "I got things I need to be doing."

"That would be a negative. Whatever you had to be doing is gonna have to be postponed for a good fifteen to twenty," said the cop as he threw a file on the table. "The prints came back a match from the safe. Your ass is up shit creek. You don't even have to explain your little boo boo on your arm." He drove both of his knuckles into the table and leaned into Travis. "I told you I was gonna put your ass away the next time your crossed my path, didn't I?"

Travis leaned back in his chair and let out a short giggle as he looked up at the ceiling. He then looked straight at the officer. "Okay then, well take me to my cell," he said while holding out his arms awaiting to be cuffed. "There ain't nothing else for us to talk about."

The officer grabbed a chair from the table, turned it backwards and sat down. "Look, Nelson, you're gonna get some time. There's no way out of that. Now the store owner said when you went dashing out of that store, someone was outside running with you. You give me a name, maybe we can knock off some of this time you're guaranteed to get."

Travis grinned, "You wanna know who was at the store with me?"

"Yup. I wouldn't be in here shucking and jiving with you if I didn't want to know. We can make this thing a hell of a lot easier for you. A little bit of an olive branch between you and me."

"You really wanna know?"

"Yes, now stop bullshittin'. This offer is only on the table just this once, Nelson," said Officer Ramsey. "We could possibly knock off enough time to where your lil' delinquent ass is still young when you get out."

Travis could only shake his head and laugh at the officer's last statement, as seeing the cocky grin on the man's face made his skin crawl.

"Okay," said Travis. "It was…"

"Say it," Detective Ramsey demanded. "Give me the name."

"It was…," he said as he let out a hard sigh. He then leaned forward and said, "Theeeeese nuts!"

The officer's face was overrun with anger. "You're a stupid son of a bitch, you know that?"

"Kiss my entire yellow ass," said Travis. "You goddamn pig."

Officer Ramsey jumped up and pounded on the door. A uniformed officer charged in immediately.

"Get his stupid little ass out of here," said Officer Ramsey. "And make sure he gets the shittiest piece of shit public defender in the whole damn city. We'll get his ass on attempted murder for shooting the clerk also."

"Come on," said the uniform cop as he motioned Travis to get up and pulled his arms behind his back. Travis grimaced at the tug on his wounded arm.

"You wanna get the full brash of this bullshit ass robbery, fine! We'll see how many fucking jokes you have when Big Tito got your ass pinned up in the cell slobbing his fucking knob in the state pen for the next twenty years."

Travis just issued the highly agitated officer a grin as the uniformed cop escorted him out of the room. Officer Ramsey swiped the folder of papers off the table and across the room.

****

The stress from seeing Travis getting hauled out of class by the cops took a terrible toll on Julius. Thoughts of them coming back and arresting him was just too much from him to bare. He needed some air and to get away from Washington High as quickly as he could. After lunch he made his way off campus and opted to walk back home the long way through town.

He couldn't get his mind off the fact that soon his fate would be the same as his friend, behind bars. The last thing he wanted to do was disappoint his mother and to hear the family telling her *I told you so*. Travis seemed to be a straight up guy and appeared to always have his back, but he wasn't certain how much of his back his friend would keep if the police tried to make him a deal to give him up.

As Julius walked down the sidewalk with his head down, he felt as if he was being followed. He looked behind himself and noticed a white Nissan Maxima creeping down the street several yards back. The vehicle seemed to be packed with passengers. Him turning around didn't stop the vehicle from approaching, instead it sped up. His eyes fell on the driver as the car drew near, and he recognized him immediately–it was Ice.

"Get his ass," Ricky yelled to Ice from the passenger side. He and the other three people in the car all carried black baseball bats in their hands. Ricky climbed out of the window at his waist and began banging on the side of the car door with his bat. "Your ass is grass, monster boy!"

It didn't take long for Julius to realize the boys wanted blood, so he quickly darted off between two buildings as the car took off behind him. The alley was narrow and congested with stray shopping carts and trash dumpsters, however it wasn't enough to stop the car packed with his enemies from speeding through it. Julius whipped through the alley like there was no tomorrow. He knew if he could make it to his hangout spot he would be able to disappear from the alley and lose them.

He glanced back a few times and realized they were losing ground due to the metal dumpsters along the trail. He took a quick right down the alleyway to his hangout spot and darted through the entrance. He backed into the door, took a moment to catch his breath and peaked out of a small hole near the doorknob.

He could hear them driving near. As they turned the corner they discovered a nearly deserted path with a few homeless people huddled about. They stopped their vehicle just in front of his building.

"Where the hell did he go?" asked Ice.

"If your ass wasn't so damn slow, you wouldn't have lost him," yelled Ricky as he slid back into his seat. "Goddamn it, I wanna beat this nigga ass so bad."

Ice looked up and around the buildings as he crept down the alley. "He must've slid in one of these abandoned buildings."

"And nigga," Ricky said, totally frustrated. "Ain't nobody going up in these crack buildings to find that punk ass nigga. Just roll. He show his ass up in school tomorrow, I'll just beat it there. I don't give a damn how many games coach makes me sit out, I'm gonna kick that nigga's ass the first chance I get."

The car sped on down the alley as Julius' eyes did their best to follow it from the peephole. He let out a deep breath, walked over to the couch and fell on it. He pulled his hands over his head and just laid back on the sofa as he realized his beef with Ricky Smith had reached a dangerous new level that stretched well beyond the school halls.

After sitting back and waiting around for about a half hour, Julius finally felt that the coast was clear and began making his way back home. He felt like the whole world was closing in on him. He pushed the only girl that seemed to genuinely like him away, his best friend was locked up for their botched robbery, and the guy that was intent on making his life a living hell was now following him home from school. Before he could ask himself what could possibly go wrong next, he briskly got his answer. As he approached his house, he noticed a cop car parked directly across the street from his home.

He tried to pretend as if he didn't see the cop stalking his residence when he approached his yard, but the officer greeted him with a "Hey kid."

Julius stopped in his tracks and debated if he should face the officer or make a run for it. He begrudgingly chose to face him. "Yes, officer?" Julius answered. When he turned to face him, he immediately recognized him as the cop Travis had told him about, Officer Tillman.

"Yeah, get over here," said Officer Tillman.

Julius slowly approached the car.

"Sir," Julius asked nervously as he bent his head down into the window.

"Get in the car." the officer demanded.

"For what?"

"You guilty of something, kid?"

"No," Julius fired back.

"Then get in the goddamn car," Officer Tillman demanded. "I got something to talk to you about."

Julius looked towards his house, realizing his mother's car was gone. He was reluctant to join the officer in the car, but he did it anyway. As he sat in the car, there was an uneasy silence.

"I know what happened," said the cop looking straight ahead.

His words made Julius feel as if he could cough up a lung. He made two fists in an attempt to hide all the trembling his hands were doing. Julius just knew he was on his way to the big house.

"We all know what happened. It's just a matter of time before we can prove what happened," he said, now facing Julius. "You see, I know what the suits don't know. I know that you were an accomplice to your man, Travis, and I get that. Do you think it goes unnoticed that you trot up and down the street with that thug day after day? I mean, your boy Nelson has a rap sheet a mile long. He has this unique way of always finding his way into deep shit. You heard about what happened to his cousin, right?"

Julius just listened as he awaited the moment for the arrogant cop to tell him if he was being arrested or not. The moment he had feared since the night before, and even more when he sat back and watched Travis get hauled away at the school.

"Why don't you make things a little easier for us all, and just tell us he persuaded you to help him. Protect yourself! You can serve a little bit of community service while your main man gets all the time he deserves," he chuckled. "Don't let him roll over on you first."

The officer's proposition brought Julius to the realization that they didn't have anything linking him to the crime at all. He also came to the conclusion that Travis didn't rat him out–not yet anyway. He then said, "Sir, I don't know what you're talking about."

The cop laughed and swiped his fingers through his short, brown spiky hair. "Yeah, yeah, I know. It's always I don't know what you're talking about. Well, let me educate you about something, sir. We're going to put you at that crime scene, and when we do, there ain't a soul on God's green earth that's going to be able to get you out of the deep shit that you've managed to allow your partna' to get you into. You understand that?"

Julius grabbed the door handle. "Can I leave now?"

"Yeah, go on. Enjoy the little time you have left, smart guy," he said as he grabbed his arm. "Just remember, I got my eyes on you. It's just a matter of time before all the truth comes out."

Julius snatched his arm away as they both exchanged unfriendly stares at one another. Julius didn't like being threatened by the officer, but there wasn't a darn thing he could do about it. He hopped out of the car, slammed the door shut and backed onto the sidewalk as the officer drove away with a smile.

Chapter 17

He sat on the edge of his bed, fully dressed in his baggy jeans and black hoodie. He had been seated in the same spot for close to an hour. He hadn't slept a wink the entire night because he feared the police would come knocking at the front door the minute he shut his eyes closed. He at least wanted to be prepared for them if they did show up.

Seeing Travis get escorted out of the classroom had him debating if he should even report to school at all. He was nearing all the days he could miss and still be able to graduate, but he held strong doubts about even being able to walk the stage with the threat of going to prison looming.

If there was one thing at all he wanted to accomplish, it was walking that stage. His mom wasn't able to do it because she got pregnant with him and it was something he always wanted to do for her. If it wasn't for his mother, with all the mess he'd gone through with every school he attended, he was pretty sure he would've dropped out a long time ago. He kept pressing on because he felt like he owed it to her. He always believed if his mother didn't choose to have him, her life would've been so much better than what it had turned out to be.

He looked down at the pistol that rested on the bed beside him. If he did go, he wasn't about to leave the weapon behind, not this time, not with the way Ricky and his crew was hounding him. He needed something to keep them up off of him whenever they decided to make their next move on him, and carrying the gun to protect himself seemed to be the only viable option he had without Travis free to watch his back.

Although it made him feel safe, the one thing he feared most about carrying the gun was getting caught with it. He didn't know what type of history Travis had connected to the pistol, and with his friend, any type of drama was possible. He couldn't believe he just took the gun without asking a single question about where it came from, or what he may have done with it. Stupid indeed, but regardless of all the negative possibilities, he wasn't about to leave the house without it. He was intent on protecting himself, by himself–for a change.

He jumped up off the bed, grabbed the pistol and tucked it in at his waist, just above his belt buckle. He draped his shirt over it and checked himself out in the mirror to make certain he looked normal with it on him.

When Felicia realized Julius was stomping through the house, she quickly darted out of the kitchen to catch him before he left. She was holding the check her stepfather had left them, and she hoped telling him about their new found fortune would be a great starting point for them to mend things between them.

"Julius... Julius," she said as the boy marched towards the front door with deaf ears to her calling. "Julius, I got something to show you..."

He stomped out of the house and slammed the door behind himself without saying a smidgen of a word. She sadly dropped her head as she did her best not to burst into tears. She had no idea on how to make things right between them, and it was killing her inside.

****

When Julius arrived at school, he was surprised to see Trey standing at the front entrance, lurking at the top of the steps. He'd never seen him waiting out there before and immediately felt it to be suspicious. As soon as he made his way up the stairs Trey approached him.

"Julius," said Trey.

"Yeah, what's up," he answered, not breaking his speed to chat with the boy as he entered the building.

"Man, you gotta watch your back," Trey said as he followed him down the hall. "Ricky, man, he's looking for blood. He's going around the school telling everybody he's gonna beat your ass for getting him suspended from the team."

"Tell me something I don't know," Julius said.

"I'm just letting you know, man, so you won't be surprised. That one dude he rolls with named Ice ain't to be played with. He's known for carrying a blade on him."

Julius turned to Trey and shoved him backwards. "What? You think I'm supposed to be scared of a nigga with a blade?"

"Nah, man," said Trey, totally surprised by Julius' aggressiveness. "I was just trying to give you a heads up."

"Well, when I need some help from you, I'll ask for it," said Julius. "Other than that, stay the hell out of my face."

"Alright, if that's how you want it." Trey gave him a slow nod as he stormed down the hallway.

****

Felecia slowly cruised her car in front of a huge white house with a beautifully kept lawn. The newly built home was one of many for sale in a freshly built subdivision that was well across town from where her and Julius stayed. The beautiful home wasn't too big and it wasn't too small, but just right for her and her son. The sight of it made her heart melt.

She jumped out of the car, jogged onto the sidewalk and simply admired the home. The house could easily be considered her dream home since she never believed she would ever be in the position to own one like it. It was everything she ever wanted for her and her son, and she had plans on making it the first purchase of her new found wealth. The beautiful structure brought tears to her eyes.

****

He entered the food court area and all he could see was happy students. They all seemed to be so happy in their coolness and separation from the free lunch hoarders that resided in the cafeteria. As he strolled around the area, he felt almost invisible. No one paid him any mind because he really was nonexistent to them. A nobody. This was the place during lunch that all the cool people hung out, near the canteen and the front office, where the people that could afford it or acted like they could, paid for their meals.

"Julius," said a voice from behind him. He knew the voice from anywhere and he immediately turned around. It was Simone.

"Hi," she added.

He didn't really know what led him into the food court, but he was hoping to see her there. Seeing her face flushed all the bad thoughts out of his mind. "Hey," he answered.

"Julius…" she said. "I don't know what my father said to you, but I apologize for it. He's just an old guy trying to keep tabs on what he feels to be his baby girl. He's always going to see me as a little girl, and I can't help that. I just want you to know that I really like you, and I don't want you to avoid being around me because of him."

He never heard another human being outside of his mother actually tell him they liked him. The words brought a smile to his face, and in his bashfulness, he bowed his head. That warm feeling he remembered from the fair was back, and it overwhelmed his heart. For a moment, no one else even existed. In a building packed full of loud and rowdy students, it felt to him like they were the only two there.

"I should've handled things better and not blame you. I'm... I'm sorry about how I acted," he struggled to say. "I was wrong."

She smiled. "It's okay, Julius. It's okay."

As he looked into her eyes, something inside of him pushed his head into hers and their lips briefly met. He backed away from her in disbelief at what he had just done, but not regretful in any way. They simply stared at each other as an array of comments and chuckles were dealt out to them from onlookers scattered about. It didn't matter what they had to say, because they had nothing to do with the feelings they shared inside.

Suddenly, Julius was hurled into her and they both went tumbling to the floor. The fall took his breath as he looked over to Simone as she laid on her bottom grappling her arm. She was wincing in pain.

"You ugly, punk ass, scrub nigga," yelled Ricky as he pointed down at Julius. "I had to sit out two games because of your bullshit, and it now it's time to pay." His homeboys Ice and Jermaine stood behind him, shaking their heads, beating their hands into their fists with smirks across their faces.

"Man, what the hell is wrong with you?" Julius screamed.

"Your bitch ass is what's wrong with me," he said.

"Julius, just get up and walk away," said Simone as she struggled to her feet. "He's not worth it."

"And you–I can't believe you put your lips on this ugly piece of shit," Ricky said while donning a frown across his face. "And to think, I was actually chasing you down."

"Whatever," Simone said with angry scowl.

"Get up, bitch," said Ricky as he turned towards Julius. "Come get this ass whoopin' I'm 'bout to give you. The felon ain't with your ass today to protect you."

Everyone in the food court began to huddle around them, yelling and screaming, as they were all thirsty to see a good fight.

The moment he saw Ricky approaching him, Julius jumped up and tackled him down at his waist. Barely mounted on top of the bully, Julius began swinging away. He knew he had to get the jump on things before the boys all tried to maul him.

The oohs and ahs from the crowd of students rang as Ricky wasn't able to get a punch off to fend himself. Before Julius could really pound on him really good, Jermaine and Ice quickly drug him off Ricky by both his arms and slung him backwards. Julius slung out a flurry of kicks as he fell backwards. He was prepared to do whatever he had to do to protect himself.

As Julius sprung back onto his feet the two boys tackled him onto the ground again. Simone tried to pull Ice away from him, but the boy slung an elbow at her that sent her tumbling to the floor. They scooped Julius back up by his arms as Ricky rose from the ground with a trickle of blood running from the corner of his mouth. The bully looked possessed in his approach.

Julius did his best to free himself from the clutches of Ricky's sidekicks, but he couldn't budge. He looked over at the crowd of spectators and recognized Trey in the bunch. When he realized Julius was staring at him, he turned his head away. The crowd was screaming for blood, and calling for Ricky to beat him down.

"You're gonna pay now, little nigga," said Ricky as he drove his first punch into Julius' gut. Ricky's buddies allowed Julius to fall backwards from the force of the punch as they all laughed.

Julius started backing away on his elbows as the trio, led by Ricky, approached him looking to do even more damage. Without thinking twice about it, Julius whipped out his gun from under his shirt and pointed towards Ricky. Each of their mouths dropped as they froze like a trio of icicles.

"Gun! He's got a gun," yelled a few students as they all began to scatter like roaches. The area was nearly cleared out in mere seconds as the students fell over themselves in their attempts to make it to the exits.

"Whoa, whoa, whoa, dude," said Ice as he held his hands in the air. "Whoa."

Julius scrambled to his feet without taking his aim off of his nemesis, Ricky.

"Hey, man, you ain't gotta bring no gun into this," Ricky said nervously. Julius could hear the fear in his voice. Seeing the pistol was all it took for Ricky to reveal the true coward he believed him to be.

"Julius, what are you doing?" Simone asked. When she got back onto her feet, she wasn't sure if she should approach him or run away like the rest of her peers. She never thought of him to be the type to carry a gun, but she understood just how much Ricky and his crew was pushing him. "Julius they're not worth this. You gotta put that gun away before Principal Benson sees you with it."

"Yeah, listen to her, Graves," said Ricky. "We were just fuckin' around with you. We can squash this, man."

"Shut the fuck up!" Julius said while grasping his gun.

"Cool man, cool. Whatever you say," Ricky said nervously.

The mere sight of Ricky disgusted him. All he could think of was all the times the jerk harassed him since the first day he stepped foot on the campus, but now he wanted peace, now that he sees his life flashing before his eyes.

"Mr. Graves," yelled Principal Benson. "Just what do you think you're doing out here with that weapon. Put it away now." The man began marching towards them. "And I mean now."

"Stay back," Julius demanded as he swung his gun in Mr. Benson's direction.

The principal quickly halted at his request and said, "Now, Mr. Graves, somebody can get hurt by the way that you're swinging that thing around at people. I don't think you took enough time to think this thing through, with all the consequences of what you're doing right now. I know we can talk this thing out. No one needs to get hurt."

"People already hurt," said Julius as he returned his aim to Ricky. A tear slid down his face. "You people make all these demands while you have assholes like this one right here right up under your noses making life a living hell for people that don't even want to be bothered." Julius squeezed the gun and said, "What the hell did I do to you, huh? What the hell did I do?"

Ricky couldn't say a word. He realized he was in a position where it could be the very last moments of his life.

"Mr. Graves, this is not the way to handle this. This is not what your mother would want," Mr. Benson said.

"My mother," Julius said sarcastically.

"Listen to him, Julius," said Simone. "Just put the gun away. He's not worth all of this."

"I will do everything in my power to make sure no one, not even Mr. Smith, bothers you ever again, Mr. Graves," Mr. Benson assured him. "This just isn't the way to handle this, son."

"Then what is the way?" Julius yelled. "You didn't want to listen to me before. When this piece of shit and his buddies beat me down in the bathroom and poured piss on my head. Where were you then, Mr. Benson? Why weren't trying to play problem solver then?"

The principal took a deep breath and brought both hands down his face. "Mr. Graves, I didn't know about any of this."

"That's the problem. You people never know. You don't wanna' know," said Julius as he pulled back the hammer.

The moment Julius pulled back the hammer on the gun, Ricky wet himself. Julius could see the moisture spreading at the boy's crotch area.

"Julius, don't do this," Simone cried. "Don't do it."

While pointing the gun at Ricky's face, he thought back to Travis' words about the hardest nigga turning bitch at the sight of a gun. He thought about Mr. Bass and the words of wisdom he always seemed to have for him as encouragement, and finally his mother–his rock. No matter how much wrong he's done in his short lifetime, she always stood beside him. He then glanced over to Simone. She had both her hands covering her mouth and tears running down her face. He could see the fear in her eyes.

He returned his focus back to his enemy and lowered the gun. He hated everything about Ricky and what he represented, but he didn't hate him enough to pull the trigger.

Mr. Benson immediately pushed out a deep breath. Ricky and his goons didn't move one inch as they feared Julius would have a change of heart and set his sights on blasting him again. They soon realized, Julius had other aspirations in sight.

Julius rapidly ran towards the exit leaving them all behind. The principal quickly called out for someone to make sure that the police were on their way. Simone remained still, without a clue as to what her next move should be. She simply watched Julius flee the building at the front. After a couple of minutes of standing dumbfounded as the teachers and staff members moved into the food court, she took off to follow her love.

With the rush of adrenaline running through his body, Julius did not tire. He had to get home. He had to get away from it all. With each step he thought about all the bad things that had happened to him.

The smirk on Vince's face when he drew the pistol on him...

The firm warning he received from Simone's father about not seeing her again...

The way Simone's friends looked down on him every time they saw him...

The idea of his mother being intimate with Principal Benson...

The constant fighting with Ricky Smith and his crew... and his family..

Being the unwanted offspring of a rape...

Travis, his only friend in the world being locked away in jail somewhere...

The robbery!

It all consumed his mind simultaneously. Life was swallowing him up, and there was nothing he could do to stop it. There was no escape in his mind.

He barged in through his front door and didn't even bother to shut the door behind himself. After trampling down the hall, he kicked open his room door and froze midway into the room.

The front of his head began to just thump. His ears began to thump, also. He couldn't stop his hands from trembling. The room felt as if it was spinning. It was hard for him to catch his breath. Too hard. As the room's spin began to slow, he felt his heart nearly beating out of his chest. He gazed across the room and saw a reflection of himself in a small mirror on the wall. It was the reflection of a face the world seemed to a hate so badly. A face he himself despised. He scooped up a stapler machine from his desk and slung it across the room, shattering the mirror in pieces.

He could hear hoards of police sirens down the street at the school. He knew they'd be at the house shortly. He wasn't going to run. He was tired of running. He was tired of everything. A rage sparked within him. That rage ignited throughout his entire body. *Why me?* He asked himself. *Why does my life have to be so bad? So cursed? I just want to be left alone.* "Why won't they leave me alone?" he screamed.

Everything surrounding him intensified his anger. He went for the wall above his desk first, grabbing and ripping every single sketch he ever drew from the wall. He broke his desk apart and slung his chair across the room. Then to his closet, he ripped every article of clothing from his closet and slung them across the room. His sheets–he unpinned and slung them to the floor. The sketches over his bed, he trashed them, also.

He made his way to the wall next to his window and ripped sketch after sketch from it but paused at one. The one he loved the most. The one he drew of Simone. It calmed him. He just stared at the sketch, imagining it was really her standing before him watching him create his mess. It was the most accurate drawing he'd ever created, and he felt as if it still wasn't enough to capture her true beauty. Her sketch brought tears to his eyes as he thought of the moments he shared with her. The only happy moments in his entire life. He took a few steps backwards and plopped down on the edge of his bed. He removed his gun from the small of his back.

Simone wasn't very far behind Julius but she was far enough to lose sight of him. She'd never been to his house, but she knew he lived down the street from the school. As she walked at a fast pace down the sidewalk, she looked from house to house for any sign of Julius. She knew he lived near the bus stop and she was getting close, but no sight of him.

She then approached a little white house just a few yards up from the bus stop, and she noticed the door was wide opened. She just knew Julius had to be in that house. She hurried across the yard and jogged up the porch steps. She was nervous about entering, but if she had to get cursed out by somebody for entering their home to check on Julius, she felt it was well worth the embarrassment. She entered the house.

"Julius…," she said softly.

As Julius sat in a trance with the pistol in his hands, he felt the only way he could be free from the pain of this world was to remove himself from this world. He slowly raised the pistol to his head.

Simone crept down the hall of the house and walked to the first open room door. To her surprise she saw Julius sitting with his back turned with the gun at the temple of his head.

"Julius!" she yelled.

"Simone," he said frantically, as he hurled from the bed and whipped around to face her, not removing the pistol from his skull. "Get out of here, Simone."

"Julius, what in the world are you doing?" she asked. Seeing him that way watered her eyes immediately as she feared what he may do with the weapon. It was obvious to her he wasn't thinking clearly. She knew she had to come up with a way to get the pistol out of his hand.

"I can't take it no more, Simone," he cried. "I can't."

"Julius, you can't do this. This isn't right," she said. "Please don't do this, Julius. We can talk. We can get some help."

"I'm tired. I'm tired of them," he said with tears pouring down his face. "They're always messing with me. I don't bother nobody. I don't."

The police sirens were getting louder and closer. They could tell law enforcement was on their way. Felicia pulled into the driveway and immediately knew something was wrong from the way her door was opened. She jumped out of the car, and looked down the direction towards the school. The loud sirens made her worry. She was even more concerned about who was in her house with the door wide open. She immediately thought it must've been Vince, since it was too early for Julius to be home. She rushed up the porch steps and hurried into the house to kick him out again.

"Who's in here?" she asked. "Vince? Julius?" She soon realized there was chattering coming from Julius' room and headed that way.

"Ms. Graves," Simone yelled out with her hands out to Julius.

"Who in the..." Felicia said as she stomped into the room. Her eyes nearly jumped out of their sockets when she saw Julius standing across from her with a pistol pointed at his head. "Julius... What in the wor... baby put that gun down."

"Nah, ma... I'm tired," Julius said to his mother. "I'm tired of them calling me names. Hurting me... I'm so tired."

"Julius, this ain't the way to handle this son," Felicia said frantically. She feared getting any closer to him because of his tight grip on the pistol. "Please put the gun down, baby."

"Julius, please listen to your mother," Simone added. "You do this, and they win. Don't you see?"

It was almost like Julius couldn't hear a word they were saying. He cried, "Why won't they just leave me alone? Can I get a break sometimes?"

"Julius, come on baby," Felicia said as she burst into tears. "Don't do this to momma. We got better days ahead of us, baby."

"Ma...Ma.. I can't do it no more," he cried. "They won't leave me alone. I just wanna' be left alone. I don't bother nobody!"

"Baby..."

Before she could get another word out, the gun went off. Splattering of blood and Julius' flesh plastered across the wall and onto the sketch of Simone. When his body tumbled to the floor, it was almost like it did so in slow motion to them. Neither one of them could believe what they had just witnessed.

"Julius," Simone said while covering her mouth.

"Julius!" Felicia screamed out in a scream that went from loud to silent. Her mouth remained opened as the pain made her voice go mute. Her face was draped with tears as she ran to his body and slowly dropped onto her knees. She couldn't believe what her eyes were seeing. She couldn't believe what her child had done to himself. She pulled his limp body into her and cradled him tightly, rocking him back and forth.

"You were better than everyone else, baby," Felicia cried. "You were better."

Simone couldn't move. It terrified her to see Julius' bloody body nestled in his mother's arm. She just couldn't believe what had just happened.

The sight of the picture of her draped in red spots and small chunks of flesh from the young man she had grown to love nearly sent her to the floor. She covered her eyes and turned her head. She slowly walked outside and took a seat on the edge of the porch. The police had arrived and were surrounding the house. She placed her hands over her face and began to cry.

THE END

UGLY

UGLY

Single Again (Preview)

By Rod Cornelius

A wise man once told me that a man needs a woman in his life like a turtle needs the shell on his back. Well, he wasn't all too wise. As a matter of fact, he was this old, drunk guy that I met at this bar a couple years ago, weeping about his wife leaving him with nothing but the shirt on his back. At the time, I couldn't understand what in the world would make him come up with such a weird comparison—turtles and relationships. I just took it as the alcohol talking. Besides, that was when I was in the prime of my mac-daddy days. Relationship jargon was just that—jargon! And in reference to what my Uncle Jim once told me, I was young, dumb and always trying to find some. By no means was I trying to feel any kind of a relationship, or more blatantly, anything lasting longer than a one night stand. So at the time, I didn't know what that guy meant, why he was saying it, or why in the hell he was saying it to me.

But like I stated earlier, that was back in the prime of my player days, which virtually ended when I met Brandi Brown. Brandi, by far, was the woman of my dreams. Never in my life had I met a lady like her. To me, she was all that a man could want in a woman. But out of all the places in the world I could've met her, I met her at a club. I first laid eyes on her in the midst of celebrating my boy Rex's birthday at this little club we hit frequently called the Hot Spot. We walked in, chillin', like we normally did, and unexpectedly, we both spotted her at the same time.

"Man, look 'a here!" yelled Rex as his eyes zeroed in on her in the middle of the dance floor. "You ever saw her in here before?"

"Hell nah," I quickly replied.

She was dancing all by herself wearing this tight, black body skirt that revealed every perfectly placed curve on her body. She had long, thick, black hair that dangled down to her shoulders, a lightly tanned complexion, and luscious, plump lips. She freely swayed to the jazzy tunes that played as if she was the only soul in the joint. This chick was so hot, not a guy in the club had the nerve to approach her. You could literally look around and view every guy in the house sneaking peaks at her when their women turned their heads, or if they were by themselves, they just lustfully stared. I even caught a glimpse of a couple of envious females looking her way with frowns on their faces.

"Damn!" I grunted under my breath.

"Now that's dangerous," proclaimed Rex.

"You gonna holla', birthday boy?"

"Hell nah, she's too damn scandalous!" he replied. "You holla'."

I grinned, "My game's good, but I don't know about that."

"Just do it for me. Show me what I taught you."

"What *you* taught me?"

"Yeah, you know I taught you everything you know about the opposite sex."

He was just scared his ego was going to get hurt. "Whatever, Rex." As I continued to stare at her, something overwhelmed my body, perhaps just hormones, but I became strangely determined to meet this lady. Not just that, but something was telling me that I had to say something to her as if it was my destiny. Suddenly, I became transfixed on kissing those luscious, full lips of hers while sliding my hands up and down her slender back, drawing her firm, naked body against mine. Yes indeed, I was going to approach this precious victim of Godly beauty. I truly felt it would've been an opportunity missed if I'd done otherwise. "You know what?" I took a deep breath. "I'm gonna do it."

He smiled, "Do that thang, pimp-a-licious."

"Pimp-a-licious, gonna do that thang, man!" If only I was as confident as I sounded. But I had to do it. I had to meet this lady. So I loaded all of the mental weapons that my brain harbored, and I strolled to my destiny.

I began bobbing my head to the music, trying to look as hip and slick as I possibly could. I'd bagged many fine females in the past but not as gorgeous as this one. As I drew near, she noticed me approaching her. "Hi!" I nervously blurted out.

She gave me a slight nod, still grooving to the tunes. I quickly realized she was going to be an arrogant one. "So, are you dancing by yourself?" Sometimes the obvious should never be put into question form. Again she said nothing. I looked back at Rex. He had grabbed himself a chair in the corner, steadily observing my actions like a gospel stage play. Man, I couldn't let him see this woman get the best of me. I would never hear the end of it from him. I quickly turned to her. "Do you mind if I dance with you?"

She stopped dancing and examined me from head to toe. A petite smile appeared upon her face. Nervous and dumbfounded, I smiled right back at her. And that's when she approached me. Before I knew it, her lips were against mine. Instantly, my mind went haywire.

"I don't feel like dancing anymore," she softly replied into my ear. Her sweet voice had a hint of an English accent in it.

With my mind on sabbatical, I could only come back with, "Well, what do you wanna do?"

She grabbed me by my hand. "Come on, love."

I looked over to Rex whose mouth had virtually fell in his lap as my feet mindlessly followed this woman off of the dance floor. I didn't know what to do next as I simply followed her lead. In a matter of seconds, we were outside in the middle of the parking lot.

"I hope your friend drove tonight," she threw a set of keys into my hands as we walked down a row of cars.

"He did," I said. Really it didn't matter who drove, because if I did, he was gonna be out of luck this night. And I knew he'd do the same to me. If he were me in the same situation and he was walking out of the club with such a beautiful lady and I was going to need a ride home, he would just leave my ass hitchhiking. But fortunately for him, he drove because I would gladly return the hypothetical favor.

We stopped at a red convertible with the top down. I opened the passenger door for her, and I anxiously jumped in on the driver side. Never had something so spontaneous happened to me with such a beautiful lady. I just wanted to get to wherever she wanted us to go, however quickly we could get there and see where things would go from there.

She gently placed her hand on my thigh. "Go straight down Main, take a left on Brenton, and pull into the driveway of the third house on the right."

Straight and direct, just what I liked. As I pulled out of the parking lot, I realized I didn't even know what this woman's name was. She just stared out of the window like she didn't even care. I could've been Charles Manson for all she knew, but even worse than that, she could've been.

"Hey, do you have a name?" She didn't answer. She blatantly ignored me, just like she did when I first approached her in the club. Now see, it's things like that, that makes a man think with his brain and not his jimmy all of the time. But then I took another glance at her body and quickly realized how much more powerful a man's jimmy is than his brain. As a matter of fact, it is his brain. Besides, this chick was a perfect ten. A ten, then some. And those are just too hard to come by at times.

Her directions led me straight to a two-story brick house smack-dab in the middle of Brenton Avenue. "Keys," she chillingly requested. A brief thought of being stranded in the middle of nowhere swiftly raced through my mind. I gave her the keys. "Come on," she said. Thank you, Jesus. I couldn't bare the thought of walking all the way back to that club and trying to quickly compose a lie to Rex as to why I was perspiring so badly.

I jumped out of the car and shadowed her tracks like a starving dog sniffing for a meaty bone. She opened the door to the house and flicked on the lights beside the entrance. As I stepped into her crib, I began to instantly think that this experience had to be some kind of cruel joke sponsored by my subconscious and somehow, I was sleeping and couldn't wake up. And the way it was beginning to feel, this was gonna be a wet one.

She glanced back at me, "Close the door." I shut the door and followed her up the stairs. The house really didn't have much in it. In fact, it looked unlived in altogether. The walls were neatly entangled with an assortment of oil paintings but not much furniture consumed the home. Nonetheless, my primary concern rested on just one piece of furniture in particular––the bed!

We walked into what had to have been the master bedroom. It was humongous. An exquisite Persian rug laced the floor. There was a huge floor-length window open, and the nightly breeze blew her finely-silk draperies into the room. Most significantly of all, she had this massive king-sized bed in the center of the room.

I looked around, not trying to seem overly-amazed. "So this is yours?"

"Nope!" she said as she walked alongside her bed, slowly sliding her fingers across the satin sheets.

Damn! I knew she had to have a man, somewhere.

"Well, it is for now. My agency is leasing this place for me until I find some place to live down here," she said.

"Oh," I said relieved that there was no sign of any manly presence in her life so far. "All this for you, huh?"

She grinned. "Yeap."

I walked over to the window and gazed down at the dimly lit street. I didn't want to seem too anxious for what she had to offer. "Nice view."

"I'll say," she replied.

I could almost feel her eyes cutting through my back. I turned around, thinking maybe I could slip a little bit of my own arrogance in there. "I was referring to the street."

"I was, too. What else would I be referring to?"

Ooh, low blow, and can't say that I didn't deserve it. As she took a seat on the bed, I just stared at her, not having a clue to where things were headed. But if I knew anything, I definitely had to have them go the direction I wanted them to.

"So," I took a deep breath. "Why did you bring me here?"

"Why did you come?" she quickly combated.

"What? You grabbed my hand and led the way."

"You're a grown man. I'm quite sure you could've stopped me."

"I could've, but why would I want to stop you?"

"Uh, because you have respect for yourself and you wouldn't want to become victim to a one night stand."

Playing it witty, I quickly turned my head acting as if I was surprised, "Is that what this is, a one night stand? Well, I have never..."

"This is not a one night stand," she said, really surprising me.

"It isn't?"

"No."

"Really?" I threw my hands up, looking side to side. "Then what is this?"

She grinned. "It's a show!"

"What, you talking about like Candid Camera, or something?" I began looking around, searching for any hidden cameras I hadn't noticed. I knew the whole get-up was too good to be true.

"No, silly," she laughed.

I was severely intrigued. "Then what type of show are you talking about?"

"A strip-show."

Suddenly I had a smile the size of Texas on my face. "Oh, for real?" I quickly planted myself onto a chair next to the window. "Go ahead."

"You don't get it, do you?" she walked to me and stood in front of me.

I looked up at her like a little boy, waiting for his mother's response to a request to go outside and play. "What am I not getting?"

She pulled me up on my feet. "I'm not stripping, silly. You are."

First Degree Sins (Preview)
By Mirika Mayo Cornelius

"So his name is Nathaniel Cylinders?" I ask, but I don't expect Candyce to answer. Therefore, I give her my own plan. "That's a great plan, Candyce, but before you get out, I'm taking my half of the money. What's mine is mine. I'm no thief." I know it sounds stupid as hell, but I'm really not a thief. A reactive killer as of recent, but not a thief. "You might just try to get away with him but remember, if you take off in that car without me, Smack will be laying smack on that ground like some smack." Truth is, I'm just calling Candyce's bluff. I've never been offended in Smack. I really do love the dog, so I'm leaning on Candyce believing me based off of my prior killings…well, the ones that she knows about. "When I drop you off at the bench, I'm going around the block where I can see you through the trees. When I see you get in the car, you need to circle the block until you see this car. When you do, let the door swing open and I'll jump in. You better remember that I have your loaded gun on Smack the whole time."

"Don't kill my baby, Lisa. Don't kill my baby," she cries, but her cries end soon as I pull up to the Waffle House. It's packed as usual, however, I don't wait on anyone to see how frantic I look, so I press on the gas to drop Candyce off at the suicide bench.

"Wait, I can't get out."

"Try your best because I can't get out either."

As I watch Candyce pull herself up by the door's handle, she pulls her hair back into a ponytail. Then she looks down at Smack with a crooked smile, and then the

323

smile fades when she looks at me. Good thing I have on my sunglasses. I look away.

"What happened? That's the least you can tell me before you let me out. You fucked my hair and face up, so go on. Tell me."

I don't hesitate to tell her. What else can she do when I have the love of her life cradled in my arms with a pistol waiting to fire? Checking the road both ahead and behind me, I make the conversation quick. That's the least I can do although I'm shaken as fuck. I have to play like I'm hard as hell so my dear friend who has miraculously survived the attack won't try anything to save her own life.

"I caught Robert in bed with one of his girlfriends after they ate the dinner I cooked for him. I'd set the table and all, but when he got home, he beat my ass, hence my black and red eye. When I left, I decided to go back. That's when I caught him in bed, both their clothes off, and he told her that he loved her. I slit her throat, stabbed his ass up and then I left. I forgot some of the other stuff, but I went shopping for Smack some food. Then you called me on the road when I was pulling your car in the garage, saying you were being late. Then, when I got in, I had to make a run for it because the cops and everyone on the street was in front of my house. I left your car there and took my car elsewhere. Now, we're here and you're getting out to come pick me up in a different car." I turn my eyes back to look her in the face and her mouth is wider than an elephant's head. "Bye." I turn to face the road, ready to drive ahead. "I'll see you in twenty minutes." She hands me my sum of money and takes the left over in her bag. Then, she looks outside the window.

"This is suicide bench."

"Get out of the car!" I scream directly inside of her beat up face. I can even see traces of ash from the ashtray on her cheekbone as she stares at me like I'm not supposed to let her out at the bench. "What?" I yell. "It was your man's idea! Get out!"

More Akirim Press Books

Books by Rod Cornelius

Diggin' Gold

The Trusted

Single Again

Ghetto Eyes

The Best Kept Secrets

When It Comes Around

Books by Mirika Mayo Cornelius

Secret

Colored Lily: Poppa Took My Innocence

Ain't Quite What I Thought

Ain't Quite What I Thought 2

Sunny Sides of My Shade

First Degree Sins

Inside The Gates Of Doons

Paton

Books by Cyan Deane

Dead Man's Mayhem

Execution's Karma

UGLY

www.ingramcontent.com/pod-product-compliance
Lightning Source LLC
Chambersburg PA
CBHW051335250626
47155CB00007B/2611